POCKETFUL

PEARLS

POCKETFUL

of

PEARLS

A Novel

SHELLEY BATES

WARNER
Faith

New York Boston Nashville

Warner Faith
Hachette Book Group USA
1271 Avenue of the Americas, New York, NY 10020
Visit our Web site at www.warnerfaith.com

Warner Faith and the "W" logo are trademarks of Time Warner Inc. or an
affiliated company. Used under license by Hachette Book Group USA,
which is not affiliated with Time Warner Inc.

Printed in the United States of America

First Warner Faith edition: August 2005

10 9 8 7 6 5 4 3 2

Library of Congress Cataloging-in-Publication Data

Bates, Shelley.
    Pocketful of pearls / Shelley Bates.
        p. cm.
    "One woman's struggle to escape an abusive cult and make a new life for herself" —
Provided by the publisher.
    ISBN-10: 0-446-69491-6
    ISBN-13: 978-0-446-69491-9
    1. Abused women—Fiction. 2. Cults—Fiction. I. Title.
    PS3602.A875P63 2005
    813'.6—dc22

                                                                    2005005029

For Joanne

ACKNOWLEDGMENTS

Thank you from my heart to those courageous women who shared their stories with me, and in the process gave Dinah a body and a soul. Marge Reynolds, your ministry is an inspiration. Mum and Dad, your support means everything.

Thanks go to Kati Carthum for connecting me with her cousin, and to Peter J. Kesling, attorney at law, for telling me what Tamsen's options were. My thanks, too, to fellow author Margo Maguire, RN, for the information on victims of stroke.

Jennifer Jackson, none of this would have happened without your belief in me. Thank you. Leslie Peterson, your keen eye and good humor have made this process a pleasure.

I'm indebted to Dr. Dan B. Allender for his book *The Wounded Heart: Hope for Adult Victims of Childhood Sexual Abuse* (NavPress, 1995), which gave me Dinah's path to healing; and to Stephen Arterburn and Jack Felton for *Toxic Faith: Experiencing Healing from Painful Spiritual Abuse* (WaterBrook Press, 2001), which helped me find mine.

Last but not least, thanks to Jeff, who now schedules his annual fishing trip during the final week of deadline. I love you.

POCKETFUL

PEARLS

"Neither cast ye your pearls before swine, lest they trample them under their feet, and turn again and rend you."

—MATTHEW 7:6

Chapter 1

THE VAGRANT CAME to the back door the night of Morton Traynell's funeral, just as Dinah was trying to organize food for the hundred or so mourners who filled the front rooms of the old farmhouse.

The knock was so soft she would have missed it if the group of women helping her hadn't left the kitchen just then, loaded down with plates of rolls, neatly sliced vegetables, and casserole dishes.

She jerked open the door and stared at the man on the steps. He held a knitted cap in both hands, squeezing it as though it were a washrag. The harsh overhead light gave his skin a yellowish cast under a ragged beard.

A stranger. With a jolt of fear, she stepped back and swung the door nearly closed, its comforting weight between herself and him.

"I'm sorry to bother you, ma'am," he said softly. He had some kind of foreign accent, but Dinah was too frightened to take the time to identify it. "I wonder if you'd have a bite to spare a hungry man."

There were enough bites in the front room to feed an army of hungry men, but food given to a stray off the street deprived one of God's chosen, who could use it for God's work.

"This is a bad time." The words came out rushed, almost under her breath. "My father was buried this afternoon, and everyone is here for the supper. I'm sorry."

The gentle hope that had filled his eyes drained out of him as though he'd been punctured. "I'm sorry for your loss," he said. "Sorry to trouble you." He bent his head and turned to go.

Her loss? Her heart began to pump painfully as she hesitated between fear and pity. "Wait."

He had been looking down the road for the lights of the next place, but there was nothing down there except the Hamilton River, swollen, brown, and rushing with spring runoff. At the thought of what the river had come to mean to her, and what it could mean to a sad, hungry man who was obviously at the end of his own resources, Dinah felt a chill of apprehension.

"I'm sorry. I shouldn't have said that. Let me get you a plate."

He came back up the steps as cautiously as a deer. A starving one, in whom fear had been brutally displaced by hunger. "I don't want to be any bother."

"This house is full of food. You're no more bother than any of the rest of them."

Leaving him on the steps, Dinah shut the door and snatched two paper plates off the table. She stacked them one on top of the other and loaded the reinforced result with vegetables, hamburger casserole, pasta salad, and bread, taking a bite for herself between every spoonful for him. She filled a plastic bottle with cold water. The man looked dehydrated. Ready to drop. And Alma Woods's casseroles were notoriously salty.

She shouldered the door back open and handed him the plate, fork, and bottle. "Don't let anyone see you."

"Thanks, ma'am. Bless you."

Dinah restrained herself from telling him that he had nothing to bless himself with, much less anybody else, as he faded into the darkened yard. She supposed she'd find the water bottle out there somewhere in the morning.

She turned back to the kitchen and removed the plastic wrap from a tray of sausages, stuffing two into her mouth as she did so. It wouldn't be so hard if Tamara were here. She should have been allowed to come back to help during the crisis, to handle their mother with her particular knack. But instead, at the age of seventeen, her sister was as one dead. Still struggling to finish high school, she'd been put away for her sins, and Dinah was on her own.

One of the women came back for more food, and took the plate from her. "How are you holding up, Dinah?"

Just for a moment, Dinah thought about telling her the truth, but she was in the service of God, separated unto himself, with a veil drawn between herself and even his people, the Elect. She had to remember that. It was the only thing that kept her going on days like today, when fear painted the future in dismal, watery shades of gray and black.

She swallowed the last of the sausage. "Pretty well," she said. "Better than Mom, I think."

The woman's expression teetered between sympathy and disapproval of someone who would admit in public that she wasn't grieving her father's death as much as her mother was.

Then again, Mom had chosen Dad.

The woman settled on sympathy as being more appropriate to the occasion. "Why don't you go out front, dear, and be with your mother. I'll hold the fort and see that everything gets set out."

What if the vagrant came back? He looked like he could tuck away three plates of food and still be hungry, but she had sensed a painful politeness that wouldn't let him ask for more. Dinah didn't want this crowd of clean, well-fed people to know she'd spoken to him. "Touch not the unclean thing," they'd say, and they'd wonder what on earth she was thinking, to let an outsider—someone potentially dangerous—anywhere near the door.

She was a vessel filled with love. Or so said Phinehas, the senior Shepherd over God's flock in the State of Washington. She had grown up in the one true way, whose people gathered in house churches instead of in worldly temples made with hands, and whose Shepherds went out in faith and love, caring for the flock unencumbered by a permanent home, belongings, or salary. But one should demonstrate love by encouraging people to hear the gospel, not by giving them handouts that only made them dependent on charity instead of on God.

"It's okay, thanks," she told the woman who, after all, was just being kind. "I know where everything is." And if she had to acknowledge one more expression of sympathy, she wasn't sure she could hang onto her composure.

The woman nodded and laid the plate of sausages on her inner arm, then picked up a platter of vegetables in one hand and dip in the other. As soon as the hem of her black dress flicked out of the kitchen, Dinah opened the door and peered out. The backyard was quiet and utterly dark beyond the circle of familiarity cast by the bare bulb mounted on the wall over the lintel.

"Are you still here?" she asked the dark in a voice that was closer to a whisper than a call.

Something winked near her feet, and she glanced down. The empty water bottle stood on the top step, the fork laid neatly beside it. The latter was as clean as if it had just come out of the dishwasher. Had he wiped it on his shirt?

"Hello?"

But no one answered.

"Dinah, is someone out there?" Her mother came in with a couple of empty trays. "The boys aren't parking the cars back there in the dark, are they? They'll never get them out of the mud."

"I was just checking." It wasn't quite a lie. She'd been checking the vagrant's whereabouts, hadn't she? "Mom, you're not supposed to be serving. These people are all here for you."

Her mother looked so fragile that the trays drooped in her hands. Her hair was beginning to come out of its neat bun, and she hadn't bothered to wipe away the tracks of tears on her face. Not tears for her husband's death, which Dinah was perfectly aware was God's will, but tears of gratitude for the kindnesses of others.

"I hope not. They're here for Morton. Out of respect. And don't put the sliced roast beef out yet. Save it for when Phinehas comes."

"Phinehas is coming?" The blood halted in Dinah's veins, and then began to crawl, slowly, pumped by a heart that had momentarily forgotten how to work. "When?"

"He was in Spokane when he called. Missions might be very successful there at the moment, but when he heard of our need, he practically dropped everything. He should be here anytime."

Anytime. After two months away from Hamilton Falls, overseeing other congregations, encouraging lost souls to God with his preaching, he would be coming back. Tonight.

Her knees twinged, their usual ache prodded into urgent life, and she grabbed a handful of carrot sticks, crunching into them as though someone were about to take them away from her.

She'd thought the waiting bad enough before, when she didn't know when it would end. The waiting was the worst. But suddenly she realized that time could be compressed into short, painful bursts when the end was finite, and the waiting could actually, physically hurt.

PHINEHAS ARRIVED AT seven o'clock, parting the crowd near the front door like Moses at the Red Sea. At the sound of his voice, sonorous and as full of authority as Moses's must have been, Dinah ducked back into the kitchen. The kitchen was women's territory; the closest Phinehas got to it was her father's chair at the head of the dining room table.

Better yet, she thought, as the women who had been washing up the dishes dried their hands and smoothed their hair before going out into the living room to greet the Shepherd of their souls, she could step outside and check again to see if the vagrant had gone.

She pulled on a flannel work shirt with a quilted lining—the one she covered her dress with when she fed the chickens.

It wasn't that she wanted to talk to the homeless man. He could be a prison escapee, or a burglar, or any one of the things that people became when God wasn't in control of their lives. But somehow she had the feeling he was too weak to burgle, and too malnourished to attack.

No, she just wanted to make sure he was no longer on the property. The last thing she needed was another man to deal with, with his needs and demands and authority laid over her like a suffocating blanket. She'd had twenty-four years of it, of being taught that women were created to serve God and others first and themselves last, and special women like herself were created to love. That didn't mean Dinah needed to take on the responsibility of another needy person. Her mother filled that department all on her own.

He wasn't in the yard. The gravel Dad had laid down last year crunched under her shoes. In the barn, the truck stood empty, too, though it would have made a comfortable place to sleep. What would they do with a practically new work truck now? It wasn't likely either she or her mother would be hauling firewood or feed or even the animal trailer, though they could if they had to. Maybe they could sell it. It might bring enough to pay for her tuition at the college.

College. A dream as far off as the Promised Land. At this rate it would take her forty years to get the rest of her two-year degree.

Sheba, her darling and the solitary joy of her life, murmured sleepily when she let herself into the part of the barn they used as a chicken coop. She caressed the hen's feathers, enough to comfort but not enough to wake her completely.

The truth was she didn't care where the vagrant was. Nobody would think to look for her here.

She settled onto the plastic lawn chair she kept near the roosts, and Sheba and the other chickens fluffed their feathers and went back to sleep. As far as they were concerned, she was one of them. She let the undemanding acceptance of the birds and their soft, reassuring murmurs calm her as she sat in the dark.

Until, behind the bales of hay, somebody snored.

She leaped to her feet and snatched the flashlight from the niche near the door where she kept it. The snores didn't miss a beat as she played the narrow beam over the sleeping form of the vagrant on the other side, curled in the hay like a calf.

He had moved into her space, the only place that was utterly hers on the whole planet.

Now what was she supposed to do?

Shake him awake and order him off the property? He might be dangerous if he were wakened suddenly, and no one knew she was out here. Not only that, they were two miles from town. There was nothing out here but the river and the mountains and the cold March wind. Their nearest neighbors were worldly people, unlikely to provide a haven for a homeless man.

Dinah realized with an uncomfortable start that the Traynells were just as unlikely to do so. It gave her pause. What did it say about God's chosen people that they would sooner brush this man off the back porch with a broom than give him a place to sleep? Because of the way he looked, she had automatically assumed he was reaping the fruit of a wicked life, and had judged him without thinking. What did it say about her that she had so little compassion, that she saw him as a problem to hide rather than a human being in need?

The poor man deserved his rest in a place that, thanks to a hideously expensive building contractor, was airtight and warm.

She backed away as quietly as she could and got an old blanket out of the tack room no one used anymore. Gently, she shook it out and laid it on the thin form. Slipping out of the barn, she went around to the back, the side that faced Mount Ayres.

She'd come to a pretty pass when simple compassion became an act of rebellion. But she refused to send that man out into the night just because of the raised eyebrows of a flock of old crows. It was just a fact that the Elect looked inward in doing their charity, following the Shepherds' advice about keeping themselves separate from the world. In it but not of it. There were plenty of worldly churches to take care of worldly people, so God's chosen took care of their own.

Maybe this sleeping man was dangerous. Maybe he was a lazy, dishonest person whose own actions had brought him to this. But at least for tonight, his fate was up to her. Right or wrong, she could take control of something for once, could make a decision and act on it, and no one would be the wiser.

With that thought, she tucked her skirts between her aching knees, bent over, and stuck her finger down her throat. Soundlessly, neatly, she purged herself into the bucket that stood against the wall.

Chapter 2

MATTHEW NICHOLAS, PHD, assistant professor of English, author of two books, voted most popular lecturer of 2001 by the students of the University of California campus where he'd once taught, opened one eye and found himself nose to beak with a chicken.

The bird made a sound like water bubbling in a pipe, as if to acknowledge that he was awake, and turned its back on him.

How appropriate.

Matthew moved his head. The cramped muscles in his neck screamed, and the rough edge of the blanket scratched his cheek.

Blanket?

Fully awake now, he sat up and pushed an ancient wool blanket—gray with a red stripe, smelling faintly of horse—off his shoulders. He was allergic to wool, but that didn't make him less grateful for it. He was in no position to be fussy. He'd discovered, in the seventeen days since his ancient Volvo had given up the ghost a hundred miles north, that simple human kindness was a commodity more often found in books than in reality.

Admittedly, he deserved it from no one. Which made it even more surprising when he found it.

He folded the blanket carefully and placed it on a crossbeam where hopefully the chickens that seemed to overrun the barn would not sit on it and leave a deposit. Having never been this close to chickens before, he stood for a few moments and watched them.

The only thing he knew about poultry was that they pecked and had an order. Looking at the crowd milling around the nearby metal feeder, he could see the first fact was true. There were more outside. He could hear them talking. Crooning, to be more specific.

To be more specific still, someone was crooning to them.

Cautiously, unsure whether to expect the young woman in the black dress or some fresh threat, he peered out the door he estimated opened closest to the voice.

"Pretty birds. Good morning, my darlings. There's my good girls. You eat lots and stay fat and healthy, my pretty birds. Pretty birds."

The woman's voice was hypnotic. No wonder the birds were clustering fearlessly around her feet, busy at a second metal feeder. Except for the black-and-white one on her shoulder that was busy demolishing some vegetable delicacy cupped in her hand.

It was a scene straight out of *Witness* or a *National Geographic* special on nineteenth-century cultures living anachronistically in modern times. She was dressed in unrelieved black, even to the bulky lumber jacket she wore, and her brown hair was twisted up in a bun from which it appeared curls and wisps were trying to escape. But there was no white cap on that hair, and from what he'd seen of the kitchen behind her the night before, no shortage of modern electric appliances, either.

So, she wasn't Amish. Was she Mennonite? Hutterite? Doukhobor? Some other rural sect about which even *National Geographic* knew nothing?

It didn't matter what she was. What mattered was this was the same woman who had answered the door. Who had lost her father. Who had fed him.

"Good morning," he said, and she looked up.

For a moment fear stamped lines on her face that hadn't been there when she'd been singing to the chickens. Then she seemed to realize who he was, and the lines smoothed away. She stood a little straighter, and the bird on her shoulder adjusted its grip.

"They seem very happy," he went on, when she didn't speak. "I've never been close to chickens. One woke me up just now."

"That was probably Schatzi," she said. Her voice was low and sweet and wary. "You were sleeping where she likes to lay."

"Do I have you to thank for the blanket?"

She said nothing. Instead, she tucked her skirts behind her knees and squatted. When she held one arm out, the black-and-white hen sidestepped down her sleeve like a tightrope walker and hopped to the ground.

"I apologize for using your barn without permission," he said. "It was inexcusable of me, but I—"

"It's all right." She stood and shook her dress out. "We're the last place on this road. You didn't look like you would have made it far."

"No. Thank you again for the supper."

"When was the last time you had proper food?" She pulled the flannel shirt she wore closer around her, though the weak sun was warm.

He thought for a moment. "Wednesday?"

"This is Saturday."

"Yes."

Most people would have asked him what he thought he was doing, wandering the roads looking like a derelict, and starving in the bargain. But she just gazed at him, bundled in her ugly black, as though to ask would be getting more personal than she wanted.

For which he could hardly blame her.

"You're going to need breakfast before you go," she said at last.

An odd feeling fluttered in his chest. Gratitude? Humiliation? Whatever it was, it hurt.

"No. Thank you, but you've done far more than I have a right to expect. Please don't trouble yourself."

"It's no trouble. Biscuits and eggs, that's all. I'm making them anyway. My aunt and uncle are still here. And Phinehas."

He had no idea whether Phinehas was a man or a rooster. "No, I can't."

"Of course you can," she said briskly. She picked up a bowl containing eggs in more shades than he would have thought possible—green, blue, brown, buff. "You're going to fall over where you stand. Don't let false pride get in the way of being sensible."

A little on the curt side, maybe, but correct.

Matthew watched her latch the gate to the chicken yard behind her and walk across the graveled expanse between the house and the barn. When the back door closed, he looked around.

The black-and-white hen cocked her head and regarded him with a beady eye. Then she bent and pecked at his shoelace, yanking at it as if it were a worm. He bent and retied the lace, and the hen scuttled out of the way.

The least he could do was to find some chore to perform before she came back out and humbled him once again with food. He might not be good for much, but he could clean up after chickens. Inside the barn, he found a wire brush and a rake standing against one wall. He soon found out what the brush was for when he saw the layers of waste under the poles on which he supposed they roosted. Some brisk elbow action took care of that, leaving him slightly out of breath and confirming that too many days between meals could do serious damage to one's physical condition. A plastic bucket that had once contained paint and now contained what looked like vomit did duty as a trash receptacle, and what didn't fit he raked into a pile.

He rested on the rake, panting. After days of hunger and rejection, it felt good to take control and do something constructive. Even if it was only shoveling chicken manure.

"What are you doing?" The woman stood in the doorway, fists clenched, the light behind her outlining a shape that practically shook with rage. "What are you doing with my bucket? And my birds?"

The rake tilted out of his hand and landed on the floor with a clatter. "I'm not doing anything with them. I'm—"

"Get away from there! How dare you?"

Matthew spread his dirty hands. "I wanted to do something to repay you for—"

It wasn't rage, he saw as she stepped out of the glare. It was fear.

He was no good with rage. But he could do something about fear. After the last couple of months, he was well acquainted with it.

He lowered his hands and moved away from the area she obviously considered hers alone. "I wanted to repay you for your kindness," he repeated quietly. "I don't have anything but labor to give you, and I saw that you'd probably have to clean the roost area before long, so I went ahead and did it."

"The chickens are mine," she choked. Her hands lay flat against the wall next to the door, not clenched now, but looking as though they were holding her up. "Mine."

Perhaps she was an only child, and not used to sharing.

"Of course they're yours," he said. "They're beautiful birds. Well brought up. Even Schatzi was polite when she asked me to move this morning."

She regarded him for a moment. A smile fought briefly with the downturned corners of her mouth, and lost. "There's a plate outside, here," she said. "A paper plate, with breakfast. Please take it and go."

He nodded over his shoulder at the fallen rake and the overflowing bucket. "I'll just pick up after myself."

"No. I'll do it. Good-bye."

Matthew dusted off his right hand. "Let me introduce myself on my way out. I'm Matthew Nicholas, from Cornwall via California. And I'm very grateful to you."

She kept her gaze on his face until, awkwardly, he dropped his hand.

"Dinah," she said at last. "Dinah Traynell from right here."

He couldn't tell if the quiet words held regret or resentment. It was none of his business anyway. His business was to move on without further imposition on her time or kindness.

The plate of food was warm in his hands. With all the self-control he could muster, he restrained himself from wolfing it down on the spot. "Do you mind if I eat this here?" he asked. "It's difficult to eat and walk. I'll go right away after I do justice to it."

She nodded and picked up the bucket and took it outside. As soon as she was out of sight, he sat on the nearest bale of hay and practically inhaled the food. As fast as he chewed, he could still appreciate the flavor of fresh scrambled eggs containing bits of red pepper and onion and warm biscuits with butter melting down their sides. He could not remember the last time he'd tasted butter, much less a biscuit as fluffy as these. Months ago, possibly. In another life.

For a moment he considered not licking the plate, and then discarded that notion as ridiculous. He licked it with relish.

"I can get you seconds." Dinah Traynell's voice was dry as she set the bucket down and began to refill it from the pile he'd made. She seemed to have recovered from whatever had upset her. Or perhaps he had reassured her by not invading the chickens' area again and sitting in the plastic chair.

A flush burned into his cheeks. "No, that's not necessary. I'm completely full."

"It's nice to see someone enjoy their food."

Was she blind, or were the effects of homelessness not as obvious as he'd thought? "*Enjoy* is not the word. Every molecule I ingest now will take me a step further down the road before my appetite gets the better of me again."

"Before you get hungry, you mean."

"Well, yes." He had no doubt she thought he was pathetic, but she hid it well. Possibly a woman who dressed as she did was used to feeling ridiculous and, as his students used to say, she could relate. "I suppose you're wondering how I came to be in this position?" he asked.

She swept up more dry balls of manure and tipped them into the bucket. "It's none of my business."

"I feel as though I owe you something. If not labor, then at least an explanation."

Eyebrows with the shape and tilt of bird wings drew together over her eyes, which he now saw were brown and devoid of makeup.

"You don't owe me anything. All I ask is that you keep yourself out of sight until you get on the main road."

Hints didn't come much broader than that. "You don't want anyone to know you harbored a vagrant?"

"No. I'd never hear the end of it."

"Why? I would think giving a homeless man a bit of food and a bale of hay would be seen as admirable."

She shot him a quick glance and bent to pick up the bucket. "Your blood sugar must be rising or you'd never be able to talk like that."

"Sorry."

"You're not one of us. The Bible says to help a brother, which would be one of the Elect."

"Elect?"

"Yes. The Elect of God. His chosen people. Us."

Not just a cultural anachronism, then, but possibly a cultic one as well. And yet, she had fed him. The red peppers were still sweet on his tongue.

"I see. So you would be consorting with publicans and sinners, then."

"Yes. Not keeping myself separate."

"You must come in contact with the outside world occasionally."

"Of course. But you were going to tell me how you got into this position."

He rolled the paper plate into a tube, and she took it from him and stuffed it into the bucket.

"I thought I didn't owe you anything."

"I changed my mind."

He rather thought she wanted to talk about her church less than she wanted to hear about him.

"It started out as a . . . well, as a quest of sorts. To find myself."

Another dry look. "That's very California. Were you lost?"

More like thrown away. He got up and paced slowly to the wall and back. With two square meals, the muscles in his legs no longer trembled with the effort to hold him up. "Yes, you could say so. Very lost. People do walking tours of Cornwall all the time, so I thought I would do the same, starting in the Pacific Northwest."

"At the tail end of winter? Not very sensible, Mr. Nicholas."

For a woman who put so much stock in being sensible, she seemed to have some odd beliefs about the nature of believers in God. He shook off the thought and answered her question.

"In February, actually. After . . . an event that precipitated my course of action. But I didn't count on that wretched transmission going out about a hundred miles north of here. So my walking tour became a reality, especially after my wallet was stolen."

"Oh, dear. Couldn't you get a job? Or call someone to ask for help?"

"No." He looked away. Somehow the lack of someone to call made him feel poorer than ever.

"Anyone can get a job," she said. "You could check groceries. Clean motel rooms. Until you get some money for the next leg of your tour."

"And where would I sleep and eat while I waited the week or two before my first check? It's not as simple as it looks. What do you do for a living, Ms. Traynell?"

The hurt cascaded over her face like a bucket of cold water, and he regretted the impulse behind the question, though it had been phrased kindly.

But before he could apologize for the impulse, not the words, a voice carried over the yard outside.

"Dinah! Where are you?"

The rake clacked against the bucket and she gathered both into her hands. "I'm in the barn," she called. To Matthew, she said, "Hide somewhere. That's my mother."

"What are you doing in there?" the voice demanded. "Phinehas is down and waiting for his breakfast."

"Everything is on the counter, Mom." The woman—Dinah—went to the barn door. "All you have to do is heat up the pan and pour the eggs in. The biscuits are in the oven."

Her mother made an impatient noise that Matthew could hear from behind his hay bale. The little gold hen called Schatzi hadn't moved from the niche between the bales that was her nest, despite his abrupt arrival. She glared at him and covered her newly laid egg protectively, spreading her wings low. He returned his attention to what the unseen woman was saying.

"Phinehas would like his breakfast from your own hands,

dear. I suggest you get in here now so you don't keep him waiting any longer. The work of God comes first."

The kitchen door slammed and Matthew peered above the hay to see Dinah silhouetted against the light.

"I'll be back," she said. "To hear the rest of it."

"I thought I was supposed to go," he whispered.

"There might be leftovers. Phinehas is a holy man, but his appetite is a little on the picky side."

"I'll be right here."

Her hands gripped her thighs for a moment, as if she were willing her legs to move, and then she walked out the door. Each step looked so painful she could have been walking on ground glass.

That was odd. He had been talking with her for fifteen minutes and hadn't seen any sign she was in that kind of pain.

But then, he was notoriously bad at reading body language. Which was part of the reason he was sitting in an empty barn, his only companions a chicken and a strange woman, both of whom wanted him gone.

Chapter 8

"HERE SHE IS, Phinehas. Honestly, I don't know what was so important out there that it would keep you waiting."

Dinah hung up the flannel shirt and edged into the kitchen. Through the archway, she saw the two of them sitting at the dining room table with the good Royal Albert china mugs in their hands. "Good morning, Phinehas. I'm sorry I—"

He waved her apology away with genial grace. "No apologies necessary, Dinah. I've been enjoying your mother's excellent coffee, and I'm sure you had chores to do before breakfast."

She'd made the coffee before she went out, but it would draw attention to herself if she said so. Dinah scrubbed her hands at the sink, turned on the gas under the skillet, and pulled the beaten eggs out of the fridge.

"I'm glad I could spend this first morning with you. The loss of husband and father, even though we've been expecting it since they diagnosed the cancer, is always tragic." Phinehas watched as Elsie Traynell bowed her head and sniffed. "But he's in a better place now, worshipping at the throne of God, and we are left to make our way as best we can. What will you do now, Elsie?"

Dinah handed her mother a tissue and turned the eggs with a spatula.

"I don't know." Elsie blew her nose.

"Did Morton leave you provided for?"

"Yes. He was very clever with the stock market, though it's a mystery to me. And of course, there's his pension."

"Strange how the devil's playground can be turned to the good of the kingdom, isn't it?" Phinehas mused. "Microsoft and General Electric will never know how God's work has been promoted through your father's gifts."

"You can be sure they will continue," Elsie said hastily. "Dinah has the head for figures. I don't."

"She does, does she?" Dinah felt his gaze on her back. "I am much comforted by that."

She got two biscuits out of the oven, put them on his plate, and spooned eggs beside them. As she leaned over to put the plate in front of him, he reached for his coffee cup, and his sleeve brushed her breast.

She had been schooled in discretion, though every cell in her body leaped and the muscles in her jaw flexed.

Her father's brother and his wife came out of the downstairs guest room just then, and as Elsie's mouth quivered and Aunt Margaret bent to hug her, Dinah caught Phinehas's eye.

Just as quickly, she glanced away. Maybe it had been accidental. But with Phinehas, it seemed, nothing ever was. Every word, every physical movement, every item of clothing, he'd once told her in a private Visit, was examined for effect, for correctness, for suitability under scrutiny. It was probably second nature by now. God watched them constantly, it was true, but Dinah often felt she'd prefer that to the vigilance of the Elect on the subject of their example. One's example to a lost world included dress, speech, possessions, entertainments—everything, in short, that was visible from the outside.

That was why her own was beyond reproach, and why, she

supposed, none of the other girls in the Hamilton Falls area liked her. Even Julia McNeill, who came from as favored a family as the Traynells, which you would think would give them something in common, hadn't been all that friendly. She and Julia and Claire Montoya were all around the same age, but even in school Claire and Julia had been chums and Dinah had followed them around feeling left out. Last summer Julia had shocked everyone by dumping Derrick Wilkinson, to whom she had practically been engaged, going Out, and then running off with a biker who had an illegitimate child. So her judgment was obviously flawed to begin with.

"Dinah?"

She came out of her thoughts with a jolt. "Yes?"

"Phinehas asked you for more coffee."

"Sorry," she apologized with a smile. She had to pay attention. It was important that everything be done just right, that everything be perfect for the Shepherd of her soul.

She handed him his cup, filled with the special blend they kept for his visits and made strong and black the way he liked it. As he reached for it, he murmured a word of thanks and the back of his hand again brushed the side of her breast. This time there was no escaping it or rationalizing it away.

She knew.

He caught her eye a second time, over a conversation about the many ways money could be used in the service of God.

Crippling pain in her knees made her stagger, and she fell into a vacant chair at the table. Her mother blinked at her.

"Try not to be so clumsy, dear. When you bump the table, it spills the coffee."

"Sorry, Mom."

Dinah bottled the urge to run, to lock a door, to set off down the road and never come back. Instead she stayed at the table, toying with a slice of orange and pretending to listen to her aunt and uncle encouraging her mother to be strong for the Kingdom's sake.

If only Tamara were here.

She and her little sister were seven years apart in age, and a thousand years apart in experience. Tamara had had to leave when she started to show, of course. You couldn't have a family member in the house when they were shunned, anyway. It was just too difficult, not to mention the sheer logistics of trying to communicate over meals and laundry. Better that Tammy had gone to Spokane to Aunt Evelyn's. Dinah had never met her father's sister because she'd gone Out years ago, but Evelyn had taken the girl in with only a minimum of argument and invective hurled at Dinah's parents over the Elect's method of dealing with sin.

At least it was dealt with. Real sins were, anyway. And you couldn't get much more real than Tamara's. It wasn't just the fornication that had resulted in the pregnancy. It was the disgrace she'd brought on an Elder's house. Dinah knew there were people who wondered if there was some flaw in their upbringing, some fault in Morton or Elsie that had made their daughter turn out so badly.

If they only knew how strict that upbringing had been. How little room there was for flaws of any kind.

Gradually Dinah became aware that the gaze of Phinehas lay on her, as tangible as a shadow and as cool.

She got up, despite the pain, and began to clear the dishes. She ran hot water into the kitchen sink, squeezed some dish soap in, and buried her shaking hands in the clouds of bubbles.

"Would you like me to come with you to the lawyer's office Monday, Elsie?" her uncle asked.

"Thank you, John." Her mother's dress rustled as she took Uncle John's hand. "You're the executor, of course, and I know what the will says, but it would be nice to have someone there with me."

"What does it say, Elsie?" Phinehas inquired.

"Why, that the ranch is mine, of course. Nothing will change, Phinehas. You're as welcome to use our home as your refuge as ever you were."

"You're a marvel," he said affectionately. "Always putting the servants of God first."

"Of course." Elsie sounded a little surprised.

"There are those who don't, I'm afraid," he said. "Those who are unwilling to give. What they don't realize is how their behavior affects their reward in heaven."

"Isn't it the truth," Aunt Margaret sighed.

Dinah kept her back to the dining room, submerged the skillet, and began to scrub it. He'd seen her unwillingness in her face. But her father had been dead only four days, and he'd come the moment he'd heard how vulnerable she was. She was a vessel of love. He'd come to give her comfort.

That was all it was.

Comfort.

She finished the dishes and wiped up the counters, then dumped the remainder of the eggs into a bowl to feed to the chickens, who were partial to red bell peppers. As she pulled her quilted jacket off its hook, her mother gave her a puzzled look.

"Where are you going, dear?"

Where was there to go? Nowhere.

"Out to the barn," she said instead. "I'll only be a few minutes."

Elsie turned to the people at the table and extended her hands. Three people reached to take them, and she chose the warm, patrician clasp of Phinehas. "I declare, that girl spends more time in the barn than in the house," she complained. "If it isn't the chickens, it's some project she's got going. She should have been a boy, and then I wouldn't have to worry about the heavy work."

Dinah closed the door on Elsie's querulous voice. She really should be more charitable toward her mother. She wasn't being very comforting, it was true. But Elsie had three people there to comfort her. All Dinah had was Sheba.

Pain shot up her legs as she struggled to get across the yard without collapsing. In the chickens' area of the barn, she sat heavily in the plastic chair. All was quiet. Schatzi still nested in her little niche in the hay. The hen would have been too agitated to settle if the vagrant were still behind the bales, so that meant he'd probably gone.

Sheba came in through the hen door and walked across the floor like the Queen inspecting the troops. She paused at Dinah's feet and looked up, waiting for an invitation. Dinah patted her knee and the hen flexed her powerful haunches and vaulted up into her lap, wriggling under the barn jacket to the warm, secure place beneath Dinah's arm.

She cuddled the bird, finding relief and comfort. Hugging the Silver-laced Wyandotte was like hugging a big silk pillow that talked back. Dinah would do anything for Sheba, including giving her the leftover eggs when all she wanted to do was bolt them down herself. Never mind that she'd made herself a full breakfast before she'd brought a plate to the vagrant.

Sheba murmured something in the depths of the jacket and Dinah opened it. The bird backed out a little and then sat companionably on Dinah's thigh, within the circle of her arm, keeping a vigilant amber eye on her kingdom.

"Is it safe to come out yet?"

Dinah jumped, and Sheba scrambled to her feet. The hen's head swiveled toward the hay bales as the vagrant poked his head above them.

"I thought you'd gone." Dinah stroked Sheba's feathers until she settled down again, but Dinah could still feel the tension in her feet as they gripped her skirt.

Probably a response to the tension in her own body.

"You asked me to stay here. I wasn't sure if you meant it, but if it means getting more of those eggs, I'll take the risk."

He was gazing at the bowl she'd meant for the chickens, and compunction nudged her. She hadn't even thought about her promise to bring him seconds. The sight of Phinehas had driven him completely out of her head.

She picked up the bowl and held it out to him. "They're probably cold."

He climbed over the bales and she noticed that Schatzi didn't move. How odd.

"They're protein," he said. "Doesn't matter whether they're hot or cold." In seconds the leftovers were gone. Sheba gave him the evil eye.

Dinah felt rather the same. "You were supposed to share."

The hen hopped down, offended, and stalked out the hen door.

"If she hasn't eaten since Wednesday, I'd be happy to share with her." He scooped the last particles out of the bowl with his fingers. "Besides, in her case there are more where these came from. I didn't realize chickens ate eggs."

"They eat chicken, too. They prefer it baked."

"How can chickens eat other chickens?"

"It isn't personal. Like you said, it's protein. Those eggs have to be built from something."

He folded himself onto a hay bale a little distance from her and regarded Schatzi, who gazed placidly back. "I am reduced to the level of a chicken," he said sadly. "My only thoughts are for protein and not getting killed by the nearest predator."

"You've had trouble with predators?" She pulled her jacket more closely around her and made sure her black skirts covered her legs to the ankle.

"Yes. The two-legged type. They had a bit of fun with my credit cards before I could find a phone and cancel them. I never realized before how difficult it is to find a phone that doesn't require money."

"Do you still need to use one? There's an extension out here." She nodded toward the door, where the phone hung.

"No, thank you. I'm obliged to be moving on."

"Not immediately."

She gathered her thoughts together for an idea that had just popped into her head fully formed. Or maybe it was the logical result of the last twenty-four hours. In any case, the more she thought about it, the angrier she got, and the better she liked it.

He gave her a long look. "I don't understand."

"How would you like a job, Mr. Nicholas?"

He stared at her in astonishment. "I thought we discussed this before. Having a job requires a place to live, which requires rent, which requires a job. A vicious circle that defeats me at the moment."

"A place to live comes with it."

He got up and then sat again, as though his legs wouldn't carry him far enough to get him out the door. "Please explain. The protein hasn't kicked in enough to allow my brain to work."

"You need a place to live and something to do," she said. "I need someone to do the heavy work around here that my father did up until the cancer made it impossible. Either I hire a boy from Hamilton Falls and have to deal with his social life cutting into his work time, or I hire you, ready and available to start immediately. What do you think?"

"I think you would not be getting your money's worth. I can no more do heavy work right now than that chicken there"— he indicated Schatzi, who had left another blue egg in the niche and was preening her feathers—"could pick up this bale of hay."

"A few solid meals would take care of that."

"And you know nothing about me except that I'm not very capable of managing a walking tour."

"Possibly. But whether you can manage a grazing lease and feed cattle concerns me more."

"I know more about chickens than cows, and that's only because of you."

"You can learn. And it's interesting you should mention the chickens. You don't frighten Schatzi."

He glanced from the bird, who had finished preening and had hopped down to the feeder, to Dinah. "What has that to do with it?"

"Schatzi is very easily frightened. But she's not frightened of you."

He sighed, and one corner of his mouth lifted in a rueful smile. "All the credits in the world, and I'm reduced to a character reference from a chicken."

"You've got ground to make up with Sheba, though, after not sharing your breakfast."

"I will endeavor to do that." He sounded as if he were trying not to laugh. "Since Sheba's opinion appears to matter to you."

"Sheba matters deeply to me." She got up. "One thing."

"Yes?"

"My aunt and uncle will be leaving Monday afternoon. I have no idea how long Phinehas will be here, but it could be several days." She pushed the thought away. "You need to keep yourself hidden out here until I can tell my mother I've hired you. Come on. I'll show you."

She led the way back to the tack room and heard his slow steps behind her.

What am I thinking? He could hurt me.

She fought back the panic. He had all he could do to get up and walk. And there was Schatzi, who had not been afraid. She took comfort in that and tried to calm the irrational fear.

She pushed open a door and stood aside. Matthew halted on the threshold and gazed at the room.

"Who is this for?" he asked at last.

"When we had a hired man, he stayed here." She avoided touching him as she passed and indicated the kitchenette. "You could do your own cooking if you wanted, but once everybody leaves it's probably more convenient to eat with us. That's the living room. The sofa's kind of old, but it's comfortable. There's a bed through there, and a bathroom with a shower."

"I had no idea this was here."

Guilt prickled, and she shook it off. "Now that you're no longer a vagrant, you shouldn't be sleeping in the hay."

"I don't know about that. Schatzi and I came to an understanding. But are you sure?" He turned to her with such an expression of pain that she stepped back in spite of herself.

"Sure?"

"That you want to do this for me. You've been so kind and I—" He stopped and made a gesture of futility with both hands. Emotion worked in his throat. "I have no way to repay you."

"You'll be working," she said briskly. She absolutely could not handle his emotion. She warded off his thanks with her tone. "I'll bring your meals for now. You can use the time to build up your strength."

"Right." He took a long breath. "Hidden away in luxury. I'll be our little secret."

She stared at him, and the remnants of distress in his face turned to alarm.

"What? What did I say?"

"Nothing," she choked out. Then she turned and, as pain lanced through her legs, walked as quickly as she could out the door.

OUR LITTLE SECRET.

Throughout the rest of the day, the words echoed in her

head. By afternoon the voice was no longer that of Matthew Nicholas, but of Phinehas.

You're a vessel filled with love, poured out in secret.

It took her two hours to prepare dinner—two hours of cutting vegetables and preparing spices, two hours in which she was far too busy to think or to acknowledge the fact that Phinehas was in the living room visiting with her mother and aunt and uncle.

Your calling is strictly between you and me and God. Our secret.

It was two hours in which to eat. She managed to sneak outside twice, under the guise of taking the compost out, and purge herself. After dinner, it took another hour to wash the pots and clean the kitchen. It was even necessary to scrub down the sink with cleanser and clean out the wells under the heating elements on the stove. All the while the spring of tension inside her wound tighter and tighter.

Come to the secret place and let us worship together.

She demolished most of the leftovers in the fridge, and afterward, in the upstairs bathroom, wondered how she was going to explain their disappearance. She'd always been able to blame it on Dad and his midnight snacks. She went down and considered cleaning the oven, too, but at nine o'clock her uncle came into the kitchen to get her.

"Dinah, Phinehas is starting to call you our little Martha, you're so busy out here. Come and be Mary for a while, and have a Bible study with us. It's the Lord's day tomorrow, you know."

She had no choice but to go.

Fortunately, the Bible study lasted an hour and fifteen minutes, during which it was perfectly acceptable to keep her eyes on the Bible in her lap while she listened to Phinehas interpret the Scriptures. Her fingers, under her Bible's worn leather covers, were rigid and cold.

After a final prayer, she slipped into the downstairs spare

room where her aunt and uncle were staying—Phinehas slept upstairs, in the large front bedroom that overlooked the river—and took a couple of blankets out of the closet. Then she pulled the last of the funeral leftovers out of the fridge. When everyone was busy getting ready for bed, she stacked the food and the blankets on one arm and slipped out to the barn.

The chickens murmured when she passed them, but she didn't stop to stroke Sheba as she normally did at night. Her feelings would communicate themselves to the birds and their eggs would be bumpy and stressed in the morning. She knocked on the door of the hired man's apartment.

"Mr. Nicholas?" she whispered.

He opened the door, an indistinct dark shape. "Please, call me Matthew."

She'd rather not call him anything. "I brought you some blankets. And some casserole. It's cold, but there's a microwave in the kitchenette."

"Thanks very much." He took them. "I'm sorry if I offended you earlier."

"Offended me?" There was no room in her mind for such petty things as offense. Not when the spring under her solar plexus was wound so tightly she'd begun to have difficulty breathing.

"Yes. I think I said something that upset you. I'm sorry."

She shook her head. She couldn't even remember what they had talked about. Silently, she went back to the house and climbed the stairs to her room.

There was no point in locking the door.

She hung up her dress and folded her underclothes neatly into their drawers, then got the embroidered white batiste nightgown from the bottom shelf instead of the comfortable black flannel one she usually wore in the winter.

There was no point in getting into bed, either.

The slow moments ticked by while people used the bathroom and brushed their teeth. The toilet flushed. Bedsprings creaked. The moon had moved halfway across the expanse of her window and she could hear Uncle John snoring when it came at last.

Her door breathed open.

The floors in the ranch house were solid and thick and did not creak. Neither did any of the hinges. She'd made sure of that.

The lock snicked. The spring inside her uncoiled with a snap and she began to tremble.

" 'Behold, thou art fair, my love; thou hast doves' eyes.' " The whisper was smooth and confident. "Say it."

She was silent while the spring uncoiled the rest of the way and she began to float.

"Say it, Dinah."

" 'I would lead thee,' " she began, and her throat closed up.

" 'And bring thee into my mother's house,' " he prompted.

There was no help for it. " 'And bring thee into my mother's house, who would instruct me: I would cause thee to drink of spiced wine of the juice of my pomegranate.' "

The moon was so lovely. She would float out the window and up into the moon.

"Two months is far too long."

His breath was warm on her neck, but she was no longer in her body. She was drifting up toward the moon, so clear, so cool, so far away.

"Undo the buttons, Dinah."

But she was gone, and in the end Phinehas had to undo the buttons on her nightgown himself.

Chapter 4

THERE CAME A point when even the most disembodied person had to admit that the moon had hard edges and it was too bright to sleep.

Not that she ever slept afterward.

When Dinah came back into her body, she was lying crossways across her bed. Her hair hung down in a tangle off the edge of the mattress and trailed onto the floor. He insisted that she take it down beforehand, as though they were some kind of married couple, and she complied only because when she didn't, he wasn't quite so careful about not hurting her.

She stirred, and this time, when she tightened her thigh muscles and pulled her knees together, it worked. Sometimes she wondered how long she could stand the pain in her legs caused by years of futile attempts to keep him from pulling her knees apart.

But neither could she imagine trying to explain it to a doctor. Particularly when the doctor all the Elect went to in Hamilton Falls, Michael Archer, was one of themselves, and a member of Phinehas's flock.

Her pillow was gone. She crawled to the edge of the bed, snagged it off the floor with one hand, and curled around it.

What she wouldn't give to be holding Sheba right now, alive

and warm and unquestioningly loving, giving affection because that was what they both did—giving and receiving in a single current that went in both directions.

The pillow would have to do.

But first, she had to get rid of the nightgown. She rolled off the bed and stripped it off, throwing the disgusting thing in an arc like a sail into a corner of the room and pulling the comforting black flannel over her head.

Black, the color of the burned sacrifice. The color of coals, not completely consumed but ready for the match. The color every Elect woman wore in public to signify the death of her human nature.

She had no idea where he'd found the white nightie, with its tiny tucks and narrow-edged lace. Probably in a mail-order magazine specializing in quasi-Victorian garments, and sent to a P.O. box in a town where his presence at the post office wouldn't be noticed. She hated the wretched thing, covering her from throat to ankles while its fragile fabric exposed her so cruelly to his hungry, possessive gaze.

And yet there was no way to stop it other than running away, and after the family's humiliating disappointment with Tamara, she couldn't do that to her mother. She was the good daughter, the capable one, the one who didn't run when the going got so bad that running or death were the only options.

Running wasn't possible. Death was.

So she died a little every time, offering up her body as a living sacrifice so that he'd be appeased. So that this wouldn't happen to anyone else.

Only her.

It had begun when her period had started, when the private studies and special times she'd had with Phinehas as a child had lost their affectionate innocence and changed. He'd always touched her with love, and the novelty of it had made her hungry for more. A hug after a long absence, a caress on the hand or the cheek when she'd shared a particularly lovely thought from Scripture with him. She'd been his special princess, from the most favored family in the district, and that alone, he'd said, had set her apart from the other girls.

Even Madeleine and Julia McNeill, who in Dinah's eyes had everything she did not, were not as spiritually lovely as she was. Or so Phinehas assured her, and she believed him. She certainly never heard such things from her parents. For them, all that existed were rules and restrictions and do's and don'ts. With her father, the Elect always came first—before himself, before his wife, and certainly before his daughters. In the Elect, you lived within a structure of biblical traditions and found beauty and protection inside it. But her parents, it seemed, wanted to make sure the fences were good and strong, to protect her from the wiles of Satan.

At fourteen she'd become the confidante of Phinehas, listening as he shared his most intimate thoughts and longings. Things he could never tell another living soul—only Dinah and God knew. She learned from him how difficult was the celibate life of the Shepherd, how he had sacrificed the possibility of home and family to travel the state, bringing the gospel to hungry souls. She learned how difficult it was for a man to get close to God when his body's demands drowned out his ability to pray.

Her melting sympathy and desire to help him had been the catalyst that had begun it. It was her fault, really. He said he couldn't resist her, and after that first kiss, the first touches, she had learned that she liked being needed. Liked feeling special, even beautiful.

And she learned to make it easy for him. She learned which stairs to oil, and how to spritz WD-40 on hinges so they wouldn't squeak.

Because when she didn't make it easy, all the love went out of her existence. He could withhold his care and approval as easily as he gave it, and the winter that descended on her young soul the first time he ignored her withered her so cruelly that in the end, during his very next visit, she had not been able to bear it any longer and had gone back to him, begging his forgiveness.

Yes, she had gone to him. Because she had wanted something for herself. Because she had wanted to feel beautiful and needed. And for that selfishness God had punished her—with pain, with isolation, with a continuing struggle with the ambivalence of knowing it was wrong, of hating every moment of it, but wanting it anyway. She kept this dreadful secret she could never share with another living creature . . . except Sheba, who could give love but not sympathy in return.

Dinah curled miserably around the pillow. A glance at the clock told her there were still six hours to endure before she could get up. She couldn't even go downstairs for a shower. Her mother might not hear the water running at midnight—Dr. Archer's pills would take care of that—but the guest room was right across the hall from the bathroom, and Aunt Margaret would be sure to wonder what she was up to.

After ten years, she still marveled—in a faint, hopeless kind of way—that no one knew. She had kept their little secret. The ugliness. The pain and degradation. All were locked inside her body with no way out. No way to ask for help. And so, of course, no one saw—or wanted to see.

No one cared.

Not even God.

Hours later, Dinah watched the sky fade from black to gray and when the alarm clock told her no one would question it, she threw back the covers and tiptoed downstairs to the lower bathroom to shower. It made more sense to use the upper one, but she couldn't bear the thought of being naked and defenseless with Phinehas just on the other side of the wall. She stood under water so hot it steamed and scrubbed her abdomen and thighs with ruthless disregard for the redness of her skin. Then she dried off, wrapped her rose-sprigged dressing gown around her, and returned to her room, where she dressed swiftly.

For a woman of the Elect, clothes were a burden and the source of much moaning and discipline. But unlike the local girls, Dinah couldn't buy clothes in the stores in Hamilton Falls. Part of the reason was that hardly any of them stocked things in black that had the two additional qualifications required by Elect women—they had to be reasonably attractive while at the same time maintaining a woman's modesty with high necklines and long sleeves.

Dinah had a third qualification. She was so slender things literally fell off her. In the case of skirts and dresses, she usually wound up making her own. That was another reason she had envied Julia McNeill when they were teenagers. Julia could flit off to Spokane for a shopping trip whenever she liked, where Dinah was trapped helping her parents, who were older than most, with the home place. Just getting to the fabric store to make something for herself meant careful scheduling and juggling of other people's priorities.

Even putting food on the table meant work. They had the money to buy pickles and canned fruit until the end of time, but Mother insisted that they put up their own, the way she had learned in her own mother's kitchen. And Dad had fixed ideas about what constituted women's work that were even more firm than the general Elect view. So there you were.

On the rare occasions when she got to the library to indulge in the sin of logging onto the forbidden Internet and checking her father's stock portfolio, Dinah would surf the Web and look longingly at all the professions a woman could take on if she had the training. But for a woman of the Elect, going to college and getting trained for something other than husband and family was, if not frowned upon, then certainly not supported. What man would marry a woman who was better trained and possibly even making more money than he was? Who would be the head of the household in reality, no matter what they were in a spiritual sense? The two heads had to be embodied in the same person, or chaos resulted.

At the rate Dinah was going, though, she'd graduate with a PhD in nuclear physics long before she'd ever be a wife and mother. The thought of being married nauseated her. And of course, without the *wife* part, the *mother* part was impossible.

Her own depressing thoughts drove her down the stairs and into the refrigerator, where she pulled out some eggs and bacon and quickly made herself her first breakfast, the one she could eat all by herself before the family and Phinehas appeared around eight o'clock.

She would not think about Phinehas. She had learned to put him in a compartment and lock him in there while she went about her work. Otherwise she would wind up down by the river, screaming. And that would hardly be becoming to a daughter of one of the favored families, would it?

At least today was Sunday, and she wouldn't see much of him. He would take her father's place and lead Gathering in their living room, and then later today he would take Melchizedek's place at Mission and lead it, too. Between both obligations he would be sequestered in his room, preparing to preach the Word of God, and she would be free of the gaze that was like an invisible leash, tugging at her, controlling her, making her go where she didn't want to.

When she went out to feed the chickens, Dinah remembered who else was in the barn, and shook her head at herself.

Lovely, Dinah. Hire the man, hide him, and then forget to feed him.

She turned back to the house and fried some more eggs and bacon, slid them on a paper plate, and added an orange and a cup of coffee.

Sheba ran to greet her when she pushed open the barn door, craning her glossy neck to see what was on the plate.

"Sorry, darling. This isn't for you." Sheba didn't listen. She hopped up and down on both feet, thrilled at the prospect of something besides lay crumble for breakfast. "No, pet. This is for Mr. Nicholas."

As if she'd called him, the man appeared from the direction of the hired man's apartment. His skin and hair were damp, and his face glowed above the collar of a shirt that was as filthy as it had been the day before.

"Is that for me or for Sheba?" he asked by way of greeting, his gaze fixed on the plate as hungrily as Sheba's had been. The hen had given up and stalked off to make the best of the lay crumble.

"For you. But she's upset about it."

She handed him the plate at arm's length and watched him gobble its contents down.

"Thank you," he said when he was finished. This time he didn't lick it clean, so he must be feeling better.

"I need to ask you about my duties," he went on. "If cleaning up after the chickens isn't a possibility, you might give me some instructions. I had a marvelous sleep on that very comfortable bed in there. I think I'm able to start today."

"Oh, no," she said. "Sunday is a day of rest. And tonight we'll be leaving for the Mission hall at about six thirty. So if you wanted, you could go into the house and do your laundry. You'd have two hours before we got back."

His fingers curled a little into the hay on which he sat, but she didn't know why. Anger, perhaps? But at what?

"Thank you. Thanks very much. I feel like seeds are going to sprout at any moment out of the pockets of this shirt."

She smiled. Not anger, then. But she couldn't imagine what else it might be.

"After all our guests leave, I'll introduce you to my mother. Then you'll have the run of the place. Do you have any clothes besides those?"

Carefully he set the empty plate beside him on the bale. "A

few things in a rucksack, equally as grubby." He sipped the coffee slowly, breathing in the scent of it between each swallow.

"Wash it all tonight." She paused, then made up her mind. "My father was a bigger man than you, but you might be able to use something. Once everyone has gone we can look."

"I wish I could do something besides continually thank you."

She backed away from his gratitude. "You will. Once you start work, you will."

Leaving him there, she escaped into the chicken yard, made sure the birds had all they needed for the day, and went around to the back of the barn. There, she neatly disposed of her first breakfast and covered up the evidence with compost. Then it was time to prepare second breakfast for the family.

With Aunt Margaret helping, Dinah was able to get the table cleared by nine forty-five, which left her fifteen minutes to put her hair up properly and put on a good dress. An Elect woman's hair was supposed to be her glory, but Dinah hadn't received much in that department. In response to the flapper haircuts of a hundred years ago, the Shepherds had decreed that a woman's hair should be long enough to wash the feet of Jesus, as Mary the sister of Lazarus had done. At the same time, they said, the hair must be modest and a means of sacrificing vanity, so it had to be put up. Some of the women, like Madeleine Blanchard, could do an effortless French roll and look as elegant as any worldly woman while still maintaining the standards of modesty required by Phinehas—and by extension, God. But Dinah's hair, while thick enough and as healthy as ordinary shampoo could make it, was uncontrollable. You'd think that with a head full of curls, it would curve prettily around her face and temples. But no. It went in whatever direction it felt like going in the morning, and sometimes the best she could do was wrap it into a bun and hope for the best.

Promptly at ten o'clock, the first of the cars began to roll into the yard for Gathering. Phinehas was already in his chair in the place of honor by the fireplace, head bowed as he prepared to lead the flock in worship. After a hymn, Phinehas indicated the Gathering was open to sharing. One by one, the men got up to say what God—or their wives—had given them to speak.

Dinah found it hard to concentrate in Gathering on the best of days; today, with Phinehas at the front of the room, it was impossible. How could she be grateful for the love of God when because of it she could barely get downstairs and into a chair without biting her lips from the pain?

There were two Gatherings in Hamilton Falls each Sunday, in the homes of the favored families. Owen Blanchard led the other one. Poor man. His wife, Madeleine, was still in the hospital—or wherever she was after the doctors had finally diagnosed what was wrong with their little boy, Ryan. Owen faithfully got both his kids ready for Gathering by himself, now that his sister-in-law Julia had gone off with her biker and was no longer around to help. The kids seemed to have adjusted fairly well without their mother, but a number of the women were pitching in. The Bible said you were supposed to help a brother in need; as an Elder, Owen was certainly that.

Thinking of this, Dinah made a mental note to take a couple of dozen eggs by their house and offer her help. It wouldn't do for the Traynells to be seen as doing less for the Blanchards than anyone else.

Phinehas announced the closing hymn, and she realized with a start she had daydreamed the entire service away. Well, at least she had looked involved and interested, and that was what counted.

When everyone milled around the living room greeting each other after the hymn, people offered her their sympathies. She responded as best she could. She had learned to ignore the sidelong glances of the teenaged girls, especially the two oldest Bell girls, who thought they were little somebodies now that they had turned thirteen and fourteen. Dinah concerned herself with giving the other women as little to talk about as possible. Her hems were the longest, her heels the lowest, her conduct irreproachable. She no longer bothered to make herself attractive to the opposite sex by wearing blouses with ruffles and lace collars. And she would never dream of buying something fashionable in store-bought colors and then dyeing it black at home, the way Linda Bell allowed her daughters to do. That, in her opinion, was deceitful.

At the door, Phinehas greeted people as they filed outside, shaking hands and exchanging words with a smile. Dinah touched Phinehas's hand and let her own drop casually. To an observer, it would look like modest respect. No one could know her very skin was creeping off her bones and only pride kept her from taking off for the barn at a run.

Her body shook as she waited quietly by the kitchen door for everyone to leave, and she concentrated hard on controlling it. Which was why she jumped when a voice spoke next to her.

"How are you, Dinah?"

Derrick Wilkinson, whom rumor reported was getting over the abrupt departure of Julia McNeill and starting to circulate, offered his hand. For a wild moment she considered running into the bathroom and locking the door, but that would make him question what was wrong with her, and that would never do.

If he was circulating in her direction, she would put a stop to it right now.

"Fine, thanks." She touched his fingers briefly so he wouldn't feel the tremors in hers.

"It's wonderful for you that Phinehas came to help you through these first few days."

Yes. Wonderful. She nodded, and added a smile as an afterthought.

"Your mom must really appreciate it."

"She does. We all do."

"Listen, Dinah. I know this is probably terrible timing, but I wondered . . . if you wanted to . . . for a change of scenery, maybe you'd like to go for a drive and have lunch with me?"

Her stomach turned over. The rumors were true. Thank goodness she'd purged herself of her second breakfast or she'd have disgraced the family right here in the dining room.

"I'm sorry, I can't," she managed past the tightness in her throat.

He looked a little embarrassed. "I know. It is terrible timing. I'm sorry."

"No, not because of that," she assured him, casting about wildly for a reason not to go. "It's just that I promised Rebecca Quinn I'd go over and visit her this afternoon."

Now she'd have to do that, on top of everything else. Why did she have no imagination when it came to inventing excuses? *Because you've had so little practice,* a voice in the back of her head answered. *You're not exactly prime date material, are you?*

Dear God, she hoped not.

"You could still have lunch beforehand," Derrick said, hope plain in his eyes.

Was the man so obtuse he wouldn't take no for an answer? It was obviously her lot in life to be surrounded by men who were simply not interested in her plans or wishes.

She made a deprecating movement with the hand that wasn't holding her Bible and hymnbook. "I need to help Mom with lunch. We have Phinehas and my aunt and uncle staying, and big meals are a bit beyond her right now."

They were a bit beyond her at the best of times, but Dinah would never say that aloud.

"Oh. Okay." This time he seemed to get it. "Maybe another time, when you don't have so many obligations. I know how it is."

You have no idea. Any charitable thoughts she might have had toward Derrick Wilkinson were incinerated in a sudden burst of anger. How dare he presume to know what her life was like? A man could never know. Never. He fatuously thought he was making her drab little Sunday better for the space of a lunch, did he? He'd give her one brief hour of happiness in his wonderful company, right?

Yes, and then think what Phinehas would do if he found out she'd been with another man. She'd pay for that hour. Oh, how she would pay.

Her alternatives had never looked so bleak. Run—or accept. Die to herself.

But maybe there was another alternative.

She'd often toyed with the thought of the river, in the way a child toys with a weapon in daddy's closet without really understanding what it means. The Hamilton River was high with runoff now. High and violent and fast.

Dinah watched Derrick shake Phinehas's hand and walk outside with eyes that saw neither of them.

Maybe the river was the best alternative of all.

Chapter 5

PHINEHAS TOOK HIS Sunday duties seriously. Between that and serving everybody lunch, Dinah managed to not be alone with him or anyone else until he had gone upstairs to spend several hours preparing for the evening Mission service in town at the hall. As she cleaned up after lunch, she took inventory. She knew every ounce of food in the fridge—how much each shelf held, how many oranges there were in the bowl, how many slices of lunch meat remained in the meat keeper.

She hoped Mr. Nicholas would take her suggestion and come in to do his laundry and have the sense to help himself to the food. Poor man. She was glad her aunt and uncle were leaving tomorrow after going to the lawyer's office. Then she wouldn't be so likely to forget she *had* a hired man. If only Phinehas would leave as well. Then she'd be free.

Well, at least for this afternoon, she was relatively free.

Oh, wait.

She'd said she was going over to Rebecca Quinn's, so she'd better do it. With her luck, Derrick would mention her proposed visit next time he was in Rebecca's bookshop, and when he found out she hadn't gone, that it was just an excuse not to go to lunch with him, his feelings would be hurt.

A daughter of the favored family did not go about lying and gratuitously hurting people's feelings.

No, she had to go, when all she wanted to do was hide in the barn with Sheba and have a nice, long cuddle.

Her mother beamed when Dinah told her she needed to take the car into town to see Rebecca. "You do that, dear. Visiting the elderly builds up treasure in heaven."

By that reckoning, Dinah's heavenly account was in great shape. She had to smile at Elsie's description of Rebecca as "elderly." They were only half a dozen years apart, and in Dinah's opinion her mother was a lot closer to "elderly" than Rebecca Quinn, who ran her own business with calm competence and lived in a beautiful house. The thought of the sunny, spacious apartment on the top floor recently vacated by Julia McNeill was enough to set Dinah's teeth on edge with envy. What she wouldn't give to be able to live independently. If she lived in Rebecca's apartment and got a job again in town, Phinehas wouldn't be able to come and visit. He wouldn't be able to stay with a single woman on her own the way he stayed at her parents' house, and if she were working, the most he'd get out of her would be lunch at a local café.

She would never have to be alone with him again. Ever.

Dreams.

She sighed. She'd given up on dreams. They were as insubstantial as worldly people's cigarette smoke and just as harmful.

REBECCA WAS A little surprised to see Dinah on her doorstep, but she hid it well. Evidently she'd had a lot of practice at being the recipient of Sunday afternoon visits.

"How lovely to see you, Dinah." She shook hands cordially. "Are you here to ask about the apartment? Because if you are, of course, I can't transact business on the Lord's day."

Dinah stared at her. Was she so transparent? If she showed her feelings about something as simple as an apartment, what might she show about things that were terrible in their importance?

"N-no," she stammered. She sat down a little heavily on Rebecca's English chintz couch. If she ever were to have an apartment, she'd have furniture just like this. Comfortable, with beautiful roses printed on it. And lots of yellow. She would love to be able to live with yellow, even if wearing it wasn't permitted. "I just came by to—to bring you some eggs and see how you were."

Eggs. I need to take some to the Blanchards, too. Mustn't forget.

"How kind of you." Rebecca took the eggs and stowed them carefully in the refrigerator. "But really, I should be visiting you. How is your mother?" She sat in the easy chair opposite Dinah.

"She's holding up as well as can be expected. Aunt Margaret and Uncle John are a great comfort to her. And so is Phinehas, of course."

She felt like a parrot, mouthing the same lines to everyone she met.

"And what about you?"

"Me?"

"Yes. How are you doing? I imagine the burden of making everyone comfortable is falling on you."

Dinah wondered if such graceful honesty was the product of age or experience. She wished she could say what she thought, just once. What a relief it must be to take control of your own words and scatter them where you wanted to, without fear of the consequences.

"I'm all right," she said at last.

"It's a pity you're not interested in the apartment," Rebecca mused, her alert blue gaze never leaving Dinah's face, her spine straight, her hair a perfect cloud of silver around her head. "I need a tenant and most of the girls in town are too young."

Temptation opened its sharp jaws and bit Dinah hard. "I have no way to pay the rent, Rebecca," she choked out. "I had to leave my job at the bank when Dad got so bad."

"I'm in need of an assistant at the bookshop. Julia gave me lots of notice, and I've had a number of applicants since she went to Seattle, but I've been waiting for just the right person. Not everyone can put up with me, you see."

She smiled, and Dinah's throat closed with sorrow and gratitude and frustration at the unfairness of life. Rebecca was offering her everything she wanted as casually as some people said "Pass the butter." And she had no choice but to refuse.

But not just yet. In a moment. She wanted to savor the sweetness of the offer and its possibilities, just for a moment.

"Do you hear from Julia?" she whispered.

"Yes, regularly. I do speak to people who are Out, you know, dear. They were married in January, she and Ross. Did you know?"

Dinah shook her head.

"And little Kailey, his daughter, was flower girl. It was very small and private, with just me and his family there, but they're so happy it filled the whole room. I took lots of pictures, if you'd like to see them."

Dinah stood abruptly. "Thanks very much, but I need to get back home. And thank you for the job offer, but I have so much to do with running the ranch and looking after Mom that I just wouldn't be able to handle working in town as well. I do appreciate your thinking of me."

Barricading herself behind the formal phrases, she got herself out the door and away from Rebecca's concerned, confused gaze. Halfway home she pulled over to the side of the highway next to the lake, in a graveled space where fishermen parked their vehicles. Gripping the steering wheel like a drowning person, she wept all her grief and frustration and envy out into the cooling silence of the car.

It was a well-insulated car. None of the fishermen even looked up.

It took about twenty minutes before she got herself under control, and then a glance into the rearview mirror told her she'd better give it five more. It would be just her luck if some of the Elect passed her on the highway, and what would they think of her red-rimmed eyes, wet face, and trembling mouth?

Maybe they'd think she was grieving her father. But maybe not. She couldn't risk any gossip.

When she finally got home, she found that—a miracle— Elsie had taken it upon herself to start dinner. Wrung out from the emotional storm, Dinah set the table on automatic and only came to life when the roasted chicken, green beans, cauliflower with cheese sauce, and mashed potatoes were dished up and set in front of her. Then she discovered she was ravenous.

After supper, she glanced into the laundry room and remembered she needed to take Matthew Nicholas a plate instead of dividing the leftovers between herself and Sheba. She filled one, covered it with a sheet of plastic, and smuggled it outside under the jacket laid over her arm.

The chickens came running at the happy prospect of a sunset snack, but Sheba was not among them. Dinah convinced them that the plate was not meant for them and tossed them a handful of scratch. Even when she called, "Sheba! Treats!" the black-and-white hen did not appear to take first dibs—the right of the alpha hen—on the snack she loved.

Dinah searched the barn, calling, but her darling was nowhere to be found. Finally, she knocked on the apartment door, and when Matthew Nicholas answered it, handed him the plate absently and said, "Have you seen Sheba? I can't find her anywhere."

As if to remind himself that he had to answer the question

before he could eat, he spread one hand over the plastic. "No. I've been reading all afternoon. Shall I help you look?"

Dinah frowned. "No, I've searched all over already. You don't suppose she got out of the pen, do you?"

"She might have. But the fencing seems very secure."

"I'm going to look. You stay here. My mother would have a fit if she looked out the window and saw a strange man rambling around the place."

"I did shave," he said, straightening. "I look relatively human."

But she was in no mood to trade gentle jokes with him. Sheba was missing. *Please, God, don't let her have been eaten by something. Help me find her. I'll be good, I promise. Just help me find her.*

A search of the yard that extended out to the edge of the woods proved fruitless, but she didn't find a heap of feathers inside the tree line, either. That was a positive sign. Maybe Sheba had gone broody and was hiding a clutch of eggs somewhere.

A second search of the barn turned up some stray eggs, but no Sheba. Someone had to have seen her.

"Mom?" Inside, she pushed open her mother's bedroom door and found her lying back on the pillows, a cloth over her eyes. "Have you seen Sheba anytime today? I can't find her anywhere."

Elsie stirred and moaned. "Keep your voice down, dear." Her voice was weak. "I did a little too much this afternoon. My head hurts. Who or what is Sheba?"

"My alpha hen. The big black-and-white Wyandotte. She seems to be missing."

"You have names for them?"

"Mom, of course. They all know their own, too. Chickens are smart. But have you seen her anytime today? Like when you went outside?"

"If it's that big black-and-white one," her mother sighed, "yes, I've seen it."

"Oh, good. Where did—"

"I had Uncle John butcher it for dinner. The Bible says we're to provide our best for the Lord. That bird was so big and fat, and you know how Phinehas loves a nice roast chicken."

THE SCREAM FROM inside the house pierced even the walls of the barn.

Alarmed, Matthew dropped the ancient issue of *Western Cattleman* he'd found in the tack room and leaped off the bed. In the open area of the barn, the chickens were standing up on their roosts and murmuring uneasily.

The back door slammed and he ran to the nearest window, being careful to keep out of sight in case the person running down the steps was not Dinah.

But it was. Her arms flapped, her legs pumped, and her mouth was frozen in a silent scream as she tore across the yard and around the corner of the barn. He dashed to the door that opened on the side facing the mountain and yanked it open in time to see Dinah fall to her knees on the rubbish pile with a howl that made the hair stand up on the back of his neck.

She vomited violently on the ground. She didn't even bother to wipe her mouth as she reached over the rubbish heap and picked up a limp object with both hands, cradling it as if it had been a child or a small creature.

He stepped outside and moved closer to get a better look. With a jolt, he realized what she held.

It was the head and neck of a chicken. Black-and-white feathers covered it. Feathers that were still glossy and thick.

Sheba.

He had known she was attached to her birds. But he hadn't known that attachment went this deep. This was the grief of a mother for her child. Or of a lonely child for her only friend.

Oh, God. Oh, dear God. Tell me what to do.

He moved without thinking, putting himself between the unknown threat and the trembling, weeping woman in the rubbish who was stroking the bird's head with gentle fingers. The warm, sharp smell of vomit and rotting vegetables billowed into his nostrils as he knelt beside her. He hesitated, then placed an arm around her shoulders.

"Dinah."

With a shriek, she jumped to one side and scrambled to her feet, clutching the limp object to her chest with hands that were streaked with its blood.

"They *killed* her! They killed Sheba, my sweet girl, the only thing in this whole world that I care about—they killed her and served her up to him for dinner!"

"I'm so sorry. How is it possible?"

She glared at him, wild eyed. "Why didn't you stop them? Why didn't you do something? You must have heard them catch her and take her away!"

The last thing he wanted was to be shoved into the enemy camp. "I must have been asleep. I did nod off this afternoon while you were out. And even if I hadn't been, I'm not supposed to show myself, am I?"

"Who cares?" she shouted. "You could have saved her life!"

He couldn't explain the futility of a homeless man attempting to stop a property owner from butchering one of her own chickens in her own yard. But neither could he say such a thing to Dinah.

"I'm so sorry," he said again. "I should have done something." What else could he say? He'd had his moments of feeling inadequate and voiceless in the past, but not like this.

"No," she moaned, the fire dying as suddenly as it had roared into hysterical life. "I should have been here. It's my fault. I let myself be tempted by the apartment and this is what happened. My poor, poor darling. She was punished instead of me." She stroked the pitiful remains of her pet, and even though he didn't quite understand what she meant, Matthew's heart squeezed with compassion.

"Come," he said. "We need to give her a decent burial. She deserves better than the rubbish heap."

"Yes," she whispered. "She does."

As Dinah sat on a fallen log and crooned over her lost bird, Matthew dug a deep hole near a big rock in the trees, where no one at the house could see what was going on. When he finished, he leaned on the shovel and took a brief inventory of his vital signs. His strength must be returning. He wasn't even panting.

Dinah wrapped Sheba's remains in a cloth she'd found in the barn and laid the little bundle in the hole with careful tenderness.

"Would you like to say a few words?" he asked. "Or shall I pray?"

"No," she said, still on her knees. "Even though she was more human than those people down there."

"I think that might cover it." His smile was gentle and sad, and she held his gaze. Sorrow and anger fought with a newborn sense of recognition in her eyes. Recognition of what, he wasn't sure. Companionship, perhaps? Complicity?

He held a hand out to her, and she took it and got to her feet. Then her face seemed to waver and dissolve and she began to cry, with the huge, heaving sobs of a small child who has not yet learned control, hugging herself and rocking back and forth.

Matthew filled the hole in much less time than it had taken to dig it, tamped the soil down hard, and leaned the shovel against the rock. Then he stepped over to Dinah and wrapped his arms around her. He wasn't sure whether she would accept his comfort, but something in her complete abandonment of control made him offer what little he could.

She sobbed against his chest for a few seconds, then seemed to recollect where she was. With a gasp, she jerked away. She would not meet his eyes. Wiping her cheeks with the heel of her hand, still hiccuping a little, she set off across the field to the house and did not look back.

I'M HERE FOR *you,* the river whispered.

Dinah made sure the windows were locked so she couldn't hear its siren call, and then, for the first time in years, locked her bedroom door as well.

She stood on the hooked rug in front of the bed and stared at the white chenille bedspread with loathing.

What good was prayer?

She didn't want to talk to anyone, especially not God. God was a big angry man in a toga, sitting on a cloud and throwing lightning bolts and disaster at people. No matter how often you crawled to him, no matter how often you begged for some good thing, you never got it. He just kept dishing out the punishment until finally there was only one thing left to do.

She was going to take her life away from him.

Sheba had been practically the only thing tethering her to the earth, anyway. And now that Sheba had been murdered and served up to the one person whom Dinah hated in all the world, there was absolutely no point in staying.

But first, she had to do something.

"Dinah?" Aunt Margaret tapped on the door. "It's time to go to Mission, dear. Are you ready?"

Dinah glanced at the clock and realized she'd been standing immobile on the rug for fifteen minutes. "I'm not going, Auntie."

"Why not, dear? Are you sick?" Sickness or death were the only reasons for not going to Mission. Anything else was self-indulgent and sinful. "Elsie isn't going," her aunt went on. "A migraine, poor dear. She can't even lift her head."

Dinah's mouth thinned. "No, I'm not sick."

"If it's about your chicken, dear, Uncle John is very sorry. But think of it this way: you gave of your best to the Lord."

She'd been giving her best to the Lord her whole life, and it had netted her nothing but the demand for more. She'd offered her pearls to the swine again and again, and all they'd done was dash them from her hand and trample them in the mud. Well, it was time to pick them up and, if she couldn't wear them openly, at least she'd put them in her pocket where they'd be safe.

"I understand you might be angry at your uncle, but Mission is a good place to forgive and find forgiveness."

The platitude scraped Dinah's feelings like fingernails on a blackboard. She gripped her self-control. "Give my greetings to Melchizedek, Auntie."

"You're sure you're not coming?"

"I'm sure."

A silence. Maybe Aunt Margaret didn't know how to deal with such obvious sin. "All right, dear. I'll think of you in my prayers."

Sinful people needed to be prayed for. Dinah refused to feel guilty at the gentle rebuke. She waited, as motionless as the rock standing guard over Sheba's grave, until both Phinehas's car and her aunt and uncle's sedan pulled out of the driveway and hummed off down the road to town.

Then she went down the hall and pulled open her mother's bedroom door.

Elsie peeked out from under the cloth over her eyes. "Dinah? Why are you still home? Are you sick?"

"Neither of us is really sick, Mom."

Her mother groaned and let her head fall back on the embroidered pillow. "You can't even imagine how awful these headaches are. Sometimes I don't think I'll survive until morning. The pain is just blinding."

"Blinding. That pretty much describes it."

Elsie pulled the cloth away and frowned at her. "What's the

matter, dear? If you have one, take one of these pills Dr. Archer prescribes." She indicated the bottle on the night table.

"I don't want a pill. I need to talk to you."

"If it's about that chicken, I have nothing more to say. We did the right thing in God's service, and if you weren't so selfish, you'd see that." Elsie shook the cloth out and refolded it lengthwise.

"Serving up my best friend to Phinehas was the right thing?"

"Chickens are not meant to be friends. They're farm animals. You set your affections too much on things of this earth, Dinah, and then you get upset and blame other people when you have to sacrifice them."

"When other people sacrifice them for me, you mean."

"Can you run cold water over this for me, dear?"

"I need you to listen to me."

"Dinah Miriam Traynell, I don't like your tone."

"Sorry, Mom, but I'm at the end of my rope. You know why you have these migraines?"

Her mother eyed her with dislike. "I suppose you have medical training, do you? If Dr. Archer couldn't tell me, I don't suppose you can."

"How about willful blindness, Mom? Maybe you're getting blinding headaches because you've blinded yourself to what's going on."

"What?"

"Oh, come on. Don't tell me you don't know. That you haven't known for years."

"Know what? Honestly, Dinah, I don't know what's wrong with you. This chicken business has unhinged you."

"Maybe that's a good thing. Maybe some hinges need to come off some closed doors around here."

Her mother moved fretfully. "I don't understand one word you're saying. If you're not going to help me and get me a cold cloth, then go back to your room until you can talk sense.

Goodness knows I don't want you behaving this way when John and Margaret and Phinehas get home."

"Mother, look me in the eye and tell me you don't know what Phinehas has been doing to me. That he's been using me as his mistress for years. Tell me you didn't know."

Elsie stared at her. "What?"

"Tell me why you never once came to help me. Tell me that you never heard him in my room. Or saw him touch me." Her voice shook.

"You are saying wicked, wicked things," her mother hissed. "How dare you say such things about a man of God?"

"He isn't a man of God. He puts on that holy face on Sunday and you'd never know how much he hurt me Saturday night. He raped me for the first time when I was fourteen, Mom. And he's continued to do it every time he visited. You keep inviting him back and he keeps doing it. I don't set my affections on the things of this earth, Mom, but I sure wish you would."

Elsie clapped her hands over her ears. "I will not allow you to say such things!"

Dinah pulled her mother's soft hands away and hung onto them. "You're going to put a stop to it now. I want you to send him away and never let him stay here again. I want you to stand up for me for once in your life. Please, Mom."

"You are a wicked, sinful girl. You should be praying for him, not saying such horrible things. If you let things like that into your mind, you let them into the Kingdom. Think about that, Dinah!"

Dinah flung Elsie's hands to the coverlet. "It's already in the Kingdom. You've known about it right from the start. You never stopped him when we had our private little Bible studies together, did you? You and Dad never let yourselves hear him going down the hall to my room at night."

Her mother's mouth worked, but no sounds came out. Her eyes were wide with shock and betrayal.

"It hurts, Mom." Dinah fisted a hand over her heart. "It hurts worse than anything, to know that you could have stopped it and didn't. What I'd like to know is, why?" She dragged in a breath and said it at last. "Why didn't you act like a proper mother and protect me? Do you hate me that much?"

Elsie's eyes bulged, and her skin, normally pale from too much time indoors, drained of color even further and turned gray. "You—woman—stop it—" she croaked.

"First you send Tamara away, and now it's my—Mom?"

With a groan that sounded nothing like the invalid moan she'd pretended to make earlier, Elsie toppled sideways. Her head clunked the nightstand with a dreadful sound that brought Dinah out of the red haze of rage.

"Mom?"

Staring, horrified, at her mother's awkwardly bent body, Dinah found the phone by touch alone and dialed 9-1-1.

Chapter 6

FOR THE SECOND time that evening, a screaming sound brought Matthew up off the bed. He dashed over to the window that overlooked the yard. This time it wasn't a human. The ambulance skidded to a stop in the gravel and EMTs leaped out, prepared their equipment, and hustled up the steps.

Not Dinah.

Then he saw her silhouetted in the light from the kitchen doorway as she let them in. He watched and waited, wondering what in the world was happening, wondering if he should go and offer his help. Ten minutes later they came out again with someone on a gurney.

He had no idea who it was, but it wasn't Dinah.

Matthew wasn't quite sure what made him think she'd need an ambulance. She'd seemed calm enough after they'd buried Sheba's . . . well, after they'd buried Sheba. But he knew enough about fear and grief to believe that a calm exterior could hide towering agony, made worse because it couldn't be shown. Oh yes, he knew all about that.

But it wasn't just the volcano of emotion he'd seen inside a woman who looked fragile enough to be damaged by a single touch. No, it was this whole ranch. Anxiety and rage seemed to hover over it, even when the sun came out from behind the cloud cover that bumped up hard against the mountain. Look at the last few days. There had been a death, a funeral, a wake, a murder of sorts, and now some other tragedy in the form of a medical emergency.

He was getting a little tired of hiding while hell broke loose all around him. He pulled a jacket off a nail in the tack room—probably her father's—and crossed the yard to the house.

"Dinah?" He knocked gently on the screen door, and when no one answered, pushed it open. "Are you here?"

No reply.

He entered the kitchen cautiously, though he knew her relatives had not returned yet. "Dinah?"

Moving more quickly now, he looked into the dining room, the living room, and even the bathroom and the spare bedroom. Then he climbed the stairs, worry blooming under his breastbone with each step into the upper darkness of the house. A quick look in all the rooms proved them to be empty, but the disarray of the fussy embroidered pillows and the quilted coverlet of the one in the back told him that it might have been her mother who had gone in the ambulance.

He was positive she had not gone with it. The car was in town with her aunt and uncle. That meant she had to be here somewhere.

In the front bedroom, where a single suitcase lay on the floor, its contents as orderly and neat as a shop window, he glanced out at the view. The moon had come up, and by its light he saw a small, dark figure march across the road in the direction of the river.

In just that way—grimly, a woman on a mission—she had walked away from him across the field, and mayhem had been the result.

"Oh, no," he breathed. "Lord, what is she doing? Help me get there first, dear Father."

He took the stairs three at a time and burst out the front door without bothering to close it behind him. He made a few seconds' time on the asphalt of the road, but the trees that stood between him and the river, though sparse and thin, held him up. The tussocky grass and the uneven banks where the river had changed direction deceived and tripped him.

He was still fifty yards away when, in the hard, silver moonlight, he saw her kick off her ugly, low-heeled shoes and toss her barn jacket on the sandbar.

"No, Lord. Don't let her. Please don't let her do it."

His breath scraped in his chest like shards of ice, and he heaved and gasped as he staggered toward the sandbar. He wasn't going to make it in time.

"Dinah!"

The rushing of the river drowned out his voice, and she waded in without glancing back, totally focused on whatever dreadful thoughts were in her mind.

The water burst around her knees and then her thighs, pulling relentlessly on her dress. She could hardly keep her footing. Then she spread her arms wide and dropped into the current as gracefully and inevitably as a tree falling.

There was no room in his head for a thought of his own danger. Matthew dragged in as much air as his lungs could hold, and plunged in after her.

DINAH HAD A split second to hope that her head would hit a big rock right away before the underwater roar of the river filled her ears and somersaulted her like a rag doll. Something whacked her ankle, hard, and she fought the temptation to curl into a ball to minimize the damage.

It didn't matter what happened to her body. Should she breathe in, was the question. She was holding her breath by instinct, but that defeated the whole point.

Ouch! Her shoulder scraped the gravel on the bottom and she felt a sudden freedom that meant the sleeve had given way. Her skirts had reversed up over her head.

Can't breathe. Need air.

No. Breathe water. It will be over soon.

Something grabbed the fabric wrapped around her neck and jerked violently. Oh, good. A snag would hold her down.

Over soon.

Alive. Whatever was holding onto her was alive. Animal?

She pushed at it and it pushed back, and suddenly her head broke the surface, but fabric was pasted to her face like a mask. With a groan, she tried to drag in a breath and got a mouthful of wet material instead.

"Dinah! Stop it!" somebody said, and suddenly she was upended face down, her cheek mashed into cold gravel. The sopping mask was torn away and she gasped and coughed, heaving on the ground, sucking in sand and pine needles with every breath.

She coughed and spat out a mouthful of water.

"Are you all right? Can you speak?"

Matthew.

A burst of anger so hot it was like a blood transfusion rocketed through her, and she pushed herself up on both hands. On all fours like an animal, she glared at him.

"What did you do that for?" She'd meant to scream, but it came out as a hoarse whisper. "Leave me alone."

She pushed herself to her feet and staggered toward the water. Rocks. That's what they did in the old days, didn't they? Weighted themselves down with rocks. She should have thought of that before.

She glanced around to choose a couple of likely ones, but he tackled her around the waist and dragged her back. He sat her forcefully on a beached log.

"I will not allow you to do this!"

She'd never seen him angry. He had seemed so gentle and unassuming and hopeless about life. She hadn't known he had it in him.

Well, well. Hinges were popping off doors all over today.

"If you can't think about yourself," he said, "at least think about your poor mother. And your relatives. What do you think they'll do with you gone?"

She rolled her eyes. "I don't care. And they don't care about me." She slid off the log, but he grabbed her and sat her down on it again.

"Don't touch me!"

"Don't go near the river again, and I won't."

"Who do you think you are, telling me what to do?"

That stopped him.

And then she was sorry. His eyes filled with pain.

"I thought I was your friend. If you don't care about your family, at least spare a thought for me."

"Why should I? I never knew you before this week."

Pain flickered over his face. Turning away, he crossed the sandbar and retrieved her shoes and barn jacket. She pushed sopping hair out of her face and realized that her underwater journey had only been a matter of twenty or thirty feet. The river took a curve around the bar, and the eddy had probably been the only thing that had prevented them both from washing all the way down to Hamilton Falls. It had pulled them in here and allowed Matthew to find his footing.

She hadn't thought about the geography. She should have planned it better and gone upriver a bit, to the canyon and rapids. All those big rocks would have done the job properly.

Matthew crunched and squished his way back to her and wrapped the jacket around her shoulders. The contrast between the heavy fabric and her clammy skin made her realize how cold the night was. The air fell into her lungs like snow.

"Come on. We need to get you dry and warm."

Next time, she'd make sure he was out of the way, and then she'd walk to the canyon.

It felt good to have a backup plan.

THEY LEFT A twin trail of puddles on the kitchen floor.

"In here." Matthew pushed open the guest bathroom and turned on the shower. "Get out of these clothes."

Panic exploded under her ribs, and she wrenched away. "No!"

"Dinah, I'm only trying to—"

"Get away from me." She slammed the bathroom door in his face.

"I'll be right out here if you need me. Just don't try any funny business in that tub."

She locked the door and stood in the middle of the room, holding her elbows and shivering. She'd felt such a sense of freedom when the river carried her away. No more feelings. Just the calmness of impending death. And now? Hot, angry tears pooled in her eyes as she peeled her dress, slip, and underwear away and dropped them in a pile that smelled of river weed and despair.

Stupid man. If she'd wanted to drown in the stupid bathtub she'd have done it ages ago.

Her aunt's shampoo and lavender-scented soap were in the shower caddy, so she used them. She caught herself inhaling the crisp scent with a sense of surprise. She'd always thought Aunt Margaret smelled like an old lady. Now she wondered if her aunt took this quiet pleasure in lavender soap, and that was why she used it.

Not the kind of thing you asked Aunt Margaret. She would never admit to pandering to her flesh in such a way.

Dinah rinsed and dried off, and then realized she had nothing to put on.

Was he gone?

She put her ear to the door. Silence. "Mr. Nicholas?"

A voice came from at least a room away. "I would think that the depth of our acquaintance, if not its length, would allow you to use my given name. I went and got your robe. It's on the door handle."

She unlocked the door and kept her body behind it while she felt the handle outside. Her fingers encountered soft cotton and she dragged it into the bathroom. She re-locked the door and wrapped the pink-and-white sprigged dressing gown tightly around herself.

She didn't want to go out there. The bathroom was a steamy, warm little haven, and it had a lock. Outside was a man who had ignored her wishes and made her take back her life, and she hadn't forgiven him for it or figured out why he'd done it.

"Dinah?" he called. Closer. He was in the kitchen. "Are you all right? I'm making a pot of tea if you'd like some."

Tea? Hunger hollowed her belly. She could consume an entire steak dinner and ask for seconds. But tea did sound warm and comforting.

"Dinah?"

"Yes. Please."

"And since neither of us has eaten, I took the liberty of warming up the last of this excellent casserole."

That brought her out of the bathroom. He had pushed the correct buttons on the microwave without even asking her how. In less time than it took to think about it, she and her hired hand were facing each other across the kitchen table. Matthew bowed his head.

"Lord, I'm very thankful for this food, and especially that Dinah is still here to eat it with me. Bless us both, and give us the strength to endure. Amen."

What an odd grace. But he was a worldly man, so it was to be expected.

He passed her the casserole and poured a mug of tea, stirring in milk and two spoonfuls of sugar before he handed it to her. "Now, would you like to talk about what took you down there, or are we going to be frightfully British and ignore the whole thing?"

Despite herself, she smiled. "In the most polite manner possible, I'm going to say 'Mind your own business.'"

He shook his head, and dished up his own meal. "Fishing people out of rivers makes them my business. It would be terribly unfair of you to make me go to all that work and not tell me what caused it. Was it your mother?"

Her fork paused in midair. "My mother?"

"Yes, wasn't it she who went away in the ambulance? You'll notice I'm making no comment whatsoever on your not going away with it."

"I told her something she didn't want to hear and she collapsed."

He gazed at her for several long seconds. "Your mother collapsed because of something you said?" he asked at last. "Do you mind sharing what it was?"

"Yes."

Her own chewing sounded like an army marching in her head, compared to the silent kitchen.

"Sometimes it's best to talk to an objective third party. It prevents painful things from lodging in one's insides."

"You sound experienced."

"I am."

"Tell me about it."

"I'm not the one in the river."

"Neither am I, no thanks to you. Give me that casserole, please." She eyed it, the yawning emptiness inside her demanding that she eliminate everything on the table.

He handed it to her, and she scraped what was left onto her plate.

"I'm not going to apologize for pulling you out of there, no matter how much you resent me for it."

"Just don't do it again. More tea, please."

He poured her another cup, added milk and sugar, and gave her a lie-detector sort of look. She'd never actually seen a lie detector, but a look like this demanded honesty.

"Again? Are you likely to try?"

"That's my choice, isn't it?"

He nodded, and turned back to his food. She wondered if he was going to eat it all. "Unfortunately, it's always our choice to turn our backs on God."

She snorted. "I've been staring at his back for so long I doubt he'd notice."

"You feel God has turned his back on you?"

"I don't just feel. I know."

"How?"

She set her fork down with a clatter. "Let me count the ways. He gives me my parents. Then Phinehas. Then what Phinehas does to me. Then he takes away my sister. Then Sheba. Then, when I finally get a grip and take something away from him for once, there you are, doing your heroic best to give it back to him. Can you blame me for being a little annoyed with you?"

Her throat hurt from shouting and her heart pounded. Despite the fact that her stomach was full, she shoveled more casserole into her mouth and washed it down with tea.

"What Phinehas does to you?" Matthew repeated.

She shouldn't have lost her temper. "Yes."

"Phinehas, the preacher, or whatever he is?"

"Shepherd."

"What does he do to you?" When she didn't answer, he said, "That was what you told your mother, wasn't it?"

What was the point in keeping the secret any more? Or in shoving her soul into dark closets so Phinehas could walk around enjoying God's favor? In a few days it wouldn't matter.

She would be back at the river and Phinehas could just live with the consequences of his own actions. She would be free.

"Yes," she said.

"Is he doing something you don't like?" The question was phrased so delicately that she nearly smiled.

"He raped me when I was fourteen." Her tone was matter-of-fact. "He's been raping me during every visit ever since. I'm positive my parents knew about it, but they kept their mouths shut because we're one of the favored families."

He was staring at her in horror, and she went on anyway. Punishing herself. Punishing him for asking. And yet, she had the same feeling as she had when she surrendered to the river. That same sense of freedom, just by speaking out loud the secret that had been bottled under her breastbone for ten years.

"As far as God is concerned, I was brought up to believe I have to be perfect for him. So I was. I was the best-behaved, most modestly dressed little girl in the whole congregation. I knew there were two sets of eyes on me—the Elect's and God's. Everyone thinks I have nothing on my mind but serving God, visiting old people, and bringing food to the ones that need it. The young people hate me. I have no friends. Only Sh—the chickens."

She got up and took her plate to the sink. "Phinehas told me I was set apart, a princess of Israel, a vessel made for the love of God, expressed through his most holy servant. And I believed him. Even when he made me take my clothes off. Even after the first time it happened." She turned to face him, throwing the ugly words in his face like rocks. "Then he told me it was my fault for being so pretty. He couldn't help himself. And it had to be our secret, because God told him that was my purpose. Not being somebody's wife or mother someday. My purpose in life was to satisfy him so he could keep on preaching the gospel."

"Dinah—" he whispered.

"It took me years, but I finally figured out it was a lie." She stared at him, challenging him. "You probably think I'm stupid, but you're not Elect. You don't know what it's like. Phinehas is the mouthpiece of God, so you know what? God's a liar, too. He just keeps hurting me and hurting me. But I'm going to put a stop to it. And you're not getting in my way next time."

She turned her back on him. The plate slipped from her hands and landed in the sink with a clatter, but it didn't break. She wished it had.

Ten seconds of silence ticked by. She'd probably shocked him. It wasn't Matthew's fault. He was just standing in for men in general—and besides, he'd asked. If he didn't want to know the ugliness that was her life, he shouldn't have questioned her.

She threw a glance over her shoulder.

He sat motionless at the table, his hands resting on his thighs, empty palms up.

Tears trickled down a face that was seamed with grief. His eyes were full of compassion and pain.

He was crying.

For her.

Chapter 7

TWO SETS OF car doors slammed outside. Dinah jumped. Matthew palmed the moisture from his face with one hand and pushed his chair back.

"They shouldn't find me here," he said.

"I've changed my mind." Dinah was still staring at him, wonder and confusion in her eyes, as if she couldn't quite believe he had broken down so completely. "I've legally hired you. There's no reason you shouldn't be in the kitchen."

"You'll need to tell them about your mother."

She looked away at last. He wondered how a woman could go through so much and yet show so little emotion. The only times he had seen her break out of her rigid control had been at the rubbish pile, on the riverbank, and just now, when she'd shouted her terrible truth at him.

"I know. And you'll keep the rest of it quiet, won't you?"

"Of course. But you have to call the police and report this Phinehas person."

"No!"

That was all she had time for before the back door opened and her aunt and uncle came in. When the third person stepped out from behind them and removed his wool coat, Matthew had to struggle to control a scalding spill of disgust, deep in his gut.

The man was tall and spare and carried himself with patrician dignity. His hair was silver, waving over his brow and skillfully cut to lie close to his ears. Blue eyes glanced swiftly around the kitchen, taking in its occupants and stopping, finally, on Matthew himself. His mouth, its ascetic lips folded in disciplined lines, tipped down at both corners.

"Dinah," he said. He looked her up and down, from the wet hair streaming down her back to the flowered bathrobe to the slippers on her bare feet.

She stopped scrubbing something in the sink. "Yes? Would you like some tea?"

"I understood you weren't well."

"I'm fine." She ran water into the electric kettle and plugged it in.

"We missed you at the service. God's blessing was poured out upon all of us."

Matthew stared from one to the other. With all that had happened, all he chose to note was that Dinah had missed a service?

"But I see you have company," Phinehas went on, "though you're rather informally dressed." He paused expectantly.

Matthew stood up. "Matthew Nicholas." He offered a hand, though he'd rather have extended it to a snake. At least a snake's poison had a reason for being.

Phinehas shook it. "I am Phinehas, Shepherd of the flock of God in Washington State. May I ask your purpose here?"

Matthew chose not to reply right away. The pompous wretch could wait a moment. He introduced himself to Dinah's relatives, and then said, "Miss Traynell has just hired me. I understand her father passed away not long ago, and she needs someone to do the outside work."

"Hired you?" John Traynell asked.

"Yes. It's a lucky thing she had someone here to help—I'm afraid her mother was taken ill this evening while you were gone. The ambulance came and took her to—" He glanced at Dinah.

"Valley General," she said.

"Goodness gracious," Margaret said breathlessly. "What was it? Is she all right?"

"The EMTs said it might be a stroke," Dinah said.

"What are we all doing? We should be down there. Come on, John."

"Dinah looks to be in shock," Phinehas said gently. "Someone should stay with her. I'll stay behind for now and then go over in the morning. Call as soon as you know how Elsie is."

"Thank you, Phinehas," Margaret said, and took her husband's arm. "Come *on,* John. I knew that migraine was a sign of something more serious. My stars, what a week this has been."

The kettle was boiling hard and no one was paying any attention. Matthew unplugged it, poured out the cold tea in the pot, and put in two new teabags. Steam warmed his hands as he poured the boiling water.

"Such an unfortunate shock." Phinehas walked into the adjoining dining room and pulled out the chair at the head of the table. "You'll be so thankful to have the kind of faith that can sustain you at a time like this, Dinah."

She made a noise that could be understood as agreement. Opening the fridge, she pulled out an uncut pie and dished up three portions. Before Matthew could eat more than a forkful or two she had wolfed hers down.

"What happened, exactly?" Phinehas ate his pie much more slowly, licking each crumb of pastry off his lips before taking another bite.

"We don't know anything more than what the EMTs said," Matthew answered.

"Dinah?"

Matthew set his teeth at the delicate snub.

"That's all." She took another piece of pie and ate it just as quickly. "They said she'd pull through, that it wasn't a severe one."

"Thank God for that. Are you going to the hospital?"

For the first time, she looked up. "I don't know. There's nothing I can do tonight."

"You can show your care for your mother at her bedside."

"I don't think they let people in intensive care," Matthew put in. "Not until they're stabilized. It's not likely Dinah's aunt and uncle will learn much once they arrive."

Phinehas turned a thoughtful gaze on him. Matthew returned it calmly.

"Perhaps you're right. An early night and an early start would likely be the best plan. Where are you staying, Mr. Nicholas? I believe all the rooms in the house are occupied."

"In the apartment in the barn."

"The barn?" One eyebrow rose, then fell. "Ah."

Matthew could practically see the wheels turning behind that bland expression. *You sanctimonious old fraud. Well, Dinah isn't as alone and defenseless as you think.*

"My duties include acting as night watchman," he said, keeping his tone friendly and bland. "I hope you won't be alarmed if you hear me doing my rounds during the night."

"Night watchman? What do you need one of those for, Dinah?"

She turned innocent eyes on him. "You wouldn't have heard, Phinehas. There have been cattle thefts lately, sometimes right out of the home corrals. I know most of our animals are up in the spring pasture, but it was worrying Dad before he passed away. And then the folks at the next place had their home broken into a few days ago. I'm very glad Mr. Nicholas is here. It makes me feel safe."

It was one of the longest speeches Matthew had ever heard her make. And if Phinehas had a brain in his head he'd count the cost and realize chances were good he'd be caught if he made an attempt on her door tonight.

How any human being could take advantage of a woman as physically and emotionally fragile as this one was a complete mystery to him. She deserved protection and care. She didn't deserve to be the tool that an overwhelming selfishness used for its own gratification. Matthew clamped his molars together in an effort not to lunge across the table for the man's throat.

"I'm glad," Phinehas said simply, with a fond look. He pushed his plate away. "And now I believe I'll spend some time in prayer and thanksgiving for the service tonight, and plead for Elsie's recovery."

When he left the room, Matthew turned to look at Dinah. The tension seeped slowly out of her, leaving her limp in her chair.

"Excuse me." She went into the bathroom, and a few moments later he heard the toilet flush. When she came back into the room, she smelled of breath freshener.

"Have you seen a doctor about that?" he inquired softly.

"About what?" She reached for her cooling mug of tea and swallowed it.

"I believe the disorder is called *bulimia*."

She gazed at him, her eyelids drooping with exhaustion, and didn't answer.

"In my last position we were trained on how to spot various things that affect young people, and eating disorders was one of them. I think it would be helpful if you talked to someone about it."

"I think it would be helpful if you minded your own business."

Humiliation burned his cheeks. He had only known this girl for a couple of days, and already she had driven him to extremes of behavior he would not have believed possible a week ago. Digging graves. Underwater rescues. Standing up to evil cloaked

in godliness. Her blunt words seemed to negate all that, to reduce him to . . . well, the status of a hired hand.

"I beg your pardon," he said, feeling as foolishly British as he
no doubt sounded. He put his plate in the sink and made sure
the kitchen door did not slam as he closed it behind him.

Dινah had fully expected God to strike her dead for
lying to Phinehas and making up such outrageous stories about
cattle thefts and break-ins. Or, at the very least, she had expected
Phinehas to see right into her miserable soul and catch her out.
The punishment would end up being the same.

But neither of them did. Instead, Phinehas had gone to his
room without telegraphing his usual intent, and she had known
the lie had worked. For tonight at least, she was safe. Maybe
there was an advantage to having God's back turned on her.
He'd actually missed an opportunity.

However, she'd wound up punishing herself. She'd hurt
Matthew's feelings, and now, at two in the morning, when she'd
heard measured footsteps moving around the house, a glance
out the window had told her he was holding up his side of their
unrehearsed lie and actually performing the duties of a night
watchman.

She'd be thankful if she didn't feel so bad. Okay, he was
wrong about the bulimia. She had every right to control her di-
gestive system, that was all. She certainly had no control over
anything else. Without a word being said, the expectations of
the congregation dictated how she dressed and did her hair.
Phinehas controlled her body. The only things that belonged to
her were her stomach and her mind, and sometimes she wondered about the latter.

She'd tried to stop throwing up. She'd keep meals down for
maybe two or three days at a time. But then Phinehas would
turn up unexpectedly or her father would lay down another

rule, and she'd run to the fridge to fill up the empty hole inside her, and reassert control by tossing everything up again.

Was it even possible to stop? She didn't know. And seeing a doctor was so ridiculous it just emphasized how ignorant Matthew was about their ways. Michael Archer was Elect. He was the only doctor they all went to see, and if Matthew's wrong ideas were ever repeated to him, he'd be out here visiting with her mother before you could say "mentally disturbed." Her mother would deny it and then proceed to make her life miserable with questions and complaints and lectures about how she was attracting attention to herself and bringing disgrace on God's Holy Flock.

Again.

IN THE MORNING Aunt Margaret had the report of her mother's condition. "She was in ICU so we weren't allowed to see her last night, but dear Dr. Archer said that we should be able to today. They revived her in the ambulance and she's conscious and able to speak. He says it will take a while for her facial muscles to respond, but she should recover those in time."

She and Uncle John were going back down at noon. "There's room in the car for you, Dinah. You don't need to go down there by yourself."

So of course there was no getting out of it. The last thing she wanted to do was see the wreck she'd made of her mother. She was torn between satisfaction that she'd finally made her listen and misery because she hadn't meant to give her a stroke. But that was just like Mom—to escape a reality she didn't like by getting sick. Down deep she loved her mother, wanted her approval. Somehow that was part of the problem, all wrapped into the Gordian knot in her middle—the knowledge that if her mother silently approved of what Phinehas was doing, then maybe she should allow it.

But that was sick, and wrong. And it was too late now, anyway. She'd been lucky last night. Phinehas had been taken off guard by Matthew's unexpected appearance. He would want to reassert his authority tonight. There was nothing she could do about it.

When she'd finally mustered the courage to refuse him last summer, he'd told her in the gentlest way possible, his hands soft on her skin, that she needed to be careful. Word could get out, he'd said, about her unwillingness and disobedience, and her glowing reputation would be shredded by the gossip in less time than it took to warn her about it. And then she would no longer be welcome in Gathering. She might even have to face the Testimony of Two Men—the Elect's way of dealing with profound sin—and be Silenced for seven years, like Tamara. And she'd seen what had happened to her sister, hadn't she?

Oh yes, she'd seen. She knew God hated sin, that his vengeance was severe and complete. But it always seemed that the vengeance fell the heaviest on the women. Look at Rita Ulstad and Julia McNeill, who had been driven Out. Even Tamara had done nothing more terrible than love the wrong person. Their names were not even to be spoken, although she'd noticed that Rebecca had ignored that rule. But what about the men on the other side of all those equations? Where was their punishment? For heaven's sake, Tamara's ex-boyfriend Danny Bell was right here in town, though she hadn't seen him much lately, and he was walking around unpunished and fancy free.

It was obvious God was a member of some exclusive men's club, out to grind women under his heavenly heel. And Phinehas, who was in direct communication with him in a way that mere members of the congregation could not know, was following his august example.

In a world like this, Dinah thanked her lucky stars for the river.

But first, she had to visit her mother.

She followed Uncle John and Aunt Margaret down the

bright hallway to Elsie's room and found Dr. Archer there with her. Dinah leaned over the rail of the bed to kiss her, trying not to look at the clear plastic tubing in her mother's nose and in the back of her hand.

Her mother did not look at her, either.

The visit lasted no more than five minutes, during which Aunt Margaret did most of the talking. When Dinah sat beside the bed and took her mother's hand, with a fretful movement Elsie pulled it away, murmuring something about disturbing the IV.

Well, she deserved that small rejection. She wasn't sorry she'd spoken out. Not one bit. But she was deeply sorry it had sent her mother's blood pressure through the roof and brought this on. And the worst part was there was nothing she could do to fix it. No comfort she could offer. How could she, when there was nothing inside herself but a great big empty hole?

"IT'S JUST SUCH a shame." Aunt Margaret looked out her window on the way home and her mouth set exactly the way Dinah's father's used to, even though they weren't actually re- lated. "That poor woman has gone through more in the last week than many people do in their whole lives."

Dinah sank back against the upholstery in the sedan's back- seat and tried to look invisible.

"Someone has to look after her, and Dinah can't be expected to do everything."

Dinah suddenly had a vision of caring for her invalid mother for twenty years, with visits from Phinehas every few months. Alone forever, with nothing but responsibility and care and pain, until she died.

"What's going on in your head, Meg?" Uncle John flipped on the turn signal and turned onto the highway.

"When she's released, she should come to us," Margaret said firmly. "She should get away from sad memories and recover somewhere where she has no cares and there are new faces around to cheer her up."

Uncle John was the kind of man who never made a decision on the spot. He thought for at least a mile, then glanced in the rearview mirror.

"What do you think about that, Dinah?"

Say the right thing. "I think it would be an awful lot of care and responsibility for you folks. I should look after her. It's my place."

"But you looked after your dad all those weeks when Elsie had that little breakdown, after you got the diagnosis. You need a break, and goodness knows we have a huge house all to ourselves since the kids have married and gone. There's no reason why Elsie couldn't have the downstairs bedroom. And we can take her back and forth to physical therapy and whatnot."

"Aunt Margaret, you're the kindest person in the world, but really—"

"No arguing, Dinah. You're a big girl. You can manage things by yourself for a little while. Then, when your mother is back on her feet, she can come home."

Dinah didn't dare feel thankful or even happy in case God noticed and did something to make Aunt Margaret change her mind.

"Bless your heart, Auntie Meg," she said at last. She hadn't called her that since she was a little girl. "We'll do what you think is best."

Her thoughts rabbited ahead. With her mother gone to Uncle John's, Phinehas would have to leave, and he wouldn't be able to come back while Dinah was alone in the house. It wouldn't look right for a single man and a single woman to share living quarters, even if that man was the Senior Shepherd and a man of God and the woman was a daughter of one of the favored families with a reputation that was beyond reproach. It just wasn't done, and thank goodness for it. She had at least a couple of weeks of blessed solitude, all to herself. No one to criticize what she did or said or wore. No one to manage her time and tasks. No one to make her do things she didn't want to do. She would be in control of herself and her environment for practically the first time in her life.

Suddenly Dinah felt ravenously hungry.

Chapter 8

A TINY FROWN appeared on Phinehas's forehead when Uncle John outlined their plan for Elsie's recovery.

"To your place?" he repeated. "All the way down in Pitchford?"

"It's only ninety miles," Aunt Margaret assured him. "An hour and a half. Less, if John is driving."

"But what if something should go wrong? What if Dinah has to be there right away?"

Dinah continued to straighten and tidy the living room, as invisible as a servant. But she knew what he was thinking. Oh yes. She knew. Her only hope was Aunt Margaret's stubborn loyalty and kindness of heart. That was the only thing that would withstand the roadblocks of gentle disapproval Phinehas was bound to throw up.

"It's just a matter of recovery, Phinehas. Elsie has come through surprisingly well. She's able to speak. Dr. Archer is convinced that with rest and good care, she'll recover completely."

"And her own daughter can't provide this?" The Shepherd's tone balanced between gentle amazement and subtle rebuke, though he did not glance at Dinah.

"Dinah has had enough to deal with. It's time the family

stepped in to assist. Now, I know you're concerned, Phinehas. Of course the Shepherd of our souls has a concern for each sheep in the fold. But this is the best plan for everyone."

Aunt Margaret was so sure of herself that Dinah sensed the moment Phinehas decided to back down and not press the matter. After all, he wasn't a member of the family. And if he expressed his wish that an invalid stay in the house as a helpless chaperone for her, disguising his nocturnal activities, her aunt and uncle might wonder why. And even the mildest question about his behavior was unacceptable to Phinehas. She'd learned that early on.

BY THE END of the week, Elsie was released from the hospital into John and Margaret's care, and arrangements were made for physical therapy at a clinic in Pitchford. There was no longer any reason for Phinehas to stay, and that last morning, as he packed his suitcase, Dinah fidgeted around the house with a dust cloth and a can of spray cleaner, praying that nothing would occur to stop his going. He still had not visited her room, and her fatalistic side waited for God to strike one last time.

When he came down at last, he had his suitcase in hand. She hardly dared to breathe.

"Ah. Dinah." He put the suitcase down in the hall by the front door and came into the dining room. "I'd like to speak with you."

He sat in his usual chair. She sank into a chair two places down, and balled the dust cloth between her hands.

"So. You'll be on your own, will you?"

"Just for a few weeks. Until Mom is able to come home."

"What will you do?"

She did not lift her eyes. What did he mean? "What I always do. Look after the animals. Do the books. Keep the house ready in case it's needed for the Lord's work."

"I'm glad you're still thinking about that. I've wondered at the depth of your willingness to serve, lately."

Oh, how she hated him. "I'm always willing to serve . . . God," she managed.

"Are you? Even now?"

Now? Oh, no. No. Be wise as a serpent and gentle as a dove. "Yes, now, except that I'm expecting Mr. Nicholas any minute. I'm supposed to go over the paperwork for the grazing rights with him."

"Mr. Nicholas." Phinehas's tone was thoughtful. "It looks bad, you know, Dinah."

"What does?" She lifted her eyes.

"You alone, with only the hired man for company. Sleeping here."

"He sleeps in the barn. And he's no threat to anyone."

"I wasn't thinking he would be a threat to you. Quite the opposite."

She blinked at him for a moment, trying to understand what he was getting at.

"What do you think God's people would think of you and Mr. Nicholas all alone out here?"

"I expect they would think he's our hired man."

Phinehas shook his head in sorrow. "We hope that God's people would think the best of each other. But there are always the cynical few, like the prophet Jeremiah, who see that the human heart is deceitful above all things. Wouldn't you agree?"

"Most people in Hamilton Falls think well of me," Dinah choked.

"I would hope so. But we don't want to give them any reason to do otherwise, do we?"

"No." He was going to override her choice to hire Matthew, to take it away just as her father had taken away her choices and overridden her decisions all her life. The hatred was a stone under her ribs, pulling her chest toward the table.

"Your aunt and uncle—who mean well, I know—have acted against my counsel. I'm going to think and pray on this matter. There must be a solution that will enable you to serve your God and King without stirring up any whispers among the worthy people here."

She should have known God didn't really have his back turned. He'd just been waiting for her to feel a little bit secure, a little bit hopeful, and then he would gleefully whip the rug out from under her feet. The landing was going to hurt. She knew it.

"Good-bye, Dinah." Phinehas got up and reached for her concealed hands, sliding his under the rim of the table and gripping her inner thigh. "You'll be hearing from me."

Her stomach turned over with a sickening thud, and he released her. She stood in the doorway and waved as he drove off, not because she wanted to, but because she had always done so and it would look odd if she didn't.

Then she snatched her jacket off its hook by the back door and pushed past a surprised Matthew, who was coming up the steps for his lesson in leases.

"Dinah? What—"

She ignored him and took off for the back side of the barn at a dead run.

SHE HAD ALREADY disposed of her breakfast by the time Matthew caught up with her. After burying the contents of the white plastic bucket, she stood the shovel against the wood rail of the composting box and straightened.

"What did he say to you?" Matthew felt slightly out of breath; he had a long way to go before he was as fit as she believed he was.

"Who?" Dinah set the bucket down and went around the side of the barn to the chicken pen. Matthew followed her.

"Don't play games. The only person, it seems, that can make you upchuck a perfectly decent breakfast."

"I told you before, it's none of your business."

"Dinah, can't you see I'm trying to help?"

She threw a handful of what looked like dried corn on the ground so viciously it bounced, and the chickens, who had been dancing around her with eagerness, scattered.

"Nobody can help. The only thing you can do is the work I hired you to do. My life is my business."

Matthew took a firm hold on his patience. Her rage was probably all she had to hang on to, the only thing that kept her standing. She couldn't help but use it as a weapon against people like him, who insisted on butting in and mouthing platitudes.

But something in her eyes, remnants of the despair he'd seen at the river, made him try again.

"I saw him put his suitcase in the car. How long before he comes back?"

She gathered her skirts behind her knees to keep them out of the dirt and knelt to apologize to the chickens. "Sorry, babies. It's not your fault. It's mine . . . I don't know. He's cooking up some scheme so he can stay here, but I just don't know what it is."

"Would it help if I were in the house? Rather like a chaperone?"

A dry glance told him what she thought of that idea. "If my parents and relatives sleeping down the hall don't stop him, how do you think you can?"

"I don't know. I could lie across your threshold with a rifle."

"Right. And add back pain and concealed weapons to your list of problems."

"I assume that if you could tell him to stop, you would have done so long ago. What sort of blackmail is he using on you?"

She sighed and stopped fussing with the birds. "Matthew, it's not your problem."

"You have to talk about it with someone, and I don't see your relatives stepping up."

"I don't have to talk about it at all."

"If you don't want me, there's One you could talk things over with."

"Who? A psychiatrist?"

He overlooked her bitterness and spoke gently. "I was thinking more of God."

For one dreadful moment he thought he had made her cry. She covered her mouth with one hand and whooped, and then he realized with a shock of humiliation that she was laughing. Not nice laughter, either. Derisive, mocking laughter. Directed at him, and worse, at his suggestion.

"Matthew," she said, when she'd finally regained control, "if you can't come up with something more helpful than that, you'd better stop trying."

He mustered his dignity, willing the burning blood out of his face. "You don't believe God can help you?"

That produced a roll of the eyes and another laugh. "Not likely, when he's the one who's been doing this to me. It's all one—Phinehas, God, my father. The trinity of misery. The only thing prayer would do is bring me back to God's attention, and goodness knows I've had enough of that. Attention from him is what makes me glad I've got the river."

Matthew tried to focus his reeling thoughts into words that might have meaning for someone who believed the spirit of love was an angry old man out to get her. "He loves you, Dinah. He gave the one thing he loves most so that you could have life."

She waved that away. "I gave the one thing I loved the most, too, so Phinehas could have dinner."

"But your sacrifice didn't cover Phinehas with grace and make it possible for him to look into the Father's face without sin."

"Oh, great," she said. "Is that what I have to look forward to? Eternity with Phinehas? But I suppose there he won't have to worry about sneaking around. Having girls at his disposal will be his reward. Thanks, but no thanks. I'll take my chances with the river."

Her dependence on suicide as a source of comfort frightened him more than anything else. "Please don't talk like that. The God I believe in doesn't condone what Phinehas is doing."

"He's sure allowing it, though, isn't he? Whether he's your God or mine, the result is the same."

Pain and fear and self-loathing. Those were the results of such belief. He watched her walk away and felt the grief well up in him again.

"Please help her to see you, Father," he murmured. "Use me in whatever way you need to bring that about. And Father? If it's possible, do it before she manages to get away from me and find her way back to the river."

HE MIGHT BE nosy and naïve, but at least he was smart. Matthew comprehended the ins and outs of grazing rights and property lines and cattle shipments after one explanation and re-cited how many of the neighboring ranchers' animals they grazed in each pasture in a way that told Dinah he probably had photographic memory, too.

He was smart in another way—or maybe it was just a healthy sense of self-preservation. After his ridiculous comments out at the compost heap, he left the subject of Phinehas severely alone and spared her any more of his philosophy about the love of God.

It seemed strange to have no one in the house. Well, no one besides Matthew. Even when he was there, he was so quiet she sometimes forgot about him.

Later that evening, she broiled pork chops for supper and set the platter on the kitchen table.

"I'll say grace, if you like." He sounded a little diffident, as if he thought she'd laugh at him again. She was sorry she'd laughed. She hadn't meant to embarrass him, but if the man insisted on saying stupid things, he should expect that kind of reaction.

"You say grace before your meals?"

"Don't you?" he asked.

"Of course, but . . ."

"But what?"

But the prayers of worldly people don't even reach the ceiling. That was what she'd always been taught. Matthew was worldly, true, and Phinehas was chosen of God, but there was a great gulf fixed between the way Phinehas behaved and the way Matthew did.

"Nothing. Go ahead."

She bowed her head and at the end of his simple, heartfelt grace—the man still regarded food as if it were the Holy Grail—she even said "Amen."

Which was a baby step away from collusion with the world, but still . . .

Dinah passed him the Brussels sprouts. "You have a good memory for facts and figures."

"I should do." He took exactly half of them and passed the pot back to her. "I was a teacher."

"A teacher? What grade?"

"University. Butter?"

"Thank you." He taught university. The sum total of her ambition in life was to have her own apartment and finish a two-year degree, and he had run away from independence and a university career. Was the man demented?

"What subject?"

"English literature."

"What, like poetry and such?"

"Yes. My dissertation was 'The Embodiment of Love: The Religious in Love Poetry of the Seventeenth Century.'"

"My goodness." There was love poetry in the seventeenth century? The only love poem she knew was the Song of Solomon, and she loathed every word of it. If she could, she would tape over the edges of those pages in her Bible, so it would never open there again.

"What about you? Where did you go to school?"

Now it was her turn to blush. "Hamilton High."

He cocked an eyebrow at her and mashed butter into his potatoes with vigor. "You haven't gone on?"

It was very important that she cut her chop into half-inch pieces. "No. There's no point."

"There's always a point to a good education."

"Not if I'm just going to stay here."

"Why should you just stay here? Why couldn't you move to Spokane or Seattle and go to college if you wanted?"

"And who would look after my mother and the ranch?"

"You mentioned your aunt and uncle would look after her till she recovered. And she's not an old woman. She can't be much over fifty. She has a long way to go before she becomes an invalid."

It was hopeless to explain to a man who tossed over careers as easily as she tossed out compost that Elsie wasn't capable of looking after herself. Her father had done it, her husband had done it, and now it fell to Dinah to do it.

"If my mother were left to run the ranch, every animal would wander away over the mountains, never to be seen again. My chickens would die of neglect, and the house would fall down around her."

"Oh," he said. "I see. I suppose it's rather late to teach her some life skills, isn't it?"

"Rather," she agreed, mimicking his accent.

After that he ate his chops in silence, and went away to his own apartment soon afterward. For which she was glad.

Dinah walked through the quiet house, removing the last traces of its guests. She emptied the wastebaskets in the bedrooms. Picked up a tissue from the guest room floor. Took the vacuum cleaner up to Phinehas's room and vacuumed the carpet viciously. Then she stripped the bed, holding the sheets in front of her averted face and dropping them in the washer as though they held the plague instead of merely the scent of the soap he used.

She hated that smell. Thank goodness he didn't use something common, like Ivory, that she'd have to smell all the time. His soap was some special men's blend from Crabtree & Evelyn that cost a fortune, and people were delighted to keep him supplied with it.

When she finally fell into bed, exhausted, the house was spotless and the past week might never have been. Only the results of it were still here.

She was still here because Matthew had thwarted her and yanked her out of the river.

He was here because she'd had a little rebellion and risked the wrath of God to house him.

And the house was here, still gloomy, still smelling of old wood because her dad had never let anyone open the windows. First thing tomorrow, if the sun was out, she would open them all and let a cleansing breeze blow through.

SHE'D FALLEN ASLEEP thinking of wind and freedom, and when she woke in the morning, she realized why. The south wind had come up in the night and blown the cumulus clouds off the side of the mountain. By the time she went out to give the chickens their breakfast treats, the sun had even dried the ground into lumpy ruts where the cars had made tracks in the mud over the last few days.

Maybe winter would loosen its grip on them and they'd get some warm days. With a pang, she realized that the sweetest part of a warm day would never happen now. She used to bring the plastic chair out into the yard and Sheba would jump in her lap, and for as much as half an hour at a time, the two of them would sun themselves together. Sheba would lean against her and spread out one wing to the warmth. Dinah always imagined the cherubim spreading their wings over the Ark of the Covenant the same way whenever Melchizedek preached about it.

But Sheba was gone, and what little warmth and sweetness there was in life had gone with her.

Matthew emerged from the barn. "Good morning."

She let the rest of the treats fall to the ground and palmed the moisture from under her eye with her free hand. "We'll take the Jeep up to the high pasture today," she said, ignoring his greeting. "I'll show you how far the land goes, and where the animals are grazing. You need to learn everyone's brands, too."

"That's fine," he said. "Are you all right?"

"Yes. If you want breakfast, I'm making omelets. If you're watching your cholesterol, you're out of luck around here."

"I'd be delighted to share some cholesterol with you," was all he said.

But it was kind of him to be concerned.

That was the most annoying thing about him, she thought as she mixed the omelet and poured it into the pan. Matthew Nicholas was consistently kind. There must be some sort of hitch somewhere—some point at which the outer skin of his composure peeled back and the anger under it roared into life. She wasn't sure how long it would take him to get to that point, but she was certain it would.

Men—and the God in whose image they were made—were consistent that way.

She was just dishing out the eggs when she heard the familiar sound of a car engine whining up the highway, and then the crunch of gravel as it turned into the drive.

Not Phinehas. Not so soon. Surely she'd be given more than a day before he came back?

She dried her hands on the nearest towel. Matthew came to the door behind her. "Who could that be?" he asked.

She'd never seen the car before, but she had no doubt about who was getting out of it. With a scream of pure joy, she leaped down the front steps two at a time and ran.

"Dinah!"

Tamara ran to meet her, and their bodies collided in a hug so fierce that Dinah was sure Tammy's small bones would crack. She started to cry, unable to get even a few words to string together enough to make sense.

"How—they said you couldn't—oh, Tammy, I'm so glad to see you—but how—?"

"They might have said you couldn't see me, but nobody said I couldn't come to see you." Tamara pulled away long enough to look her in the eyes. Dinah could hardly see through tears that blurred the face she loved.

"Oh, sweetie, I'm so happy. Everyone's gone. No one needs to know."

"I knew *you* would talk to me, at least," Tamara said. "They called Auntie Ev and told her about Mom. She told me, so here we are."

Dinah forgot what she was going to say and gripped Tamara's arms, looking down at her stomach.

Her flat stomach. Covered with a bright-red knitted sweater. The jeans she wore fit like a glove.

Cold horror splashed over her. "Tammy? Did you—where's the—you didn't—?"

"Right here." Tamara pulled open the back door of the four-door compact and with experienced fingers unbuckled the straps of the car seat. She hefted the baby up and held it out, feet dangling, to Dinah.

"Here you go, Di," she said. "Meet your niece, Tamsen Dinah Traynell."

Chapter 9

R ELIEF WASHED OVER Dinah in a flood. Tamara hadn't given her baby—Dinah's niece—away. She'd been told to, but she hadn't done it.

She took the baby, who was wearing a pink terrycloth sleeper under a pink quilted jacket, and laid her on her shoulder. She hadn't had much experience with kids other than Tamara, but she hadn't forgotten how neatly their little bodies fit on her arm, how they smelled, the way they snuggled.

She hugged the infant tightly and tried not to cry.

When she finally looked up, Tamara was leaning on the hood of the car, an odd, watchful expression in her eyes. It cleared immediately, and she smiled. Dinah smiled back. Tamara probably thought she was going to either suffocate or drop the baby. She stopped murmuring nonsense words and addressed a proper sentence to her sister. "How old is she?"

"Four months."

"Oh, my. Isn't she just beautiful?" She dropped kisses all over the baby's cheek, and the little face screwed up in distress. Her perfect little lips parted in an ear-splitting scream.

"Here. She's probably hungry," Tamara said. "We'd better go inside so I can feed her."

While Dinah brought her diaper bag in, Tamara dropped into

the armchair. Dishes clinked in the kitchen and someone put the kettle on the stove. In the act of pulling up her sweater to give the baby access to her breast, Tamara lifted her head like an animal scenting danger. "I thought nobody was here."

Dinah waved a hand. "That's Matthew. Sounds like he's making tea. He's English," she added by way of explanation.

"Matthew?" Tamara made the baby comfortable and stared at her. "Who's Matthew?"

In answer, he came through the door and crossed the room with one hand held out. Tamara grabbed a thin blanket out of her bag and tossed it over the baby, then reached up to shake his hand from her seat in the deep, comfy armchair.

"Matthew Nicholas. Dinah hired me recently to help out with the animals and whatnot. I'm so pleased to meet you. She didn't mention she had a sister."

Tamara slanted her a glance. "I bet she didn't. You're not Elect, are you?"

"No. I was homeless, but Dinah has rectified that."

"Homeless?"

"Yes. I came to the door asking for food, and she gave me a job instead. Much more effective."

"Did she?" Tamara sat back. The baby sucked noisily.

Dinah lifted her chin. "Somebody has to do the work around here."

"You don't have to explain to me. I'm happy you've got help. Anything that pokes the Elect in the eye, I'm totally in favor of."

"I'm not poking them in the eye. There's nothing wrong with us having a hired man. People do it all the time."

"Yeah, but most people don't have a whole town talking about every little thing they do, either."

"You sound just like Phinehas."

"I do not." After burping the baby, Tamara switched her to

the other breast and adjusted the blanket. Matthew looked away, and a flush crept into his face.

Dinah smothered a smile.

"Want some matrimonial cake? Alma Woods brought it to the funeral supper and nobody had any."

"Sure. I'm starving. You look like you could use some, too, Di."

"I will, don't worry." She ignored the underlying concern about her thinness. "Except I hate how it crumbles all over everything."

"How did it go? The funeral, I mean."

Dinah went into the kitchen and pulled out the pan. She sliced generous helpings because there was no one to tell her not to. "It was all right. Uncle John and Aunt Margaret handled most of the arrangements, and Phinehas was here."

"I bet he was."

The bitterness in Tamara's tone might have been a bond between them, but Dinah's secret was locked behind her lips, even from the one she loved best. Particularly from the one she loved best. Even though Melchizedek, Julia's father Mark Mc-Neill, and their own father had been the ones to sentence Tamara to seven years of Silence, it had been Phinehas who had advised them to do it, by long-distance phone call from Spokane.

Despite what he had done, Dinah couldn't give Tamara anything more to hate him for. It was already standing between her and God, and she feared for her sister's salvation. From the look of her clothes, it was in serious jeopardy.

Matthew poured the tea into mugs and brought them into the living room. Tamara finished feeding the baby and handed her to Dinah.

"She can spit up on your shoulder and initiate you into aunt-hood."

"Oh, thanks." Dinah armed herself with the blanket and patted the baby on the back in a relaxing rhythm.

"Er . . . would you rather I stayed, or not?" Matthew asked in a low voice.

"Stay." Tamara's voice was firm. "I've got nothing to hide."

Still, Matthew looked to Dinah for confirmation. She nodded. "If Tamsen throws up all over me, you can have her."

He perched on the edge of the sofa and watched the baby as if she were a bomb and he was deciding whether or not to run.

"So, are you okay?" Tamara asked.

Dinah shrugged. "The same."

"Do you think Mom would talk to me if I went and visited her?"

Dinah couldn't stop her face creasing with distress, and Tamara saw it. "I don't know, honey. You know how she is about the rules. If Melchizedek says you're Silenced, then she's not going to speak."

"You did."

So she had. Without a second's thought. "I love you." Too late, she realized how that sounded.

"And Mom doesn't?"

"That's not what I meant."

"I think it is. You should come to Auntie Evelyn's. She's great. She hugs everybody. She was a little weird with me at first, but then she had a meltdown about all my black clothes and we went shopping. She was fine after that."

Aunt Evelyn, whom the family treated like the whore of Babylon because she'd never come into the fold, because she'd escaped as soon as she was old enough and had never come back. The only time his sister's name had ever crossed her father's lips had been when he'd called her to ask if Tamara could come and board there.

Aunt Evelyn was the second person she'd met or heard about within a week who treated people with more kindness and compassion than the Elect. Something was seriously out of balance here.

It was dangerous to think that way, she reminded herself. The Elect were God's chosen people. They might not be perfect, but they were chosen. Her job was to fit in, to bend and blend, not to criticize.

Wasn't it?

"Tammy, are you sure you want to wear color?"

Was that amusement or derision in the brown eyes she loved? "Come on, Dinah. Say what you mean."

"Okay. Have you gone Out?"

Tamsen burped and spit up, and Dinah wiped her face and handed her back to Tamara, who settled her in the portable car seat on the floor.

"Tammy?"

"Yeah, I heard you. What do you think? I get pregnant, I get Silenced, I get tossed out of the house. Gee, I'm going to stay Silent for seven years and then come crawling back, grateful that people are going to talk to me now?"

Something inside Dinah quivered and threatened to collapse. "Don't, honey," she whispered. "You sound so bitter."

"I'm not. Not a bit. What I am is free, Di. You should try it. It feels great."

Dinah shuddered and looked at the carpet. She might not have much, but at least she had the safety and fellowship of the Elect. Out there in the world was nothing but howling loneliness and chaos and spiritual death. It nearly made her ill to see Tamara embracing that so wholeheartedly.

The way you embraced the river? whispered a tiny voice in the back of her mind. *What's the difference?*

"What do you think about all this, Matthew?" Tamara demanded in a tone that just missed being insolent.

Matthew hesitated, looking from one sister to the other. "I don't know enough about the situation to give an opinion."

"But you know about the world, probably," Tamara said. "Tell Dinah it's not such a bad place."

"It isn't. Not in general. But my experience seems to have been the opposite of yours," he said. "I came here and found a welcome. More than I'd learned to expect in the other places I've been."

"Yes, but you probably didn't have my father and Melchizedek to deal with," Tamara pointed out.

"No, I didn't. Phinehas was here, however."

"I bet he wasn't too keen on you."

"I don't know about that," Matthew said steadily. "He seemed very civil."

Dinah glanced up to find him looking at her. *Don't you say a word,* she thought.

He didn't.

"I'm going to assume our trip up the mountain is postponed?" he asked, deflecting the conversation away from danger. "I'm sure you and your sister have a lot to catch up on."

"Oh, did you guys have plans?" Tamara looked from Dinah to Matthew.

Dinah waved a hand. "I was going to take him up to the summer pasture and show him where the cattle are. But we can do that anytime. I'm not going to let you out of my sight, now that I have you."

Tamara bent over to check that Tamsen had fallen asleep. "I'm not going anywhere, Di. If you guys planned to take a ride in the Jeep, you should do that. I could use the time to sleep."

"Is she up every two hours?"

Tamara straightened. "That was only in the beginning. At night she's down for six or eight."

"When you first came home, you'd wake up screaming. When I was little I used to get scared at the sound of running feet in the night, but it was only Mom, going to get you."

"Tamsen doesn't scream, thank goodness. She does this thing like a fire engine. You know, *rrrrrrRRRRRRRrrrrrRRRRRRR*. If I don't get there fast enough, she turns up the volume. But she sleeps in my room, so it doesn't get to that point very often." She paused. "I mean it, you guys. Go do what you were planning to do. I'm going upstairs to crash. My room's still there, right?"

Dinah felt herself flush. "Yes. Dad wanted to turn it into a study, but Mom wouldn't let him. Then he got sick and had other things to think about."

"That's one blessing, then, isn't it?"

She didn't know if Tamara was being sincere or sarcastic, so she let it go. Tamara gathered the baby's carrier, blanket, and bag and toted them all upstairs as if she'd had practice at doing a lot of things at once. Her body looked small and slender with the bulky items slung all around it, and Dinah wondered if she'd been eating properly.

She was a fine one to talk. But with a start, she realized she hadn't been driven out to her white plastic bucket since yesterday. Since Phinehas had gone, in fact, and she'd cleaned him and everyone else out of the house.

She followed Tamara up to the back bedroom and found her sitting on the edge of the bed.

"Sweetie, I don't feel right about leaving you here all alone."

Tamara glanced over her shoulder. "Why? Is somebody going to come and kick me out?"

"No, no. That's not what I meant. I just . . ." She sat beside her and slipped an arm around her sister's waist. The sweater felt soft and warm against the crook of her elbow. "I haven't seen you in nearly a year. I want to hug you and drink you in and make sure you're okay and feed you and . . ."

"Okay, okay, I get it." Tamara grinned the wide, unselfconscious grin Dinah loved and hadn't seen in so long. "Don't worry about feeding me. Somebody needs to feed you. Good grief, Di, you must weigh ninety pounds."

"A hundred and ten."

"And you're five foot seven."

"Black is slimming."

"It doesn't fool me. That skirt is falling off you. The only thing holding it up is your hipbones sticking out. When are you going to get some help?"

"You sound just like Matthew."

"I knew I liked that guy for a reason. Please, Dinah. This isn't right."

"I'll be okay."

"You've been saying that for years."

"And I am okay, aren't I?"

"You are not. You're bulimic and thin and pale and—"

"Tamara."

"What?"

"Leave it alone."

"When are you going to deal with this?"

"I kept my breakfast down today."

Tamara was silent for a couple of seconds. "That's dealing with it?"

"Yes. And I'll see about lunch when we get back from the summer pasture."

"Dinah, what really makes you do this?"

Uneasiness prodded Dinah to her feet. She picked up a book from the dusty stack on the desk where Tamara used to write her research papers on sharks and poets and the expansion of the Roman Empire.

"Nothing makes me. I just don't need as much to eat as other people."

"That's a crock and you know it."

Stung, Dinah glared at her. "Don't talk to me like that. How would you like it if I asked you what made you go out and get pregnant?"

"Is that what you think?"

"That's how it's usually done, isn't it?"

"I just went out and got pregnant. Just ruined my life for the fun of it. Right, Dinah." Tamara's voice sounded weary and resigned and adult, in a way Dinah had never heard before. It frightened her. Why was she talking to Tamara this way? All she wanted to do was hold her and protect her forever, and instead she sounded just like her mother. *Don't do this. You should have done that.*

Dinah hated herself. She reached out a hand to touch Tamara's shoulder, but her sister bent down to look into Tamsen's sleeping face, and they didn't connect.

"I'm sorry, sweetie," Dinah said softly. "I sound just like Mom. I didn't mean it."

"I'm really tired, Di. The drive from Spokane was longer than it used to be. I'm going to have a nap. You go do the pasture thing. We'll talk later, okay?"

It wasn't the forgiveness she hungered for, but it would have to do. Dinah closed the bedroom door and walked softly down the hall, as if Tamara were already asleep. When she passed the bathroom door, she hesitated, but then she heard Matthew come in the back door. There was no time to purge herself, to get rid of her stomach's burden. And she didn't want Tamara to hear the toilet flush and realize she'd been right.

She found Matthew in the kitchen, and grabbed her boots from the mud room. "Ready to go?"

"You're not going to stay and visit with your sister?"

"She's probably already asleep. She said she was going to take a nap and we should do what we'd planned to do."

"With a baby so young, she probably is. Are you sure she doesn't mind my taking you away so soon after she arrived?"

"Positive. Come on, let's go."

THE BUMPY SHORTCUT across the fields to the service road normally took about ten minutes. Dinah shoved the Jeep into a lower gear and slowed for a swampy bit at the bottom of a slope, then listened to the engine drop to a guttural growl as it began to climb again. Neither she nor Matthew spoke until they reached the service road and she sped up to thirty miles an hour.

"How much land do you have?" His right hand gripped the armrest on the door as if he thought she was going to take them over the nearest cliff. Well, there weren't any of those until they got up to the top.

"Two hundred acres," she said. "It's not very big, but the leases are a bit of income."

"Cattle raising seems very . . . frontier-like."

"It was bigger in the forties, when my grandparents settled here. Now that Dad is gone we'll probably sell off our animals at auction and just let other people run theirs on our land."

"And what then?"

She gave him a sidelong glance. He'd kept all her secrets so far. There was no reason to think he would give away another. But hard-won caution kept her quiet. If he knew about the on-line stocks, he might try and control them somehow. Give advice she didn't need. Men, in her experience, couldn't seem to help themselves that way. That portfolio was all she and Elsie had to live on, and she wasn't about to jeopardize it just so he wouldn't feel concerned.

"I don't know. Maybe I'll go back to the bank."

Sure she would. Jobs in Hamilton Falls weren't easy to get. Everyone could see them coming a mile away and they were always filled immediately. Besides, Claire Montoya had her old job at the bank. It wasn't likely they'd take her back for old time's sake.

The job at Rebecca's bookshop was open as of Sunday, her mind whispered.

But Sunday made her thoughts shut down in pain, and she turned to practicalities. It was a good strategy. It had worked many times before.

They left the service road on a track that meandered across the lower slopes of Mount Ayres, and she began to point out particular meadows and landmarks. Small groups of cattle were visible in the distance, and he answered her quizzes on brands and breeds with a steady patience that told her he just might be humoring her until she was ready to talk.

But she wasn't going to talk about anything but cows. Tamara, the baby, their finances, the Silence—these were not things you talked about with your hired hand, even if he had buried Sheba with quiet sensitivity and had not laughed at her grief.

He was still humoring her two hours later when they finished their tour of the mountain and bumped back across the fields to the barn, where Dinah pulled open the double doors and parked the Jeep where it usually sat.

"I'll see you at supper, shall I?" Matthew said in his contained way. "Thank you for the tour."

"About four o'clock. Early, because we didn't have lunch."

"All right."

She watched him move into the shadows and heard the apartment door close quietly. Shaking off the sense that she hadn't done something that needed doing, she fed the chickens and went in the back door of the house.

It was very quiet. Tamara and the baby must still be sleeping. Well, they would likely be awake any time now.

She glanced out the window and noticed the car was gone.

Tamara must have moved it so it couldn't be seen from the road. But the barn storage, the only place a car could be parked other than the gravel turnaround, had only had the truck in it when they'd put the Jeep away. Had Tamara needed something for the baby and made a fast run to town?

She ran up the stairs and hesitated outside the closed door of Tamara's room. But there was no reason to wait, she chided herself. If the car's gone, so are they. You're not going to wake anyone.

She pushed open the door.

The first thing she saw was the baby bag and the baby carrier. How on earth could Tammy go to town without the car seat? That was downright dangerous.

She leaned over and moved the blanket that covered it.

Cold disbelief ran light footed over her skin. Tamsen slept the deep sleep of infancy, her little hands curled up against her cheeks as though mugging surprise.

"Wha-a-t?" Dinah breathed. Tamara couldn't have gone to town and left the baby alone in the house. She might only be seventeen, but she was a mother of four months. Surely she had more sense than that.

Dinah looked wildly around the room—for what, she didn't know. A manila envelope sat on the desk. With hands that had begun to tremble, she picked it up and saw that it was addressed to her. There were a couple of pieces of paper inside, so she pulled out the first one.

I, Tamara Elsbeth Traynell, of 1812 Mackay Street, Spokane, Washington, do hereby forever renounce my daughter, Tamsen Dinah Traynell, to the care of my beloved sister, Dinah Miriam Traynell, of Rural Route 14, Hamilton Falls, Washington.

I resolve and swear that I am not capable of providing the care and love that Tamsen deserves, and, being confident that my sister will give her both, give Tamsen into her keeping. I will not at any time attempt to rescind this gift, nor will I interfere in the upbringing of Tamsen Traynell, whom I now consider my sister's child.

Signed, Tamara Elsbeth Traynell, and dated this fourteenth day of March, 2005.

Chapter 10

FOR SEVERAL HORRIFIED seconds—maybe even a minute—Dinah stared at the document. Its words didn't change after the second reading, or the third. When they didn't change after the fourth, either, she looked up and out the side window—the one that gave a view of the road that led past the neighbors' place and down to the highway.

The road was empty. Nothing moved but a flock of magpies that wheeled over the ditch and came to rest on the fencing like a row of little judges.

Maybe she could still catch Tamara before she got to the highway. But no, she'd had a couple of hours' head start. She could be nearly back to Spokane by now.

Spokane. Aunt Evelyn. She could call Aunt Evelyn, get her to talk Tammy into taking the baby back. She couldn't give up the baby. It wasn't right or natural. A baby should be with its mother, especially since its dad wouldn't acknowledge its existence or even admit the act that had created it had happened.

She needed to stop thinking of her niece as "it."

She. She was a problem, just another in a long line of problems that Dinah had had lots of practice solving. She could solve this, too. *One step at a time.*

The first thing to do was find Aunt Evelyn's number. She'd

never spoken to her in her life, but if ever there was a time to start, it was now.

She found her father's phone directory in the top right drawer of his desk and located the number, written in his neat hand. As she waited for it to ring through, she tried to think of a way to introduce herself and break the news of what Tamara had done while still sounding reasonably adult and logical.

The problem was her estrangement from her aunt and the baby's abandonment were neither adult nor logical. But before she'd gotten much beyond that unhappy conclusion, someone picked up the phone.

"Aunt Evelyn, you don't know me, but I'm your niece, Dinah." There. Even her voice had decided to cooperate. Calm. Adult.

"Well, hello." Her aunt's voice was deeper than she'd expected. She pictured a woman in tweeds with a short, practical haircut. "The last time I heard your little voice, you were hollering for a feeding."

So her aunt had seen her as a baby. She hadn't known. Of course, since Evelyn's name was never spoken, there was a lot she didn't know.

"I'm sorry I don't remember."

"You were the cutest little thing. Huge brown eyes like melted chocolate, and glossy dark hair. And a darling little dab of a nose. I hope it didn't turn into the Simcoe Schnozz."

It took Dinah a moment to realize she meant her dad's mother, who had been a Simcoe. "No. It's a pretty ordinary nose."

"Bad enough I got it. It looks all right on boys, but it's a horror to a girl in high school. I had it done five years ago. I wasn't going to inflict it on Jim for the rest of his life."

"Done?" Jim?

"Yes. Had a plastic surgeon in Seattle take a scalpel to it. Now

I have a nice ordinary one, too. Jim says it always gives him a jolt in the mornings. Keeps things interesting."

Jim was her second husband. Dinah's step-uncle. Another name that was never mentioned.

"Aunt Evelyn—"

"I know. You probably didn't break Silence to call down here to talk about my nose. What's up? Tamara get there okay? She didn't run my car into the side of the barn, did she?"

"Yes. I mean, yes, she got here. She didn't run the car into the barn."

"Oh, good. She's a levelheaded kid, but you never know. She said the only thing she ever drove was the truck and her boyfriend's Honda. It had a stick shift."

"Aunt Evelyn, did she say anything about what she planned to do when she got here?"

"Have a visit, I think. Maybe try to see her mother. Why? Not that I'm not glad to hear from you, but calls from Hamilton Falls tend to mean either death or disaster, if you know what I mean."

Dinah took a deep breath. "I guess this falls into the second category, then. Tamara's left the baby here."

"What, and gone to find that kid she was seeing? Oh, to be seventeen again, thinking that everybody's going to pick up the slack for you. Well, here's what you do. If the baby's sleeping, let her. If she wakes up, feed her. That ought to hold you till Tammy gets back. And you can tell her from me that she'd better not pull a stunt like this again or that'll be the end of the free babysitting."

"I don't think she's coming back." Dinah saw the bedroom in her mind's eye, empty of everything but the envelope, the baby's bag, and the car seat. Now that she thought about it, Tamara had never even brought in any luggage. Had probably never intended to.

"What do you mean, not coming back? She went out there to see you guys. Otherwise, why risk the grief she'd get?"

"She left an envelope with a letter in it." Dinah read it in a steady voice, though her hand was still shaking. When she finished, silence hissed down the line.

"Ye gods and little fishes." Evelyn sounded winded. "The kid's gone off her rocker."

"When she gets back to your place, you have to talk her out of it."

"You're not kidding. How long ago did she leave?"

"I was gone for about two hours. She said she was going to take a nap. She'd just fed the baby and probably waited long enough for her to fall asleep and for us to drive out of sight before she took off."

"Will you be okay babysitting until we hear from her? My word, this just beats all. After this, I'm not letting Tammy out of my sight. I take back what I said about her being levelheaded."

"We'll be okay, Aunt Evelyn. Let me know as soon as you see her."

"No problem. You did the right thing to call."

When Dinah hung up, some of the panic lodged under her ribs had dissipated. It felt strange to have someone come down firmly on her side for once, someone who pitched in to help without throwing blame and "should-haves" along with it.

A furious howl penetrated the floorboards, and she realized she'd been hearing a noise behind her conversation without registering what it was. Tamsen had awakened alone in a strange place, and her fire-engine noise had turned into screams that even Dinah could recognize meant panic.

She dropped the phone and Tamara's letter and ran for the stairs.

Matthew must have heard them, too, all the way out in the barn, because when she got to the bedroom she found him hovering helplessly over the baby, whom he'd managed to extract from the car seat and lay on her back on the bed. Part of Tam-sen's panic probably stemmed from the sight of a strange male looming over her.

Dinah was a stranger, too, as far as that went. The baby's screams were deafening as Dinah checked her over.

"She's wet," she shouted. "Hand me a diaper, will you?"

"Where is your sister?" Matthew scrabbled through the baby bag and finally found a stack of diapers. He handed her one, and she changed the baby with hands that hadn't forgotten how.

But the screaming didn't stop.

"Is she hungry?" He stared at the writhing, roaring infant with such terror that Dinah would have been tempted to laugh if she hadn't felt the same way.

"She could be. Is there milk or formula in there?"

He produced a bottle half full of milky liquid with an air of a man triumphing at the eleventh hour. "Here. This should do it."

Dinah picked her up, sat on the bed, and stuck the nipple in Tamsen's mouth. Tamsen hiccuped and gasped around it, then after a minute settled down to suck.

"Thank God." Matthew pulled the wooden chair away from the student desk and sat as if his knees had given out. "Where is your sister?" he asked again.

"She's gone."

"Well, yes. I hope she doesn't plan to stay away long."

"Permanently, as far as I can tell." Dinah filled him in on the details, and when he didn't believe her, he went and got the let-ter himself.

"This is preposterous." He appeared in the bedroom door and held it out. "It can't be legal. It looks like a printout from one of those 'be your own attorney' computer programs."

"I don't know if it is or not. All I know is Tamara came out here on purpose to leave the baby."

"Surely part of it was seeing you."

She didn't reply. Had Tamara faked her happiness at the two of them being together again? She'd faked a lot of other things.

"So now what do we do?"

"We?"

"Yes, we." Matthew gave her a penetrating look. "Unless you'd rather I take myself back out to the barn and we divide our duties along traditional lines."

"What, women inside and men outside?"

"It may have worked in the old days but I can't see much in it now."

"True enough. But Tamsen is my responsibility."

He shook his head. "She is her mother's responsibility. The only responsibility we have is to see that she gets safely back to her."

But when Aunt Evelyn called that evening just after supper—a supper that Matthew had thrown together while Dinah was trying to bathe the baby in the kitchen sink—they found it wasn't going to be as easy as that.

"I got an e-mail from Tamara." Aunt Evelyn didn't bother with preliminaries. "TamaraT at Hotmail dot com, so we can't trace it. She says she left my car at the Amtrak station here in Spokane with the keys on top of the left front tire. She sends her love."

"But where did she go?" Dinah gripped the receiver with hands that had gone stiff and cold.

"No indication. Seattle, probably. Or Boise. Or Topeka, Kansas, for all I know."

"Aunt Evelyn, we have to do something."

"Your uncle and I will report her to the police as a runaway. I think it's better if we stay here, in case she decides to contact us again. Or come home, even. Meantime, I hope you've got lots of formula and diapers on hand."

She didn't, Dinah thought as she hung up the phone. But she wasn't going to need them.

She found Matthew at the sink, drying Tamsen off, much to the baby's disgust. "Come on," she said. "We're going into town."

"What for?"

"We're going to introduce Tamsen to her father."

THE WOMAN WHO opened the door to the modest split-level home broke into a smile when she saw Dinah. The smile wavered a bit when she saw Matthew standing behind her, and her eyes grew speculative.

"Dinah!" Her voice was welcoming, and she held the door open so that they could come in. Then she saw the baby carrier, and her smile dropped away in astonishment. "What brings you out on a cold night like this? And who have you got there?"

The door opened straight into a living room littered with toys, books, and pint-sized items of clothing. Without being invited, Dinah sat down on the couch. For lack of anything better to do, Matthew sat beside her. He wondered how the odd tableau looked to this woman. "Found Family," they could call it. Like the found poetry he'd once assigned his students, they were patched-together and accidental. But there might be some beauty they could find between the lines.

Linda Bell, Dinah had told him on the way over, had five kids of her own, ran a day care center out of her home, was the worst gossip in Hamilton Falls—and was Tamsen's grandmother. She just didn't know it yet.

"Linda, we need your help." Dinah pulled away the pink blanket that was draped over the baby, and Linda knelt to look.

"Isn't she darling," the woman cooed. "Are you babysitting? I'm so glad you came to me. I know how hard it must be, losing your dad and worrying about your mom, and now you're looking after a little one. Well, I'll help in any way I can. What's her name?"

"Tamsen. She's Tamara's daughter."

Linda drew back from the baby so suddenly Matthew thought she'd tip over and land on her backside on the carpet. "What?"

"Tamara's daughter. I'm looking after her for a little while, but I need to—"

"Why have you brought her here? My goodness, Dinah, I thought you were more sensitive than that. People already think she's—that Tamara and Danny—well, we don't want to give them anything more to talk about, do we?"

Matthew stared at the woman. So much for beauty. She stood as far from the baby as she could get, her hands pressed against her black skirts as if the child were about to climb out of the carrier and throw up on her.

"Linda, I need to speak with Danny."

"Why?"

Dinah swallowed. "He and Tamara were seeing each other. It's time he took responsibility for his actions."

"What actions?" Linda's voice was dangerously quiet.

"Please don't be angry with me. I know he said Tamsen wasn't his when Tamara was first—" She swallowed again. "—Silenced, but that was a very natural reaction. He needs to come forward now."

"Why?"

"Because—because Tamara has gone away, and a child needs at least one of its parents."

"Gone away? Where? When?"

"I don't know. This afternoon. She left the baby with me and drove away and no one's seen her since."

Matthew heard the pain in her voice at having to make such a confession about her only sister to such an unsympathetic audience.

"Left the baby. With you," Linda repeated, as if this confirmed the opinion she'd had of Tamara all along.

"Yes."

"For how long?"

"I don't know. She didn't say. But Danny should prepare himself for long-term."

"Danny doesn't need to prepare himself for anything but coming back to the Elect," Linda snapped.

Dinah stared at her. "But—"

"I suppose you've had so much to deal with you haven't had a chance to think about what's happening in other people's lives."

Matthew winced at the needle sharpness in the woman's tone. The effusive helpfulness had disappeared like steam on a hot day.

Linda Bell crossed to the window, giving the baby carrier a wide berth. "Danny left two months ago, after he heard that she—" She gestured at Tamsen, who, thankfully, was sleeping. "—was born."

"Left?" Dinah sounded bewildered. Matthew felt rather bewildered himself. There was too much going on here for him to assimilate all at once.

"Yes, left. He left his home, his family, and his church, all because of your sister trying to pin this on him. Thanks to her, he's lost his salvation. The good Lord only knows who that child's father actually is. But it isn't Danny."

Dinah's eyes never left Linda's face as she picked up the carrier. Matthew got to his feet as well. He'd be glad to see the door close on this angry woman.

"Where is he?" Dinah asked. Her hand, gripping the handle of the carrier, looked drained of blood. The only reason she hadn't dropped it was because the bones of her fingers were locked around it.

"I doubt he's run off to join her, if that's what you were hoping," Linda said. "He's living with a worldly school friend at the other end of town. The Barings. But I wouldn't recommend presenting him with Tamara's child." She leveled a look of extreme dislike at the carrier. "From what I gather, he never wants to see any of the Traynells again."

DINAH KNEW THE Barings only vaguely through . . . an uncle? . . . a grandfather? . . . who bought hay every October. A stop at the pay phone by the Jiffy Market provided a phone book with an address, and fifteen minutes after their ignominious departure from the Bells' they pulled up outside a shabby ranch home on Front Street. The street had been so named because it fronted on the railway line, back in the days when the railway had been more important than the interstate.

"It's late," Matthew offered. "Perhaps we should tackle this in the morning."

But Dinah's hands were cold and stark on the steering wheel, her mouth set in a grim line. "If she's not coming back, somebody has to be responsible."

"What are you going to do if this Danny really isn't the father?"

Dinah shifted the truck into Park and shut off the engine. "He has to be. There's no one else."

The worldly boy who answered the door wore wrinkled jeans and a black T-shirt advertising a rock concert. He eyed Dinah in her black dress and coat as if she were a sideshow act at the midway.

Not that Dinah had ever been to a midway.

He leaned on the doorjamb and chewed on the pencil that hung loosely in his fingers. "Yeah?"

"Is Danny here?" Dinah asked.

"Maybe."

"I'd like to talk with him for a minute, if he is."

"You from his church?"

"I'm Dinah Traynell. He knows me."

The kid heaved himself upright and swung the door shut without a reply. Beside her, Matthew shifted and reached for the baby carrier.

"It's no good. Let's try another time."

Dinah couldn't quite believe a stranger had shut the door in her face when she was so desperate. This was what you got with worldly people. She should have known better.

She turned away just as the door swung open again.

"Dinah?" Danny Bell flipped the porch light on and stepped out onto the mat. He wore no coat, though the air was chilly. "What's going on?"

Dinah had never seen him wear color before. He wore a green T-shirt with some kind of cartoon character on it, and his jeans looked as though they'd been bought for a larger boy. About the size of the one who had answered the door.

A borrowed home. Borrowed clothes. What had happened to make Danny Bell leave his parents?

"We need to talk to you," she said.

"We?"

Matthew stepped into the light, the carrier hanging heavily from one hand. Danny's gaze glanced off it, dismissed it, and returned to Dinah's face.

"If my mom sent you over, I can't talk right now. I'm doing homework."

"She didn't. In fact, she wasn't very keen about me coming over at all. It won't take long, and you can get back to your homework."

He leaned on the wrought-iron porch rail. It gave a little under his weight, and Dinah wondered if the flimsy thing would pop off altogether and dump him in the flowerbed, where a few cold daffodil shoots were trying to come up.

"What's up?"

"Tamara came this morning from Spokane," she began.

Under the porch light, Danny's face seemed to thin, to pinch up and harden. "I don't want to hear about her." He pushed away from the rail and reached for the doorknob.

"Danny, wait." She'd never touched him in her life other than the formal handshake of fellowship after Gathering, but extremity was pushing her to do a lot of things she'd never done before. She gripped his arm, just above the wrist, and pulled him nearer to the shallow steps where Matthew stood. "This isn't about Tamara. It's about the baby."

"What baby?"

"Hers. Tamara's and yours."

"There isn't any baby." His voice, which had started out sounding young and polite, hardened into something adult and unyielding. Suddenly Dinah saw part of the reason for Linda's pain. But it didn't stop her.

"Yes, there is. Right there." She nodded at Matthew and the carrier. "Tamara left her with me and disappeared—we don't know where to or for how long. But I'm not one of her parents. She should be with one of you. Not me."

Danny stared at her, and to her surprise, he laughed. It was a soundless, disbelieving huff of air. "And you think I'm the father."

"Well, yes. You guys were dating. Sharing a hymnbook."

"So who else could it be, right?"

"Right."

"Even if I was, Dinah, how would I take care of a baby? I'm seventeen. I've got two more months of school, finals, and gee, I'm living on a mattress on somebody else's floor. I really know how to take care of things."

"I don't pretend to know why you're not at home. But I'm sure your folks would help."

"I'm sure they wouldn't. I'm never going back."

She stood there, helplessly waiting for him to change his mind, to admit responsibility for his daughter and take this problem off her hands.

He crossed his arms over his chest. "You really don't have a clue, do you?"

She shook her head. "I don't have a clue about a lot of things."

"For once in her life, my mother didn't spill her guts?"

"About what?"

"About why I'm here."

"No. I could see she was upset about it, but that's none of my business. The only thing I care about is getting Tamsen back to one of her parents."

"Yeah? Well, you'd better talk to old Phinehas about it, then."

She stared at him. "Why?" Phinehas was the last person she'd go to with a problem like this. Sure, he was the final judge in serious problems among the flock, but this was a family matter. She could take care of it, if she could just get the baby's parents to own up and do the right thing.

"Tamara didn't tell you, either?"

"Tell me what?"

"What I said. You want to talk to the kid's father, you'd better go find Phinehas. It wasn't me. We never even took our clothes off. But Phinehas, now, that's different. Only he doesn't ask first. He just takes what he wants and leaves the girl to deal with what happens."

"What?" Dinah couldn't form an intelligent sentence—couldn't even get a breath to go into her lungs. She swayed, and the world tilted.

"I'm sorry you're strapped with his kid, Dinah. But life's not fair. Not for Tammy, and not for me. One thing I'm glad about though." He spoke in a conversational tone, as if Dinah's world hadn't just torn itself apart and was drifting on the cold air like ash. "It made me see the Elect the way they really are. Any bunch of people who could let that guy get away with what he does deserves what they get. I tried to get Tammy to say something, but oh no, she'd rather let everybody hang it on me. And if she doesn't care enough to tell the truth, then I don't, either. I'm done with all of you. As soon as school's out, I'm out of here. You can tell *that* to Tamara—if you ever see her again."

He pushed into the house, and for the second time in ten minutes, the battered front door shut in Dinah's face.

Chapter 11

MATTHEW FELT AS though he were walking in the pitch dark, on a path full of holes into which he could fall at any moment.

Somehow he managed to strap the baby's seat into the truck and maneuver Dinah into the passenger seat without dropping either one. If he hadn't, Dinah would probably have stayed on the lawn all night, staring in that eerie, unfocused way into the middle distance. He was beginning to have serious doubts about the young woman's sanity. After all, how much abuse and how many shocks could one person be expected to withstand before she broke?

He turned right onto the highway and pushed his foot down on the accelerator. She had broken once already. How could he have forgotten that terrible scene in the compost heap, when she'd lost her pet? That had led her straight to the river.

She had just learned her only niece was the child of rape— rape by the same man who had been raping her for years. Two girls in one family. And who knew how many others?

Grimly, Matthew fought down the un-Christian desire to throttle Phinehas, that white-walled hypocrite, with his bare hands. Instead, he kept both wrapped around the steering wheel and concentrated on getting everyone home safely.

It was like something out of one of those southern gothic novels his friend Paolo's wife was so fond of reading, full of incest and betrayal and family secrets going back generations. Or worse, the whole situation in her church was a breeding ground for this kind of thing. From what he had been able to gather, the Shepherds of these poor souls were accountable to no one—except God, one presumed. And with no accountability and a congregation that catered to their every wish, it was only a matter of time before human nature got the better of them and they became corrupted by their own power.

No wonder Dinah saw God as an all-powerful old man dishing out punishment. When God's representative to her was exactly that, how could she think anything else?

He glanced at her, but she was still staring straight ahead. Had she even blinked since he'd snapped the seat belt around the slender span of her hips?

He pulled into the yard behind the ranch house and got out to open the barn doors, then parked the truck in its spot next to the roofless Jeep in which they'd climbed the mountain—could it really have been just this afternoon?

With the baby's carrier dangling from one hand and his other arm supporting Dinah, he got them both into the house and upstairs to Tamara's old room, where Tamsen woke and demanded food. Dinah sat on the bed and unbuckled the baby.

"She's wet." Her voice sounded hollow.

"I'll make some tea and heat a bottle." He paused at the door. "Dinah."

She looked up.

"Change her," he suggested gently. Then he went down to the kitchen. He wished there were something stronger to put in the tea than milk. But of course there wasn't. No alcohol, no cards, no jewelry, no color in the house. Just plenty of abuse, lies, hatred, and hypocrisy.

How could any healthy thing grow up in such a place?

He plugged in the kettle, took a bottle out of the fridge, and put it in the microwave. And how could he stay, and be sucked down into all this?

Because he could leave. It would take some time and a lot of humiliation, but eventually he could hitchhike his way back to California, get his things out of Paolo's garage, and cobble together some semblance of a life. He could thank Dinah for her kindness, take his week's pay, and go.

He could, but he wouldn't.

It wasn't gratitude that kept him here, or fear of hunger on the highway. No, there was only one thing that would make him overcome his disgust at the ugliness of human nature—including his own—and force him to stay where it was manifesting like mushrooms after rain.

Dinah.

He would stay because one after another, everything a woman could reasonably be expected to trust had been taken away from her. He would stay because if he didn't, the river might get the better of her again. And most of all, he would stay because he wanted to surprise that smile, the one that illuminated her whole face—the one he'd only seen once in all the time he'd been here—into existence again.

And, since he was examining other people's motives, perhaps he should examine his own. He'd omitted a few pertinent facts in his conversations with Dinah when he'd first come to the ranch. He'd fled California because of a girl's accusations—not because they were true, but because, despite the fact that his name had been cleared by the school's investigation, everyone still believed they might have been. He had been accused of sexual abuse when he was not guilty. Phinehas had been accused of nothing, when he was guilty. If Matthew stayed, he might get the chance to even the scales a bit.

Not the most honorable of motives, but it would do.

When he came back upstairs with the bottle, the pot of tea,

and two mugs carefully arranged on the cover of a flat book because he hadn't been able to find a tray, the baby was staring around in fresh horror at her surroundings and howling. Dinah was gone.

He put the tea things down on the floor with a clank, and before the volume got much higher, he was able to get the nipple into Tamsen's mouth.

He balanced her on his left arm, held the bottle at the correct angle with his right, and went in search of Dinah. She hadn't gone far, if the retching in the bathroom were any indication. When she didn't come out after a few minutes, he bumped the door open with his shoulder.

"Dinah?"

She sat on the floor with her back against the bathtub. The tissue she'd evidently used to wipe her mouth was crumpled in one hand, and her head was bowed.

He realized with a sense of inevitability that God had led him to this town, this house, this woman, for a reason. Maybe this moment was that reason.

He folded himself into a comfortable position next to her on the chenille bath mat, taking care not to bump the baby. There was plenty of room; the bathroom was a huge, old-fashioned one with a black-and-white checkered floor. Near the head of the tub, partially concealed by a fern, were the sheared stubs of the old pipes—presumably relics of a claw-footed tub that had stood here. At least there had been that much change over the years. Much of the rest of the house looked as it must have at the turn of the century.

He wondered if the family's values had changed at all in the interval. Likely not.

"I can't believe this is happening." Her voice was a whisper of sound in the silence, broken only by the baby's energetic attack on the bottle.

"I know," he agreed. Best if he stuck to brief replies. He

wasn't sure what kind of emotional lava was bubbling under the surface. Best if she did all the talking.

"It wasn't just me," she said in a wondering tone. "All those years of sacrifice, and it wasn't just me. He said I was a vessel sanctified unto him, but I wasn't. I wasn't."

"No."

"I thought if I gave myself, if I made myself a living sacrifice the way it says in Romans, it would save the others. Tamara, girls in other cities, I didn't know. I thought if I made him come back to me, it wouldn't happen to someone else." Her breath hitched. "But it did. It still did."

The bile rose in his throat at the thought of the tall, distinguished man twisting Scripture to fit his own dark desires, convincing a sheltered, innocent girl that what he was doing to her was the will of God. The baby moved restlessly as his arm tightened around her, and he made his muscles relax. Two traumatized females in one room would be more than he could handle. One was making him feel badly out of his depth as it was.

"Nothing you could have done or said would have changed what he was doing," he said at last.

"I wanted it to," she said sadly.

"You're not responsible for what happened to Tamara and any other girls he abused. You couldn't have stopped it. No matter what you sacrificed, he would still take what he wanted. He is responsible, not you. He needs to be stopped."

"You can't stop Phinehas."

"Why not?"

"Matthew, he's the senior Shepherd."

"What about the church board? There must be some kind of governing body to hold the ministers accountable for what they do."

"Only God." From her tone, God was in on it with Phinehas, and couldn't be expected to help.

"No other authority? No church elders?"

"There are Elders, but if anyone even whispered something like that out loud, they would be put Out. It's like challenging God. Just like refusing him is refusing to do God's will."

"Dinah, God doesn't ask people to do evil."

"He asks us to make sacrifices for others. Phinehas said that if it weren't for me, he wouldn't be able to go on as a Shepherd. That my love gave him strength to give everything to the lost sheep. And if I stopped, the souls he couldn't reach would go to hell and it would be on my head for all eternity."

"That sounds like emotional blackmail." His voice was gentle, though his blood felt chilled. "He must be very good at it."

She buried her head in her arms, crossed on her knees. "I'm so stupid. So ashamed."

Somehow he managed to hold the bottle with his left hand so that Tamsen could still reach it, and slipped his right arm around her shoulders.

"You have nothing to be ashamed of, dear."

Small sounds came from beneath her arms, and her body shook with weeping. He didn't know if she could hear him or not, but it had to be said.

"Phinehas is an abusive criminal who should be handed over to the police. He took advantage of you and hurt you. None of this is your fault."

She still did not respond; in fact, he wondered if she remembered he was there. Nonetheless, he stayed beside her until his back began to ache, his arms around two of the victims of Phinehas. A clock downstairs struck a quarter after midnight and he realized that, at last, the terrible day that had begun with such joy was done.

DINAH WOKE WITH a jolt when the baby let out her fire-engine noise next to her. She stared at her for a moment, wondering how a kicking, yelling infant had got into her bed, and then the events of the previous day flooded her memory.

She clenched her teeth against the pain in her knees, pushed her hair out of her eyes, and crawled out of bed to see if she could find a bottle.

There was another one in Tamara's baby bag. It was empty. A quick search produced no formula, no expressed milk, nothing resembling food of any kind. Could babies drink regular milk? She couldn't remember, and the noise was deafening.

A bleary glance into the fridge told her there was no milk, anyway. There was nothing for it. She was going to have to go to town.

Tamsen didn't want to go to town. She didn't want to be changed. She wanted her breakfast, and when it wasn't forthcoming, she shrieked with rage and frustration as Dinah pulled on the first dress that came to hand, staggered down the stairs and out to the barn, and bundled her into the truck. She screamed down the highway. She roared in the drugstore, where thankfully the cash register was open and there was actually baby formula in stock. By the time they got into the truck and back out on the highway, hysteria was competing with exhaustion and—Dinah was convinced—the advanced stages of starvation.

Somehow the instructions on the package registered in her brain and she got the bottle filled, to the right temperature, and into Tamsen's mouth.

The silence in the kitchen was like cool cream on a sunburn.

Matthew came in with an egg carton full of eggs and took them both in with a glance.

"Was that the truck I heard?" She was too drained to do anything but nod. "You had to go to town for formula? Dinah, there are two of us here. Why on earth didn't you ask me to go?"

She looked up at him. "I didn't even think of it."

He put the eggs in the fridge. "Next time, do think of it. You don't have to do everything on your own. You don't have to take care of everyone. I'm your hired man, remember?"

"Hired men don't usually look after abandoned babies."

"Perhaps not, but I haven't done anything hired men usually do since I got here. I've fished a woman from the river and fed a baby, been a night watchman and buried a beloved companion. I haven't pitched hay or driven a tractor even once."

She couldn't help the smile that trembled briefly at the corners of her mouth. "I knew there was a reason I hired you. You're versatile."

"I have another useful skill. I can make very nice poached eggs, if you would like some."

This time the smile was a bit more solid. "I would love some."

Tamsen finished the bottle and Dinah put her on her shoulder to burp, too tired to care if the baby spit up all over what she belatedly realized was her Sunday dress.

"Better use this." Matthew handed her a tea towel from the drawer.

Tamsen promptly spit up on it, and when Dinah had cleaned her up, she sat the baby on her lap so they could look one another over.

Half of her was afraid to know, to have what Danny had said confirmed in the innocent flesh of this child. Ambivalence was a familiar emotion. She hated Phinehas, but he was the only one who paid her any attention. She'd been told that her salvation depended on loving God, and Phinehas by extension, but how could you love someone who abused you, whom you couldn't ask to stop?

That was a mystery she was too exhausted to figure out.

And now here was this baby. Her niece. Child of the girl she loved with all her heart, a child that under normal circumstances—say, if Tamara and Danny had been married—she would have adored and spoiled and been "favoritest aunt" to.

But here she was, this child of violence and power and hatred, sitting in her lap with not one single person on the planet who wanted her to exist.

When you looked at it that way, only Dinah and Matthew stood between her and an adoption agency, and for all Dinah knew about such matters, it could be a grim possibility.

"She doesn't look like him." Tamsen's gaze, which had been rambling around the room, returned to her. "Her eyes are brown, like Tammy's."

"Brown is a dominant gene." Matthew sounded absent as he concentrated on cracking eggs into the simmering water.

"Good." If she had to look into the ice-blue eyes of Phinehas every day, it would be a lot harder to love this little scrap.

The baby's nose was a turned-up dab, and she saw Tamara's wide-lipped grin and her dimpled chin. The forehead could be Phinehas's or her father's, but she preferred to think it was the latter. Bit by bit she erased any possibility of recognition from Tamsen's face.

She tickled the palm of her niece's little hand, and the baby's fingers wrapped around her forefinger. There were the hands of Phinehas, long and aristocratic. "You're going to be a piano player when you grow up, aren't you?" she murmured. Phinehas could play their old upright as though it were a concert grand. But hands weren't like eyes. You couldn't see disgust and desire and the unflinching need for control in hands.

"You are such a cantankerous little thing," she said. "How did Tamara produce you?"

Matthew buttered the toast and slid the eggs onto a plate for her. "Can you manage?"

"I don't know." She settled the baby in her lap and let her kick and wiggle while she ate.

Matthew dished up his own breakfast and sat beside her. Briefly, he bowed his head and she realized she hadn't said grace for her meal.

Grace was a habit, like washing one's hands before dinner.

The truth was she didn't like thanking God for meals when she had absolutely nothing else to thank Him for. She waited until Matthew picked up his fork, and went on with her eggs.

It felt strange, off balance, to eat with a baby on one arm. How would she manage to cut a steak, for instance? "I wonder if there's a high chair around here," she said aloud.

"That sounds like long-term thinking."

"No, just practical. Aunt Evelyn will find Tamara sooner or later and we can get Tamsen back where she belongs. But in the meantime, I guess I'd better look around for baby stuff."

"I HOPE YOU know something about caring for babies." Matthew followed Dinah up the attic stairs, marveling at how quiet the house was with Tamsen asleep. They'd grabbed the opportunity to do some detective work and see what they could find in the way of baby clothes and equipment. "What I know could fit in the nipple on her bottle."

"My knowledge is seventeen years old," Dinah confessed. She opened the attic door and stood to one side as he joined her. "A little girl's idea of looking after her little sister is trying not to poke her with the diaper pins and sticking a bottle in her mouth when she's hungry. There has to be more to it than that." She paused, surveying the room under the peaks of the roof by the light of the bare bulb overhead. "Good grief. Look at all this stuff. It's going to take all day to find anything in here."

That was just for starters. Matthew didn't know how long the family had been on this place, but there were at least three generations' worth of belongings up here. A three-speed bicycle leaned against an Art Deco-era chest of drawers. Boxes were stacked on top of boxes, all labeled *Books*. That might be interesting, but definitely not at the moment. A number of lamps missing bulbs crowded the surface of a cedar chest, and across the back of the room, a clothesline sagged under the weight of what looked like fifty or sixty dresses. He narrowed his eyes.

"Were those your mother's?"

Dinah looked up from a box she'd opened labeled *Dinah Baby*. "Those are color. Women in my family haven't worn color in three generations. Those are probably Great-Grandmother Sarah's, from before she met the Shepherd. We're a favored family because of her."

"What does that mean?"

"Well, when the original Shepherd came here, only two families would give him a place to stay or listen to the gospel he brought. So as the Elect grew, those original families were called the First Fruits of the harvest, or just favored families. We have Gathering in our home, and the men of the family are Elders, as it was in the first days. Hey, look. Here are some sleepers of mine. And bibs and stuff."

Still trying to work out the tenets of this odd religion, Matthew said, "But what if there are only girls in the family? Such as this one, for instance."

Dinah held up a crocheted, pale-aqua blanket with an old stain in the middle. "The McNeills—the other family—had girls, too. So when Madeleine married, her husband Owen Blanchard became Elder."

"Rather like British primogeniture," he commented. "Property goes to the eldest son, or the son of the eldest daughter."

"That's going to be a problem in my case." She didn't sound as if she cared much that a four-generations-old tradition was going to end with her.

"No husband, no son? How unsporting of you."

"No way." Her voice was hushed, and it sounded as though the words were being forced between her teeth. "Here's another box with Tamara's baby things. Have a look around and see if you can find a high chair. And a crib. She can't sleep in the car seat forever."

That closed that subject. Matthew didn't press her. It was nothing to him whether or not this odd group got its elder or not. From what he'd seen, the sooner it atrophied and died out, the better, starting with its leadership.

No, what concerned him was Dinah's attitude toward men and children. What did that mean for her little niece? For relationships in general? For Dinah's future?

And what made it his business, anyway? She was his employer, nothing more.

Buried under what looked like miscellaneous car parts and several lines of toasters and mixers—all in pieces—Matthew finally found a high chair. It was chrome and the seat was padded with yellow vinyl, so odds were good that it had belonged to an earlier generation of Traynells than Dinah. It would do just fine for the newest generation.

"I've found the high chair," he called over to where she knelt on the plank floor, filling a box with pastel plunder.

"And I've got sleepers, clothes, and bibs. That leaves diapers and formula from the store, right? Anything else we've forgotten?"

"How can I forget when I don't know what the requirements are in the first place?" He was only half joking. "In the absence of a Babies 101 textbook, what we need to do is to get on the Internet and do some research."

She looked up at him and began to pack the unwanted things back in their box. "The closest terminal is at the library, downtown by the post office and the police station. You get half an hour on it before the librarian kicks you off."

"Don't you have a computer?" He couldn't imagine any household in America not having one. He himself had two, back in California in the boxes in Paolo Martinez's garage. He'd considered bringing his laptop along, then discarded the idea as silly. What sane person went on a walking tour with a laptop? It would just have been stolen along with his wallet, and he'd be in exactly the same position.

"No," she replied. "The Elect believe computers are tools of the devil."

He stared at her. "Why?"

"Because the monitor is like a window, letting the world into your home, the same as television. Radio is a no-no, too."

It had been a long time since complete irrationality had flummoxed him. He tried to think of something reasonable to say. "Do you believe that?"

"Of course not." She hefted the box of baby clothes onto one hip. "But my mother does."

"So that's why you know where the nearest terminal is. But Dinah, it's going to be very inconvenient, driving into town every time we need to know something."

She shrugged. "Convenience is for lazy people."

"No one could ever imagine you being lazy. But I'm thinking of Tamsen. What if she catches a virus or something and we need to know how much aspirin to give her?"

"We call Dr. Archer."

"Is he a pediatrician?"

"Well, no, but everyone goes to him for everything."

"What if she wakes in the middle of the night in pain from teething? She's going to be doing that soon, isn't she? You can't just ring him up and ask him what to do."

"I could," she said stubbornly. "Besides, she won't be here by the time she starts getting teeth in. Tamara will have come back by then."

"Let's deal with what is rather than what we wish were the case," he said with a little more shortness than he intended. "There are loads of things we can learn if we have a laptop here. We won't have to drive to town or call someone every time we need to find out some little fact."

"I can't have a computer here. My mother would never get

over the shame that such a thing came into the Elder's house. And Phinehas would probably destroy it. He's snapped the radio antennas off people's cars before."

Was that reluctance in her tone? He pulled the high chair closer to the stairs to give himself a moment to think.

"We'll say it's mine," he said finally. "We simply must have one, and if that's the only way, then we can keep it in the barn with me. No one need know it's here."

Across the debris of who knew how many lives, they exchanged a long look. In her eyes he saw indecision and longing and a frustrated practicality.

"All right," she said.

It was the voice of a woman who realized she was on the long, slippery slope to moral compromise. As far as he was concerned, it was about time.

Chapter 12

AFTER CONFERRING WITH Matthew on the features and functions a person would need on her laptop, Dinah went to the library with her credit card and ordered one off the Internet, complete with modem cable and carrying case. Every moment she sat at the library's terminal, she kept one eye on the screen and the other on her fellow patrons. In all the years she'd been using the computer, she'd never been caught, but there was always a first time. And to be caught ordering a laptop would just add insult to disaster. It seemed crazy to spend so much money for something she was going to have to sell in a matter of weeks anyway, but she couldn't argue with the logic of it.

After the order was placed and she'd agreed to an exorbitant amount of money to have it rushed, she checked her stock portfolio and noted that she'd made enough this quarter to pay for the computer.

A comforting thought.

Then she checked her father's portfolio and let the brokerage know he'd passed away and the accounts should be transferred fully into her name. No doubt she'd have to do a bunch of paperwork, but the accounts were joint, so they weren't in probate. He may have been of the opinion that all she was good for was making dinner and cleaning house, but after the cancer diagnosis at least he'd had the sense to listen to Elsie and transfer partial control of the money to her. Of course, he did all his transactions by phone with his broker. What he didn't know was that she had had all the accounts set up online as well and could tell him as much about them as the broker could.

There were advantages to being underestimated.

THREE DAYS LATER, right on schedule, the UPS truck delivered the laptop. While Dinah hid the packaging in the barn so she could use it to mail the unit to its new owner later, Matthew set it up on the table in his little suite, talking Tamsen through each step as she watched him from her carrier installing software and inserting CDs. Dinah came in as he plugged in the modem cable and set up an ISP account.

"Now, then," he said with satisfaction as the Internet came up, "let's do some research."

As Dinah hung over his shoulder, she saw that his research skills were much better than hers. More, he had passwords to university libraries she'd never heard of. "All kinds of child psychology here," he said, bookmarking site after site. By early evening they'd learned that Tamsen was roughly on track for development in her age group and what kinds of things they could expect to begin feeding her in the next couple of weeks if they didn't hear from Tamara. And speaking of that . . .

Dinah finished giving Tamsen her supper bottle and nudged Matthew off the chair. "It may be useless, but I'm going to send Tamara an e-mail."

"I thought you weren't supposed to communicate with her? Shunning, and all that."

"We call it being Silenced. And it's a bit beside the point now, isn't it? If I can buy a computer I can e-mail my sister."

She thought she saw the corners of his mouth twitch. The

corners of her own were doing the same. She brought up her e-mail account and scanned it hopefully, but there was nothing but her usual financial digests and a lot of spam. She sent a note to Tammy's mailbox telling her that she had received her manila envelope, that Tamsen was fine, and that she hoped she'd changed her mind and was on her way back.

> Tamsen needs her mom. You know as well as I do that this isn't a good house to bring up a child in. I'm sure you can do better once you get settled and let me know where you are.

That was getting close to blasphemy, and as close as she dared come to the subject of both of them being abused. She couldn't bear the thought of Phinehas having unlimited access to yet another generation of Traynell girls. At the same time, opening up that subject over e-mail just wasn't right. She could do that when Tamara came home.

She hit "Send" and watched the screen close itself. It felt a little like throwing a ball when there was no one there to catch it, but she had to try. Someone had to make Tamara see sense.

MATTHEW PUT HIS secondhand kettle on to boil while Dinah went out into the barn to tuck her birds in for the night. He leaned one hip against the gray Formica counter and shook his head at himself. If someone had told him a month ago that he would feel such a sense of accomplishment at causing someone to sin against her church's doctrines, he would have recommended they see a doctor.

And not the medical kind, either.

But the point was he was convinced God had led him here

for a reason, and he needed to talk with Dinah about that reason. She simply couldn't be expected to live like this.

The computer monitor some kind of cosmic window to the underworld, allowing wrong into one's home . . .

The Shepherds as the voices of God . . .

Women dressed in perpetual mourning . . .

What did God have to do with all that?

If the good Lord's reason for bringing him here was to talk with Dinah and help her see how skewed her perspective had become, then he needed to step outside his own comfort zone and do it. He was not a man who minded other people's business, but it was clear Dinah was willing to let him intrude now and again, as the laptop sitting on the table proved.

Not that he was any kind of saint, himself. In fact, like Moses, he was not eloquent, and he would just as soon the Lord used someone else. But for Dinah, apparently, there was no one else. He just had to have faith that the Lord knew what He was doing.

For a moment he was tempted to share his own story with her. If she knew the losses he had suffered because of Torrie Parker's unfounded accusations, it might be a kind of bond between them. And maybe the knowledge he had gained and the research he had done on the dynamics of sexual abuse could be of some use to her. But even as the thought formed, a lump of resistance formed, too.

He couldn't. The poor girl had enough ugliness to deal with. Why burden her with more? She already knew he wasn't perfect. He was broke, the next thing to homeless, and he had holes in his socks. If God needed to use a humble instrument, he fit the bill.

No, he'd keep his story to himself. Maybe the opportunity would come where he could share his knowledge. But in Dinah's case, sharing himself would probably do more harm than good.

Dınah made sure the chickens were comfortable on their roosts before she closed the door to the outside pen. Schatzi made her contented bubbling cluck, and a pang struck Dinah as she sat in the plastic chair and no Sheba hopped onto her knee looking for a cuddle.

Fighting back the futile tears of loss, she walked back through the dark passage and into Matthew's suite. He smiled as she came in, then took the boiling kettle off the burner and filled the teapot they'd found in one of the boxes in the attic. It made sense for him to have them. He loved his tea and the only time she drank it was when she was with him.

"Everyone all right?" he asked.

"Yes." Everyone who was alive was just fine.

"So tell me something," he began. "How much do you believe in the expectations of your church?"

"What do you mean?" Dinah slid into the other chair at the cheap little table and resisted the urge to unbuckle Tamsen from her carrier and cuddle her. She should be grateful the baby was sleeping and not roaring with hunger or discomfort.

"Well, it seems to me there are all kinds of strictures and structures in place to keep order. It's almost as if you concentrate more on those than on worship."

A wrinkle formed between her brows. "I don't understand. The structure is there to keep us safe. The way we behave is our worship. It's our service to God."

"Not having a computer is service to God?"

Put like that, it did sound a little odd. Dinah had never given the structure of her life much thought. You looked a certain way, you behaved a certain way, and if you thought otherwise than a certain way, you certainly didn't say anything about it. The structure was there for a reason—to show people the beauty of worshipping God.

Not having a computer hadn't brought anyone to God, though, she had to admit. At least, not in Hamilton Falls.

"Let me ask it a different way," Matthew went on when she didn't answer. "How is God deprived if you get a computer in service to Tamsen?"

"He isn't," she replied. "But it might be a stumbling block to someone else if they found out I had one."

"A stumbling block?"

"If they saw that I gave in to temptation, they might be tempted, too."

"Even though its purpose is good and in itself, it's harmless."

"Yes." Now the preaching she'd heard against the "window into the world" was really beginning to sound silly. She'd had to accept it because the words had come from the Shepherds, who were inspired by God. "We're supposed to obey the word of God without questioning, Matthew," she said quietly. "Anything else means we're disobedient. That we have a wrong spirit that isn't Christ-like."

"Christ questioned all kinds of things," he said. "He was always making people think about what they were doing. And I think you question what you're doing a lot more than you let on."

The water had to be ready by now. Why wasn't he making the tea? "That's because I'm a bad, disobedient person. I'm supposed to be a holy vessel and most of the time I just feel like an old cracked pot that somebody threw out." And if that wasn't an invitation to a pity party, she didn't know what was. Shame and embarrassment scorched her cheeks. "Sorry. That was a selfish thing to say."

He got up from the laptop and for a horrible moment she thought he was angry. Then her panicked brain translated his gentle movements. He was just reaching for the box of tea bags in the cupboard behind her.

"You are none of those things," he said softly. He poured

hot water into the fat brown teapot, swished it out, and dropped the tea bags in. "You are a beautiful woman, with a kind, generous heart. That wretch of a Phinehas has taken what is loveliest and twisted it so you don't even recognize it any more."

Beautiful? Was he crazy? She was skinny and awkward and all her body was good for was attracting the wrong kind of attention. Rage and self-contempt burned her throat and she bent to snatch the carrier up off the floor. The abrupt movement wakened Tamsen, who began to cry.

Dinah hardly heard it above the roar in her own head and the desperate urge to flee. It wasn't until she'd run across the yard and was safely in the house that she came to herself and realized Tamsen was screaming with all the fear and rage of one who believes she will never be cared for again.

AT ONE IN the morning Dinah finally admitted that trying to sleep was pointless. A glance out the hall window, which looked out over the barn, told her she wasn't the only one—the lights in the hired man's suite were on, too. In fact, the only person getting any sleep was Tamsen, for which Dinah was pathetically grateful.

After scaring the baby earlier, it had taken an hour to calm her down enough to distract her with a bottle. Tamsen knew perfectly well Dinah wasn't her mother, so even when Dinah tried to hold and comfort her, she wasn't having any of it. Or maybe it was because Dinah couldn't relax—maybe the child felt the stiffness in her muscles, the rage in every fiber.

Dinah was convinced sheer exhaustion had finally sent Tamsen into dreamland, and she'd tucked her into the old white crib they'd brought down from the attic with a sigh of relief. Who had told her that little babies were easy to take care of? It must have been Linda Bell, who looked after other people's kids for a living. If this was the easy part, she didn't envy Tamara the later stages of motherhood one bit.

But it wasn't stress over the baby that was keeping her awake now. It was the war going on inside her and the pictures her mind played on the darkened ceiling of her room.

How could he spoil their friendship by calling her beautiful? In just the same way Phinehas had rooked her in, had shown her love and attention, and then—when she was addicted and couldn't live without it—had begun the unspeakable.

Now she was going to have to ask Matthew to leave. She couldn't bear the sight of him, knowing that he was thinking of her that way. Knowing what was in his mind the moment she let her guard down. She was alone out here, and he could begin his campaign of misery at any time he chose.

Well, she'd handled worse things than firing a hired man. She could do this, too, much as it hurt. She'd actually begun to think of him as a person, not a man, which was new in her experience. She'd even smiled at his gentle jokes and admired his skill with a computer, even if he was sort of useless at practical things like managing a walking tour on his own.

He'd protected her and even saved her life, but that was probably just part of the buttering-up process. If she saw him as her protector, she'd be more likely to let him get close, wouldn't she? *Well, fool me once and it's your fault,* she thought. *Fool me twice and it's mine.*

He'd gone and spoiled it and proven himself to be a wolf in men's clothing, seeking to devour. In the morning she'd hand him his wages and he could just go buy a bus ticket and devour somewhere else.

With a decision made, and control asserted somewhere, even if it was only in her mind, Dinah turned over and tried once again to go to sleep.

———

NATURALLY, ONCE SLEEP did come, she overdid it. Dinah cocked a bleary eye at the alarm clock on the bedside table and groaned. Nine thirty? Good grief, the baby had probably died of starvation. In fact, she must be dead or the screams of enraged hunger would have roused her hours before.

Oh, no. Oh, no.

Dinah crawled out of bed and staggered to the door, where she snatched her dressing gown off its hook and ran down the hall to Tamara's old room. By default it had become the baby's room, more because there was room for the crib and a writing desk that did duty as a changing table than for any other reason.

The crib was empty and the carrier gone.

Had Tammy come back in the early hours and taken her? But no, there was the diaper bag sitting next to the bed. Mystified and filled with dread, Dinah ran down the stairs and skidded to a halt in the kitchen doorway.

Matthew looked up and smiled. "Good morning." Tamsen lay cradled in his left arm, both little starfish hands splayed against the bottle. Her plump cheeks worked in and out, flushed with the effort of wrestling nourishment out of it.

"This is one bottomless pit of a baby," he said proudly. "We had one breakfast at six o'clock, and decided to have our elevenses early. At this rate she's going to start putting on the pounds."

If she hadn't been so astonished, Dinah would have found the scene comical. Matthew's elbows stuck out at angles, as if he couldn't quite get the knack of holding her comfortably, and he held the bottle in his fingers as if he were poking it through the bars of a cage at the zoo.

Tamsen didn't seem to mind one bit. In fact, she was a whole lot happier on Matthew's lap than she had been on Dinah's last night.

Last night.

The angry speech she'd rehearsed in her head seemed to be written in washable ink and it was fading by the second. How was it possible he'd forestalled Tamsen's crying and managed to feed her twice already without waking her, Dinah? And how deeply in need of sleep was she that she'd missed it all? Most important, what depths of consideration and care did it show in this man that he'd (a) thought of all this and (b) acted on it?

What was she going to do now?

Dinah sagged against the kitchen door jamb and tried to get her foggy brain to work.

"I started a pot of coffee." Matthew nodded toward the pot. "It isn't as good as yours, but then, your tea isn't as good as mine." His smile held all the satisfaction of a man who had put in a hard day's work and was proud of it.

Wordlessly she got a mug from the cupboard, put in some milk, and poured coffee. While she sank into a chair at the kitchen table, Tamsen finished the bottle and Matthew lifted her to his shoulder, patting her back.

Dinah hooked a tea towel from the oven door with two fingers. "Don't forget this."

"The towel is probably in better shape than my shirt." He repositioned the baby on his shoulder and continued to pat her.

She had planned to offer him some of her father's clothes, poor man. Right, and she'd planned to kick him off the ranch today, too. Which was it going to be? She buried her nose in the coffee mug and hoped the caffeine would clear her brain. Hot and strong, softened with milk, it was actually pretty good. Not bad for an Englishman.

There she was, thinking good thoughts about him again.

If the good ones outweigh the bad ones, maybe you should rethink this altogether.

As if he'd read her mind, Matthew said, "I'm sorry I upset you last night. I made personal remarks and offended you, and I would like to apologize."

He'd said she was beautiful. That was offensive, all right. To a crazy person. A normal woman would have smiled and accepted it gracefully. Unfortunately, Dinah didn't have the knack. Never had. Not that compliments came her way all that often. But still . . .

"It's all right," she said at last, awkwardly, her voice muffled in the depths of the coffee cup. The decisive tones of a woman about to give an employee his walking papers. Sure.

"It isn't all right. I caused you to question your beliefs, with the presumption that mine were somehow better."

Is that what he thought he'd done? "It wasn't that."

"What was it, then?"

She'd made such a fool of herself last night he couldn't think much less of her if she went ahead and told him. "It all goes back to Phinehas."

She'd lost him already. "Phinehas?" he repeated.

"He—he would tell me I was beautiful. For years, you know, before he . . . before. That I was his favorite among the favored families, that my spirit made me lovely in his eyes. It took a long time to realize what he was doing."

Matthew gazed at her a moment, his eyes sad. "He was preparing the soil?"

She nodded, thankful there were some things she didn't have to say out loud. "And I fell for it, like a total idiot."

"Dinah, what was it like for you, growing up?"

A breath of cool relief passed over her at the swerve in subject. "I hated being a kid, but it was nothing to being a teenager. You can't imagine how awful it is to be an Elect girl at Hamilton High School."

"The black?"

"The black clothes, the hair long enough to wash the feet of Jesus, the notes we have to give the Phys. Ed. teacher explaining why we can't wear shorts, doing our homework in a stuffy class-room while everyone else is out at the track. Even swimming in the river is impossible."

"Why?"

She thought back to past summers—the heat, the discomfort, the frustrated longing to be normal. "Bathing suits are immod-est, so we wear T-shirts and our oldest skirt, pinned between our legs."

"To swim?" Tamsen hiccuped and swiveled her head to look up at him as his voice rose.

"Eventually you give it up because it just isn't worth looking that silly."

"I can see that," he agreed. "But what was it like here at home?"

How did one describe it? "My father believed in the struc-ture. Every jot, every tittle of the law was important to him, and he made sure it was important to us, too."

"Moses's law?"

"No. God's law. The Elect's law."

"Can I see it? I'd like to become better acquainted with your doctrine."

"Oh, it isn't written down anywhere." She waved a hand. "It's something you learn by osmosis, listening to Melchizedek and Phinehas preach, watching the others, watching your parents." She paused, remembering. "Getting smacked when you don't wear your sleeves long enough or you don't put your hair up neatly enough. When you wiggle or get bored in Gathering, which apparently I used to do a lot." She shrugged. "But all of that trains you to have the right example, and that can lead oth-ers to the way where they can find salvation."

"To Christ, you mean."

She nodded, and took another sip of coffee.

His brows were creased in a puzzled frown. "But how does how you look lead people to Christ?"

"The outside reflects what's on the inside. And what's inside brings people to want that for themselves."

"It seems to me, from what you've described, what's on the inside is a lot of unhappiness and failure to measure up to the jots and tittles."

Dinah realized that, in her selfishness, she'd failed to explain this in a godly way so that he'd understand. "It—it's good for us to make sacrifices. It pleases God when we give up things and don't conform with the world. That's how we work out our salvation."

The baby spit up on the tea towel at last. Matthew cleaned her up and then held her in his lap, where she stared at Dinah, her little mouth open.

"Dinah," he said quietly, "have you ever heard of grace?"

That was easy. "Of course."

"How would you define it?"

She thought of the preaching at Summer Gathering, of the hot, airless tent and the hundreds of people packed inside listening to the word of God. Last summer there had been a lot about grace, prompting follow-up sermons about how much the people of God needed it in an unholy world.

"Grace is like grease," she explained. "It's what moves between the people of God so that they live in harmony with one another. The way engine parts all work together." He was looking a little doubtful. Had she got the answer wrong? "Why, how would you define it?"

"I believe that grace is what covers us because of the sacrifice of Jesus," he said quietly. "It's what makes it so that we don't have to work our way to heaven. He paid the price for us, and now his grace makes us worthy."

"Work our way to heaven?" She latched onto something she recognized, pleased that he could understand. "Yes, he paid the price for us, and now his death is an example of how we can die to ourselves."

Why was he shaking his head?

"That's still work. Salvation isn't performance based, like a giant corporation where you work your way to the top. Jesus paid the price once for all of us, and now we live free under grace."

That couldn't be right. If that were the case, there would be no point in wearing black, no point in long hair, no point in her whole miserable childhood and teenage years.

No point in all that sacrifice.

No point in doing what she had done with Phinehas.

No point in her life at all.

"Worldly churches use that as an excuse," she said finally, reeling back from the precipice and taking refuge in truths she'd been taught since birth. "If you believe that, you can go do what you like and grace covers you. Like—like a big old insurance policy."

Matthew smiled. "But isn't that where being born again comes in? The new woman born in Christ doesn't behave that way, does she?"

"No. She does what pleases God."

"Yes, but does that include all these things that you call the structure, or does it mean love in its fullest sense?"

"You can't put a finger on love." She glanced at the baby in his lap. He was playing a modified version of patty-cake and instead of screaming, Tamsen seemed to be enjoying it. "Love has to be concrete, like changing diapers and feeding. Love is a service."

"It can be," Matthew allowed. "But sometimes the service becomes more important than what prompts it. Like changing diapers on a baby because they're dirty, not because you love her and want her to be comfortable. Service like that gets between us and our Father. We're perfectly capable of performing the service without any love at all, as Phinehas can probably tell us."

"He would never say such a thing."

"I can see it, though."

She huffed a breath of laughter. "Don't ever let him know. If you were Elect, you'd be Silenced in a second for criticizing him."

"He isn't perfect."

"No, but the grace of God covers him. You said so yourself."

"I believe it does, but I don't think that man is walking in newness of life. If he were, he couldn't do the things he does. He couldn't abuse you."

Dinah was silent, watching the baby's tiny fingers in Matthew's hands. He was becoming more sure of himself with the baby every second. And with other things.

"You told me not long ago that God was in on it with him," Matthew went on after a moment. "I believe that Phinehas's worst crime is in distorting the way you see God."

"You have no idea what the worst is. Just like I have no idea what God is." The words fell out of her mouth before she had time to stop them. Then a hot flush of embarrassment washed into her cheeks.

"That's not surprising," he said gently.

"Oh, and I suppose you do?"

"You're right. I have no idea what the worst can be. But the Father I love gives me strength and hope and unexpected gifts along the way."

"Right, like your car breaking down." Acid etched her tone. "And those guys who stole your wallet. Those were really unexpected gifts."

"I was thinking more of you," he said. "And little Schatzi, of whom I'm becoming quite fond. And of course our little voice here, howling in the wilderness." He smiled down at Tamsen, and the baby smiled back. "Dinah! Did you see that?"

She had. "Will she do it again?"

Matthew made a big, goofy face and the baby cackled in delight. "You see?" he demanded, his face all lit up in just the same way. "Unexpected gifts."

Clearly, Dinah thought, she and Matthew believed in completely different Gods. The problem was she had no idea which one was real and which the distorted fantasy.

Chapter 13

AFTER REWARDING THEIR labors with a smile, Tamsen decided to be difficult for the rest of the morning. The dry diaper wasn't right, Dinah's attempts at entertainment weren't right, and going down for a nap was out of the question. Finally Matthew did what any reasonable man would do—he got on the Internet to look for solutions.

"It says that at four months we might try solid foods," he reported after a trip out to the barn. "We can buy those here, can't we?"

"Hamilton Falls isn't that small." Dinah raised her voice over the sound of Tamsen's fussing, which didn't help the situation. "It's pretty nice outside. Why don't I take her out while you go get baby food? You never know. It might work."

Matthew took the truck, and Dinah wrapped Tamsen in the stained but clean aqua blanket and took her out into the front yard. March had gone out like a lamb, and the early April sunshine held the promise of relief from the cold and new life springing up from the unfriendly soil. The Traynell property sloped away to the road, and on the other side of it, down to the river in a gentle roll of grass and scrub pines and weeds.

Half a dozen chickens, led by Schatzi, had found some dry ground close to the house and were busy giving themselves dust baths. Tamsen, who had fallen silent the minute Dinah had stepped out on the porch, made a sound Dinah translated as interest in what the birds were doing. She sat on a stump and told the baby all the birds' names and why dirt was flying in every direction as each bird happily hollowed out its bath and sent swathes of dust over its back.

When she heard a car's engine a few minutes later, she couldn't believe Matthew had gone to town and back so fast. Maybe he'd forgotten something.

She swiveled on the stump and saw Claire Montoya climb out of her discreet, compact sedan.

Claire?

But Claire had never come out to the ranch for anything other than a young people's meeting or Gathering. They'd bunk together at Summer Gathering, maybe, or share a booth at the café if they both happened to get the same lunch hour. But there their commonality ended. Claire Montoya had normal parents who lived normal lives. Dinah . . . well, Dinah put on an act that looked reasonably normal and kept her mouth shut.

Claire picked her way across the wet grass in her neat black pumps. Her black suit was wool crepe and cut so nicely she probably hadn't made it, but had ordered it from Nordstrom or Bloomingdale's. She worked at the bank—in fact had taken the position Dinah had had to give up when Dad got so sick he couldn't run the ranch. Her blouse was black but made of something like satin, a sensuous, worldly fabric that wouldn't escape the old ladies' hawk eyes.

From her expression, she'd already heard about the baby's arrival. Was she coming to check out the rumor before she spread it any further? Dinah supposed she should be grateful. The Elect grapevine was highly efficient, but not too picky about accuracy.

"Hi, Dinah." Claire greeted her with a smile, but her fascinated gaze was locked on the baby.

"Hi. What brings you out this way?"

"Is this your new niece? Linda Bell told me you were looking after her."

Which pretty much answered the question.

"Her name is Tamsen. It's Cornish for 'a person who is free.'" So said Matthew, anyway, who could reasonably be expected to know, since he had been born and raised in Cornwall. She wondered if Tamara had known that when she'd named her. *Free.*

Claire tickled the baby's fingers. "I never heard it before. It's unusual. But then, from what I hear, just about everything about her is unusual."

Dinah attempted to be civil. "So did you come to find out what her name was, or is there something else I can do for you?"

Claire seemed to give herself a mental shake. "I've been hearing the strangest things and thought I'd come out and have a Visit."

A Visit. Oh, dear. Not a small-v visit like most of the world enjoyed. A capital-V Visit meant that someone thought you needed encouragement or help. That maybe your service was slipping a bit. Of course, sometimes it was simply an offer of a shoulder to cry on, though she and Claire weren't really on those terms.

In any case, she didn't need Visits from anybody.

"Are you busy?" Claire asked after a moment.

"I'm trying to get Tamsen to settle down enough to have a nap. For some reason nothing is making her happy today."

"Is she hungry?"

"No."

"Dry? Comfortable?"

"Yes."

"Nothing is poking or hurting her? No gas?"

"She uses disposables and she burped after her second breakfast."

Claire nodded briskly. "Sometimes you have to just let them cry. It's good for them. Builds their lungs."

Dinah eyed her. "You haven't heard Tamsen cry. I'd have to move out and go in the barn."

This seemed to throw the switch on Claire's train of thought. "Is it true you hired a vagrant and he sleeps out there?"

Was she always this abrupt and nosy?

"I hired a former university professor and he's living in the hired man's suite."

"I heard he was a homeless man."

"Well, you might want to check your facts. He isn't." Not now. But Dinah wasn't going to go into details. Matthew's life was his own business, not fodder for the Elect women to chew on.

"But Dinah, isn't it dangerous?"

"What? Matthew? Of course not."

"Well, look at you." Claire waved an arm at the grass and the river. "All alone out here, now that your mom's gone to Pitchford. Anything could happen."

Anything could and already had happened. Matthew could only improve the picture.

"I'm not worried," she said mildly. "He's a very nice man. He's gone to get baby food for Tamsen, in case you were wondering. You'll probably pass him on the highway on your way back."

That was about as pointed as she could bring herself to be, but Claire didn't take the hint.

"Maybe he's not a physical danger, but what about, well, your reputation?"

Dinah blinked at her, and waited.

Claire had the grace to look a little uncomfortable. "You know. All alone out here with—with him. A worldly man, nice or not, is still a worldly man."

"Claire, he's an employee. We've had hired men off and on

for years." Dinah settled the baby more comfortably in her lap. "Why does it matter to you?" she asked finally. "We've never really been the best of friends. My behavior has never worried you before."

"You never gave anyone anything to worry about before." Claire's voice held something Dinah couldn't identify. Her lashes veiled her green eyes, and her hair—which curled around her forehead and temples in a way that Dinah could only envy—was pulled back in a heavy chignon at the nape of her neck. On Dinah this would have been fatally ugly. Claire could have been a nymph in a Greek frieze.

"I'm not giving anyone anything to worry about now," she said quietly. "I'm in a weird situation and I'm making the best of it."

"I believe you." The words seemed forced out of her, and Dinah frowned. "But people are talking."

"What, about me and the hired man? Good grief, Claire, I just lost my dad, my mom had a stroke, my sister dumped her baby on me, and I have a ranch to run. I don't have time to—to have an affair, if that's what people are thinking."

To her amazement, Claire lifted her head and grinned—a real grin, not the fake smile that had been holding up the corners of her mouth until now.

"Put like that, it does sound a little unbelievable."

"That's because it *is* unbelievable. Honestly, don't people have anything better to do?"

"Here, why don't you let me have her for a bit?" Dinah handed the baby over and Claire sat on the stump without, it appeared, a single thought for her wool-crepe skirt. "Aren't you the cutest little thing?" she cooed and gave Tamsen her wrist-watch to play with before returning to the conversation. "The thing is you're from a favored family, and people like to talk about them the way magazines talk about movie stars. I guess it's because we look inward at ourselves instead of outward at the world."

"How would you know what magazines say about movie stars? I'm shocked."

Claire rolled her eyes, and Dinah began to see that her motives for coming out here may have been sincere. Her suspicion lightened a little.

"There's nothing wrong with reading a magazine. Julia used to do it so she could talk about movies with her worldly friends at school."

Dinah couldn't imagine prim and proper Julia McNeill doing such a thing. But then, she'd run away with that biker, hadn't she? Obviously the signs had been there.

Then she gave herself a mental slap. What signs? Like reading a movie magazine was some kind of evil seed that had manifested itself in her behavior later? If that were the case, what would grow from her use of the computer? Absolutely nothing—except a wider knowledge of baby care.

"Speaking of Julia," Claire began.

As opposed to actually speaking to her, Dinah thought, *since she's Out and none of us are supposed to have contact with her any more.* "Yes?"

"I was talking to Rebecca about her apartment."

Something tugged under Dinah's breastbone—a sense of impending loss. Cold crept over her skin as she realized the real purpose of Claire's visit. "Were you?"

"I want to move out of Mom and Dad's and Rebecca needs a tenant." She looked up from the baby. "She said that she'd discussed it with you, but you hadn't made a decision. So I thought I'd come and talk with you about it, and see what you were going to do."

Bless Rebecca for giving her another chance. But there was no decision to make. "If you want it, you should take it, Claire. I can't leave here now. We're going to be taking the cattle to the auction pretty soon, I've got Tamsen to think about, Mom will come home next week, and . . . and I don't think Rebecca really wants a dozen chickens digging up her prize roses, do you?"

Claire smiled. "I don't know. I like your chickens."

"Yes, but Rebecca may not."

"Are you sure?"

"Completely." Somehow her priorities had changed. The apartment was no longer the unattainable haven it had been not so long ago. No longer one more thing she couldn't have. "Besides, Julia was your best friend. You're the right person to move into her place." She paused. "Do you hear from her?"

Claire looked at her from under her lashes and didn't reply.

Dinah huffed a laugh. "It's all right with me if you do. I'm not going to tell anyone. Tamara's already been here and broken Silence, remember?"

"We talk all the time. It's not like she was Silenced or anything. She's just Out."

Once again she'd underestimated Claire. "Just Out." *Just?* How many times had the Shepherds told them that those who were Out were spiritually dead and to "touch not the unclean thing"? And here was Claire, talking with Julia all this time, keeping her secret as closely as Dinah kept all of her own.

But now Claire was trusting her with this. If she could do that, could Dinah trust her to be a friend?

"She's so happy, Dinah. It's in her voice, it's in Rebecca's pictures, you just see it glowing out of her. I know she did wrong to go Out and marry a worldly man, but then when I see her so happy I wonder what the wages of sin really are. I mean, how can you be filled with so much love when you're not obeying God?"

Love, a voice whispered in the back of Dinah's mind. *It's not the works that matter, it's the love.*

"I don't blame you at all for staying in touch," she heard herself say. "I'd do the same if it were my best friend."

In the beginning she'd had Tamara, and then Phinehas. But Phinehas had spoiled everything backward and forward in Dinah's memory, and Tamara was gone, maybe for good.

Now all she had were the chickens. And Matthew and Tamsen, she thought with a little shock of surprise. She might not have a job or an apartment or a wool-crepe suit, but she had them.

Which, when you got right down to it, was more than she'd ever had before.

MATTHEW WHEELED THE big truck in close by the kitchen door feeling rather like the hunter returning with a spear over his shoulder and the week's meat supply on a travois. Well, he supposed half a dozen bags of groceries qualified, including several different kinds of baby food recommended by the young mother to whom he'd appealed in the supermarket aisle. As he hauled the bags in two at a time, he heard voices upstairs in Tamsen's room. Dinah and no doubt the owner of the little silver car in the driveway.

They came down just as he was putting the last of the fresh vegetables in the fridge.

"She finally went to sleep," Dinah reported.

"That's a pity." He indicated the neat row of liquefied carrots, peas, cereals, and other baby foods in their jars on the counter. "A woman in the store helped me find all we'd need for the next little while."

"I'm sure we'll need it when she wakes up. That kid is like a lion, seeking what she might devour," Dinah said. "Matthew, this is Claire Montoya. Claire, Matthew Nicholas, our hired man."

He shook hands with the young lady in the black suit. "It's nice to meet a friend of Dinah's."

The two young women exchanged a glance. "We haven't actually been friends, for reasons that escape me now," Claire said with refreshing bluntness. "But I hope that's going to change."

Matthew wasn't sure what to expect, but the flush on Dinah's face indicated she might be pleased about it. Had she had so few friends? Did this girl know about Dinah's struggles? Probably not. If she did, how would that change things? And what would be the effect on Dinah if yet another person turned their back on her?

But he was getting ahead of himself. If God had prompted Claire to come out here and offer her friendship, there had to be a good reason for it. He could only be grateful for those few friends who might stick by her right now.

"Thanks for doing the shopping," Dinah said, pulling out cheese and bread. "Grilled-cheese sandwiches all right with everyone?"

Claire glanced at her watch and then volunteered to make a salad, and Matthew put the kettle on for tea. When they were all sitting around the kitchen table with full stomachs and cups of strong, hot tea cradled between their hands, Claire spoke up.

"Dinah says you used to teach at a university, Matthew. What made you change jobs?"

He smiled, and sipped the brew in his cup to cover up the sudden jolt of alarm in his gut. "I planned to do a walking tour and ran into a series of problems. Dinah was kind enough to give me a job."

"Matthew was kind enough to take it," Dinah put in. "It would be pretty difficult to manage without him at the moment, especially with the stock sale coming up."

"Are you going to do it?" Claire's gaze was uncertain. "Down at the county fair, all by yourself, with all those ranchers?"

Dinah shook her head, as if such a thing were out of the question. "Of course not. I could, but I'm not going to give Alma Woods anything more to gossip about. I'll tell Matthew what to do, and I'll ask the Hendricksens over on the next place if they can trailer our animals in with theirs. If Matthew looks after the actual sales—which isn't hard, Matthew, it's an auction—then that will be the last of Dad's stock. After that I'll just run the other ranchers' cattle on our pastures and get out of the business altogether."

"It gets pretty rowdy down there, I understand," Claire said. "The ranchers aren't used to seeing Elect women in the barns, are they?"

"They weren't used to seeing us in the bank, either," Dinah said, "until you and I changed that."

Claire shook her head. "Folks have gotten used to it. Melchizedek and Phinehas just have to understand that women have to make their own living nowadays. We can't all run day cares or get married straight out of high school. Maybe that was the norm twenty years ago, but things have changed."

"Yesterday, today, forever," Dinah reminded her. "Though I agree with you."

"Jesus might be the same, the way might be the same, but we have to change."

"Why can't a woman go to a stock sale?" Matthew felt goaded to ask. "Women are just as capable as men at that sort of thing. More, in this case."

"Of course they are," Claire replied. "But it puts a woman in a public forum, and we were brought up to believe that isn't becoming. My job at the bank and even Rebecca's owning the bookshop are walking the fine line. Not that it's stopping either of us, you'll notice."

"Knowledge and using one's abilities is very becoming in a woman, I've always thought."

"Not to the Elect. We're taught that the woman runs the household," Dinah explained. "and the man goes out to work. I'm just not sure how much longer they'll be able to teach that.

Not with rebels like Claire and Rebecca around." She grinned at Claire over her cup.

"What about the woman in Proverbs 30?" he asked. "She managed her affairs very capably in a public forum, and her children rose up in the gates and called her blessed."

"Yes, well, she wasn't living in Hamilton Falls," Dinah said.

"A capable woman can be called blessed wherever she lives. And she shouldn't have to hide her talents and abilities just because Melchizedek and Phinehas say so. Are they so afraid of women that they have to keep them shut up in their homes?"

Dinah and Claire glanced at each other, and then Claire said, "I hope you don't plan on saying things like that in public, Mr. Nicholas."

"I'm not afraid to express what I think in public or in private."

"That's the difference between us, Matthew," Dinah said quietly. "In the Elect we have to think about others before we speak."

"You mean you have to think about what other people *think* before you speak."

"Matthew, don't talk about things you know nothing about."

"He's right." Claire sounded a little surprised at herself, as if someone had elbowed her in the ribs. "Listen to us. We both agree with him, we've both worked in public, and yet we still talk the talk. And don't even get me started on women having no part in Gathering."

"What?" Confused, Matthew looked from one to the other.

"In the Sunday Gatherings, only the men speak," Dinah explained. "But the wives and daughters usually talk things over with their men so everyone's thoughts can be expressed. Except—" She paused, then plowed on. "Except Dad."

"Your dad never passed on your mother's thoughts?" Claire asked. "Or yours?"

Dinah shook her head, and Claire frowned. "That's a bit unfair, isn't it?"

"Dad took his place seriously."

"Well, yes, most of the men do, but he should still have included you."

"He's gone now, so it doesn't matter," Matthew put in gently. What a strange church these people belonged to. He could no more envision women being excluded from participation than he could imagine himself selling stock at an auction.

But obviously both were reality. If not now, then soon.

"It does matter, though." Claire put her mug down. "Now Elsie and Dinah have no voice at all in Gathering. I mean, even if I move out, my dad will still give my mom and me a voice."

"Guess I'll just have to get married, then," Dinah said lightly. Matthew glanced at her and frowned when he saw how pale she was. In her eyes he saw a sardonic doubt that contradicted her tone. "Speaking of getting married, did you know that Derrick Wilkinson is back on the market again?"

"Now, there's a man who would always include you, with scrupulous attention to detail," Claire said.

"No doubt about it. But for that you'd have to live with him."

Both women laughed at whatever man they were talking about. Matthew didn't much care, because with the sparkle of laughter about her that made her forget about herself for a moment, Dinah's face became beautiful.

"Poor chap." It was difficult not to smile. "What on earth is wrong with him?"

Claire tried to explain. "Picture a man in a shirt and tie every day of the week, with pens in his pocket."

"You could be describing me, most days," he said mildly.

"Yes, but your main goal in life isn't to be the next Deacon."

"Well, no. What is your version of a deacon?"

"The Deacon is an Elder in training. An Elder leads Gathering. But in order to do that, you have to be a son born into a favored family, or married to a daughter of one. And now with Julia McNeill married to someone else, her sister Madeleine already married to an Elder, and Tamara gone, there's only one eligible woman left in town. Better watch out, Dinah. He could be getting ready to ask you out."

"He already has." The laughter faded from her eyes. "I turned him down."

His brain was getting a lot of exercise these days, Matthew thought, trying to wrap itself around all these strange customs. Maybe *National Geographic* should do an article on these people. Maybe he'd write it himself.

"Isn't that a little archaic?" Of all the questions in his mind, that was the least offensive.

Claire shrugged. "Maybe. But that's just the way it is."

"So because Dinah doesn't fancy him, he doesn't get to realize his ambition?"

"Dinah doesn't get to realize her own ambitions," Dinah put in with more than a trace of sarcasm. "Why should he be any different?"

"Because he's a *man*," Claire said with a dramatic gesture and a roll of the eyes.

Matthew began to see that, under their sober black and all the restrictions placed on them, there were two women, at least, in the Elect who were seething with rebellion. They just didn't seem to be willing to give up what they had to act on it. He felt as though he'd been transported back to the age of suffragettes, when women were still lobbying for the vote.

"I hate to break this up," Claire said with another glance at her watch, "but I need to get back to work."

Dinah got up. "Thanks for coming, Claire. And for asking about the apartment. Even though there's no way I could take it, I appreciate the gesture."

"Let's see more of each other, all right?" Claire said. "A person can never have too many friends."

Dinah smiled, and Matthew rejoiced to see it. As she waved at Claire's little car from the front porch, he cleared up the kitchen and put the lunch dishes in the dishwasher.

He heard her footsteps go into the bathroom. The door closed, and a moment later the toilet flushed.

No. Oh, Father, help her. She's been doing so well.

She came out of the bathroom and stood in the kitchen doorway, swaying a little.

"Dinah! My dear, what's the matter?"

The face that had been animated with laughter and interest just moments ago had stretched and fallen into a mask of grief. A deep sob shook her thin shoulders and tears trickled down her face. One of the side effects of bulimia, he knew, was uncontrollable mood swings. He was just going to have to do his best to help her through it.

"Dinah?" Without thinking, he crossed the kitchen and wrapped his arms around her, smelling fresh cotton and mint mouthwash. Her head fell forward and she wept into the front of his shirt. "Dinah, please tell me."

She dragged in a jagged breath, her fingers curled into his shirt. "She should never have come out here." Her voice was muffled and watery.

"Why not?" he asked gently. "She wants to be your friend."

"How long will that last?" she wailed on a long note of grief. "Why would anyone want to be friends with me? I'm ugly and dirty and used. Who wants to be friends with that?"

Chapter 14

MATTHEW'S ARM AROUND her shoulders was a small comfort as he guided Dinah into the living room. A small comfort against the wilderness of loneliness and self-contempt inside her.

He should take his arm away, she thought, palming tears off her cheeks. Why would he want to touch garbage like me?

Instead, he sat her down on the brown couch and kept her in the circle of that arm, where she cried until she was exhausted and her eyes were red and stinging. Then he handed her a tissue and waited for her to blow her nose.

"Talk to me," he said in a voice so gentle it made her tear up again. "Tell me why you think you're dirty and used."

"You know why!" How could such a smart man be so obtuse? She tried to pull away but he wouldn't let her. Finally she gave up and slumped against his side, her arms crossed over her chest. She put her shoulder toward him so she wouldn't have to see his face. "Hello-o . . . I'm somebody's mistress. Claire is pure and a virgin and I'm just one of Phinehas's whores. Not even the only one. My body is used and ugly and I'm filth in everybody's eyes, even God's." *Correction.* "Particularly God's."

"And you've taken on all the ugliness that belongs to Phinehas and appropriated it for yourself."

Shock hit her in the solar plexus. "What? What did you say?"

"Listen to yourself. Filth, ugliness, moral ruin . . . you're taking all that on yourself instead of placing it where it belongs—squarely on Phinehas. Why are you protecting him?"

"I'm not!"

"Something inside you is. Is it easier to do that than to admit the person who was supposed to care for your soul and act as your shepherd is a wicked, selfish man who should be in prison?"

"It was me that turned him," she said in despair. "He couldn't resist me. He said so. And I liked it. I liked having something he wanted, because goodness knows I didn't have much else."

"He manipulated you, Dinah. He pushed all the blame on you when you didn't deserve it. That's what abusers do, you know. They blame the victim and make her think it's her fault because they can't take responsibility for their own actions. But you don't have to believe it any more. It's all a lie. Your responsibility is to live the truth."

"I don't even know what the truth is." The confession was dragged out of her word by word. "I'm a lie, he's a lie, God's a lie. Everything's a lie."

"I'm not," he said quietly. "Tamsen isn't. Schatzi isn't."

Involuntarily, her lips twitched. "There's nothing quite so real as a chicken. Or a baby."

"Phinehas created a woman who has to lie to herself and others in order to survive. And you see that woman when you look in the mirror. But she isn't real. I want to know the real Dinah."

Dust was beginning to coat the surface of the coffee table, Dinah thought distantly. It was time to clean house again. "I'm twenty-four. It's too late for the real Dinah, Matthew."

"I'll never believe that. But the first thing you have to do is admit there is a real Dinah, somewhere under this illusion Phinehas has made. I've seen her a time or two."

"When?" How could he see someone who didn't exist?

"The first morning I was here. I saw a lovely girl with a bird on her shoulder, singing to the other chickens. That was very real."

Sheba, my darling. Dinah's throat closed with loss.

"And I saw her again, holding Tamsen, counting her little fingers. And just now, laughing at the kitchen table with a friend." Matthew squeezed her shoulders, just briefly. "That's the woman who deserves to live. The joyful one who finds beauty in a single moment and lets it shine out of her."

Beauty? Dinah could hardly remember any beautiful moments that hadn't been tarnished by Phinehas or her father. But these had happened after all that. These had happened in the present, when there was nearly nothing left of her. How could that be?

"I'll agree with you that Phinehas is a lie," Matthew went on. It was obvious he'd been thinking about this. A lot. For days, probably. "He's a 'whited sepulchre,' looking on the outside like everything a person should be, and on the inside he's dead and rotting."

She couldn't agree more. Did anyone but she and Matthew see it, though? And what good did it do them? Phinehas was holy, untouchable. Even if she said something, no one would believe her. Matthew had said she was appropriating his filth to herself. Well, that was nothing to what the church would heap on her if she dared to open her mouth.

"He's recreated God in his own image for you." Matthew's voice, while still gentle, was tight. "You told me that night at the river that God was a punisher, throwing thunderbolts at you every time you turned around."

"He is. He does."

"If you looked at those thunderbolts closely, though, my dear, I wonder how many of them really came from Phinehas's hands?"

Sheba's death. Her mother's stroke. Tamara's pregnancy and disappearance. All were connected in some way to Phinehas.

"Why would he do that?"

"Maybe he doesn't intentionally, but his actions still reverberate in your life. And God has nothing to do with it."

"But the Shepherd is God's representative here on earth." Oh, for goodness sake. Even she could see how silly it was to believe that. "Never mind."

"He might be representing the God he sees, but it certainly isn't the God I know and love. The one that loves you and whose heart breaks every time you paste Phinehas's face on him."

It was difficult not to. That God was the only one she knew—and feared and hated.

But what if it were true?

Your whole life would have to change. Somehow.

I can't. It's all I can do to survive right now. I can't change anything.

Maybe not. But Matthew sees beauty in you. That's a change.

Matthew is a homeless man who is just being nice because I feed him.

Stop lying to yourself.

All right. All right. Matthew is either pure of heart or completely naïve.

You're doing it again. Shoving him away. Putting yourself down so no one will do it for you.

Fine! So he sees beauty in me.

And?

And there is beauty in me. Phinehas took it away. Took my pearls and threw them all over and ground them into the mud. He did it. Not me.

His fault. No matter what you did, it's still his fault.

I have to be responsible for some of it.

No. The only thing you're responsible for now is what you're going to do about it.

Do? I don't know what to do.

I don't either. But if Matthew's right, there is One who does.

THE MORE SHE thought about it—and that was a lot during the next few days—the more she could see that time after time Phinehas had manipulated events and her own thinking to make her accept the blame for his actions. Maybe that was why she'd taken refuge in control—of the household, of her body. Of Matthew's fate, even. Maybe her soul was trying to get out from under the crushing burden of shame that should have belonged to Phinehas.

Now, more than ever, she longed to talk to Tamara. Between the two of them maybe they could ease the burden it was clear they'd both carried for years. At least having someone to talk to who had been through what she had would ease some of the pain.

Talking to Matthew, though, was a pretty good substitute. She could see that he carried some pain, some wound, deep in his heart, but was incapable of releasing it. However, the very fact of its presence made it easier to open her own heart, which she'd closed off from everyone in sheer self-defense. If she were patient, he might open up and tell her what it was that troubled him.

He didn't push her to talk, but if she wanted to, he listened. She watched carefully for any signs that he was judging her, but the most he did was make her think.

And hurt. That happened a lot, too, but she could hardly blame him for it.

She'd decided that since he knew part of the story, he should know it all. A little niggle in the back of her mind said that maybe if he knew it all, he'd admit she was right and she was really as filthy as she believed. Then he'd leave her in disgust and she'd be vindicated.

But the new voice inside her, the one that wondered if

beauty and realness were even possible, wanted to get it all out for another reason. Maybe if she could lance the boil, it would heal.

Right. Until Phinehas comes back. Then what will you do?

Hastily, she buried that thought. She'd jump off that bridge when she came to it.

So, over several nights and days, she immersed him in her life—as it had been and as it was. Those childhood moments when the only brightness came from Phinehas's affection. The days in her preteens when she'd been his little favored flower, receiving his caresses and special times of prayer and meditation as though they were refreshing rain in the cold desert of her family life. It took a couple of days to get through her teenage years, though, mostly because the story came out in jagged little pieces that tore and hurt, and he would gently withdraw to let her cry in peace.

Sometimes she wondered what his motives were. Why did he bother? Was he some kind of saint? Because he never seemed to ask anything from her except the necessities of life. She gave him her past and his meals, and he gave her manual labor and understanding, and somehow she thought she was getting the better side of the bargain.

Altogether, it was a strange way to treat a hired man.

Oh, face it, Dinah, he isn't a hired man.

No, he isn't. He's more like a friend.

Are you sure that's all he is?

Well, he certainly can't be any more, can he? Not with everything he knows now.

He's still here, isn't he? He's not running for the hills.

The paycheck is here, too. Don't get ideas. The last thing I want to do is have everything be spoiled by—by that.

By what?

But Dinah went outside to feed the chickens and refused to give herself an answer.

MATTHEW WAITED UNTIL Dinah had finished giving the chickens their evening treat—vegetable peelings, broken lettuce leaves, apple cores—and had gone inside. He knew how possessive she was about the birds. Well, perhaps *possessive* was the wrong word. It was more like she needed the time alone with them the way some people needed prayer. He could hardly begrudge her that, though he wished there was some way he could show her that the real thing—prayer—was a source of strength and comfort that could outdo even that of chickens.

And speaking of which . . .

He opened the door to the barn passageway. In the dimness, he heard a rustle and then a familiar sound like water bubbling in a pipe. Opening the door wider, he stood aside and a small golden hen poked her head into his kitchen, tilting her head to gaze up at him with a sharp hazel eye.

"Hello, Schatzi." He'd learned that when she greeted him, she expected a reply. In just the same manner the chickens greeted each other and Dinah . . . and for that matter, so did the people back home in Cornwall. How many times had he heard that abbreviated West Country greeting, "All right?" and answered "All right" without thinking about it? It was just what social creatures did.

With a liquid cluck that sounded like a request for permission, the hen picked her way carefully across the linoleum floor. The first time she hadn't known the floor was any different than that of the barn, and the results had been disastrous to her dignity. She'd come originally, he supposed, thinking that he was Dinah moving around in the suite, and he'd surprised her in the middle of the floor, on her stomach, feathers askew from the slip. He'd given her a handful of bran flakes to make it better, and every evening after that she'd come to visit after Dinah had gone in.

He felt a little guilty about coercing one of her birds, but where was the harm, really? He and Schatzi had hit it off from the first, hadn't they, and it was only thanks to her recommendation he'd been allowed to stay at all. Once in a while she left a small, round deposit on his linoleum, but that was easily cleaned up. Certainly she was never anything but socially acceptable when she hopped up on the back of his reading chair.

The first time she'd done that she'd startled him so badly he'd nearly dropped his cup of tea in his lap. After all, one doesn't expect a five-pound bird to suddenly land next to one's head with an energetic flapping of wings. After he'd got over the strangeness of it, Matthew began to see why Dinah and her Sheba had bonded so magically. He had never earned the trust of a bird before, never felt this feathery warmth next to his ear and the relaxing of the feet that told him she was comfortable enough to sleep. Sometimes she did catnap there, while he listened to the radio in the quiet dimness of the room or read by lamplight one of the ancient ranching magazines that were stashed in the closet. Then he'd slip his hands under her and carry her into the barn, where he'd arrange her on her roost for the night.

What would the little hen do when he left? he wondered, as she bubbled a comment and picked a bit of hay out of his hair. Not that he was leaving, mind you, when Dinah had said herself that she needed him. But at some point her mother would return and he would need to settle whether he was going to stay or take his small earnings and make his way back to California and his old life.

Part of him wanted that old life. Part of him missed the summers of research and the rush of September with new classes and new students and new piles of paperwork. He missed the long talks with Paolo Martinez, the theater prof, on whether John Wilmot, second earl of Rochester, was a syphilitic clown or a real poet who had been underappreciated during his lifetime and ignored by history since.

Another part admitted that that life was gone forever. Yes, his name had been cleared and Torrie Parker exposed as mentally unstable, using him as a stand-in for the father who had abused her. But academic circles were small and tight, and a scandal like that had spread far and wide even without the help of the newspapers. Technically, he could work if he could get a position. But why would someone hire an assistant professor who came dragging such baggage when there were hundreds of fresh-faced PhD lecturers available for half the price?

His options were to stay here on the ranch until the Lord only knew when, hiding from life, or start over again on the lowest rungs of the academic ladder in an attempt to make the best of it in another state.

Washington, perhaps. Where he could be within visiting distance of Dinah.

Is that what you want? something deep in his mind whispered. *To visit?*

Well, yes. She's in no shape for anything else.

But what if she were? This Derrick Wilkinson person is already in line, it seems.

She isn't giving him the time of day.

She gives you the time of day, doesn't she? More.

During the past few days he'd been exposed to more pain and ugliness than he'd known existed in the days of his youth and innocence. But then, under the veneer of civilization, it was hard to say what, exactly, was normal. The point was Dinah had shared with him secrets she'd never told a living soul, and while it had been agonizing for both of them, he could see that just saying such things aloud was helping to lift the burden somewhat.

He couldn't flatter himself that being around him was going to cure her. Far from it. But by being a sounding board and drawing on his experience and research into sexual abuse during the whole awful hearing process, at least he had been able to ask the right questions. And some questions, at least, might lead to answers for her.

Schatzi made her hookah-pipe sound next to him, as if asking a question of her own.

"What should I do, little one?" he asked, then smiled at himself. Dr. Nicholas, pride of the British university system, talking to a chicken. Well, she had more sense than many a department chair he'd known. He and Paolo had had their share of laughs at the head of the humanities department and his idiotic policies.

"What do you think, Schatzi? Shall I ring up old Paolo and give him a coronary?"

Schatzi fluffed her feathers and did not reply, though she kept one eye on him in case the sounds he was making indicated a treat was in the offing.

Matthew pulled the phone closer and dialed the familiar number.

"Martinez. *Hola.*"

"You're home. I thought you'd be in rehearsals."

A stunned silence hummed down the line. "Mateo? Is that you? Where in the world are you? Are you all right?"

He laughed with the sheer pleasure of hearing his friend's voice again. Paolo, at least, had stuck by him during the worst of it. Paolo had tried to stop him from leaving, and once that had proved fruitless, had agreed to store Matthew's books and his few possessions in his tiny garage until he returned.

"Yes, somewhere southwest of Spokane, Washington, and yes. It's good to hear your voice, Paolo."

"You could have heard it sooner. What kind of friend disappears for weeks and doesn't call? You could have been dead in a ditch, for all I knew."

"You sound just like my mother."

"No surprise there. I'm practicing to be a dad."

Matthew grinned with delight, though of course Paolo couldn't see him. "A dad? Is Isabela pregnant?"

"Four months. Which you would have known if you'd stuck around. How are you going to be godfather when you're some-where southwest of Spokane? And how did you get there?"

"It's a long story."

"Isabela's in bed already. I have the time."

Briefly, Matthew outlined the circumstances that had brought him to Hamilton Falls, leaving out the hunger and the despair, which would only distress his friend more than he had been al-ready.

"A handyman," Paolo said at last. "You're working on a ranch as a hired man? Am I having auditory hallucinations?"

"No, you're as sane as I am, though that isn't saying much."

"Why on earth didn't you call me, *amigo*? You know I would have come up there and brought you back. Lent you our other car. Done whatever. Not left you to thumb your way across half the state!"

"I couldn't."

"You could have called Pastor Schultz, then. You know there would have been a money order wired up there the same day. You should hear the prayers, man. A Sunday doesn't go by that somebody doesn't lift you up and pray for your safety."

In a moment of sudden clarity, Matthew saw that his pride had not only been the means of his own destitution, it had put a burden of worry and concern on the people in the little church under the redwoods where he and Paolo and Isabela worshipped. He hadn't meant it to happen, but then, he hadn't been thinking of anyone but himself, either.

"You're right." He sighed. "But I thought if I did things on my own, I wouldn't be a burden to anyone. Looks as though I was wrong."

"It's no burden to pray for someone we love. Or send them a money order when they're in trouble. And we won't even go into how well equipped you are to be a ranch hand, my friend.

You're not the one who grew up on fifty acres of scrub in New Mexico."

"As a matter of fact, you'd be surprised."

"What? You mean you're slinging hay bales and roping cattle?"

"Well, no, but I am supposed to be managing a stock auction. Somehow. I'm not quite sure about that, yet."

The silence on the line told him Paolo and Claire Montoya might find something to agree on there.

"But that's not what I meant," he went on. "You know I could never understand why, out of all the faculty, Torrie Parker picked me to work her destruction on."

"I still don't understand it. Not when that sonofagun Beiler is still keeping his sexual activity under the radar in the science department. If anyone deserved destruction by Parker, he did."

"I think I know now. I think it was part of God's plan."

Another pause. "You're going to have to explain that one to me," Paolo said at last.

"There's a woman here. Dinah, my boss. The daughter of the family that owns this ranch. She's a victim of abuse at the hands of this preacher type who apparently is the top dog around here."

"Yes?" Paolo said cautiously.

"She's in this weird and toxic church that believes this guy, Phinehas, is the mouthpiece of God and infallible."

"Uh-oh."

"The poor girl has been his unwilling mistress for—get this, Paolo—ten years. Ten *years*."

"Why doesn't she do something about it?"

"I don't think she can. Not by herself, anyway. But we've been talking for days now, nonstop, and it's all coming pouring out of her like she's never had anyone to talk to before in her life."

"She probably hasn't. Imagine what the risks would be."

"Exactly."

"And this is the plan of God how?"

"As you know, I spent a lot of hours in the research library studying this very thing. I think I can help. At the moment I'm not doing anything but listening and mucking out chicken manure, but I think somehow I can help."

"Is that why you're not on the next plane headed to San Francisco? It seems like you are very involved with this woman."

"I am, Paolo. But not the way you think. If God went to all the trouble to educate me and bring me here, I'm going to stay and find out what he wants me to do."

"If you say so, *mi hermano*. I'll pray for you."

"I appreciate that. Now, if you'll excuse me, there's a chicken on my chair, and I need to put her to bed."

Amid Paolo's laughter, Matthew hung up. When he picked up Schatzi and took her out into the barn, he was still smiling.

Chapter 15

JUST BEFORE LUNCH the next day, the phone rang.
Dinah and Matthew were in her dad's room so Matthew
could try on a few of his clothes. In the middle of the bed,
propped up on the pile of shirts, pants, and sweaters, Tamsen lay
in her little terry sleeper, kicking happily and gumming the
spotless cuff of what had been Morton Traynell's best Sunday
shirt.

Dinah's father had been a heavier man, but he and Matthew
were about the same height. Dinah held one of his newer shirts
up against Matthew's chest. "This one might work," she said.
"Try it on while I get the phone. And keep an eye on Tamsen.
She rolled over on the changing table this morning and you
never know when she's going to do it again."

She jogged into her mother's room, where the only upstairs
extension was, and grabbed it on the fourth ring. "Traynells."

"Dinah, it's Auntie Meg."

Oh, dear. What was going on down in Pitchford? "Hi, Auntie. How is everyone?"

"We're all fine, dear, including your mom. That's what I
called to tell you. Elsie has been thriving, I'm happy to say, to
the point where she's getting restless."

"Is she able to use her hand?"

"Mostly. And except for what they call asymmetric loss of movement in her face, you'd never know she had a stroke. She's been doing exceptionally well."

Dinah was used to feeling ambivalent about a lot of things. The thought of Phinehas had evoked revulsion and fear mixed with a helpless need for his approval. Same with her dad. But her feelings for her mother had been less those of love than of the knowledge that she should love her—and felt instead an odd balance of tolerance and dismay, with a little frustration mixed in.

What kind of horrible person felt like that about her own mother?

The kind that suspected she had collaborated in some awful way with Phinehas. Or, if *collaboration* wasn't the right word, then at least turned a blind eye to what was going on. The night she had given her mother a stroke was burned into her memory, as was the knowledge that her mom thought she'd brought Phinehas's behavior on herself.

Great. Thanks for the support, Mom.

"Dinah, did you hear me?"

"Sorry, Auntie Meg. I'm glad to hear mom is doing so well."

"Uncle John and I feel she's ready to come home now, dear."

What?

"We'll be driving up after lunch, so we should see you around three."

"Today?"

"Of course, today." Margaret's sharp voice softened into humor. "Why, have you let the place go to rack and ruin since she's been gone? Better get out the vacuum."

Right, as if her mother ever did anything more exhausting than the dusting and the dishes. Dinah was the one who kept the place spotless, and with the house sitting in a sea of gravel over spring mud, that wasn't easy.

"Thanks for the warning," she told her aunt. "See you around three."

"Don't you want to talk to your mother?"

"I'll catch her up when she gets here," Dinah said hastily. What could she say? *Gee, Mom, Phinehas is gone but he threatened me before he left. Tamara left her baby here, and Linda Bell is spreading gossip about it as fast as she can. Oh, and I hired a literature professor while you were out.*

No, the truth was she had nothing to say to her mother that she wouldn't see herself once she got here. "I'm off to do the vacuuming," she told her aunt. "Bye."

Matthew looked up when she paused in the bedroom doorway. "What do you think?"

He modeled her dad's shirt and a pair of the pants they'd bought when the pounds had started falling off him. Matthew had cinched the waist in with a belt, but on the whole, the corduroy pants fit pretty well.

"Those are good." She nodded with approval. "So is the shirt. If you turn up the cuffs you won't notice the sleeves are a bit short."

Matthew was putting on weight, she noticed. And not in a bad way, either. He'd lost the hopeless look and stood straight in front of the mirror as if he liked the person he saw.

She liked that person, too. The very fact that he was so pleased to have these castoff clothes made her smile.

He cocked an eye at her. "Was that Pitchford on the phone? How is your mother?"

Her smile dropped away. "She's coming home this afternoon."

"That was fast. It hasn't been two weeks yet, has it?"

"Two weeks yesterday. Apparently everyone is very pleased over her recovery."

"Except you?"

Dinah went to the pile of clothes on the neatly made bed and began to sort through them without disturbing Tamsen's little nest. There had to be more shirts and maybe some work pants in here that Matthew could wear.

"Dinah?"

She threw a pair of brand-new jeans back on the pile. "What do you want me to say? That I'm happy she's coming back? That I'm looking forward to apologizing for giving her a stroke?"

That was the problem with Matthew. Now that she'd told him everything, she had nowhere to hide. And he'd been there that night. Had dealt with her suicide attempt. She'd told him what had happened and he hadn't judged her. When was he going to start? Now?

"Do you really think it was you who caused her stroke?" he asked gently. "Do you think you have the power to cause blood clots?"

"Of course not."

"So what do you have to apologize for?"

"For bringing it on!" she shouted. Tamsen started, and her face crumpled up to cry at the harsh sound. Dinah rubbed the baby's stomach and tried to lower her voice. "For upsetting her so badly she turned gray and passed out."

He shook his head. "Not logical. Odds are the stroke was waiting to happen, if that migraine was any indication. Your confronting her was a coincidence in timing, not the cause."

"I still upset her."

"I don't doubt you did. You may need to deal with the fall-out from that."

That was a truth Dinah had already faced. She still wasn't sure he was right about her not causing the stroke. He hadn't been in the room, hadn't seen Elsie's eyes bulging with suppressed fury and pain. If she wasn't responsible for that, who was? Anybody? God?

"What do you think upset her?" Matthew took the pair of

jeans she'd thrown down and began sorting through the pile for more possibilities.

She gave him a dry look, sat on the edge of the bed, and pulled Tamsen into her lap. "It was either me accusing Phinehas of rape or me accusing her of allowing it to happen. She didn't act like a mom once in all those years. She still doesn't. The night you came, he came to my room two doors away and she never made one move to help me."

"She has as much to lose by speaking up as you do, doesn't she?"

"She isn't the one being raped, Matthew." She slung the ugly words at him, perversely hoping they'd hurt him as much as they hurt her.

"I didn't mean that. Of course she isn't. But whether she speaks up against him or you do, what would the result be?"

It was hard to stay furious at a man who so obviously put her interests first—and more, was willing to say so out loud. That was more than anyone had done for her, ever.

"What would happen if we spoke?" The consequences were so dire and so numerous it was hard to get them all in one reply. "No one would believe us, for starters."

"The widow of an Elder? And the daughter of one?"

"Phinehas is our Shepherd. They're set apart, given special gifts from God in order to do His work."

"That doesn't make them immune to criticism. Or criminal liability."

"It makes them immune in other ways, though. We'd be accused of having a bad spirit, of being malicious and evil minded. Gathering would be taken out of our home, though it might be anyway, since there isn't an Elder here anymore." She looked up from the baby. "And our reputations would be trashed. My reputation is pretty much all I have right now."

Tamsen made a cooing noise and reached for Dinah's nose.

She talked around the little hand that explored her face. "The worst that could happen, though, is that we'd be Silenced."

"What does that mean?" Matthew asked.

"It means no one can speak to us for seven years. There are degrees of it, but that's the bottom line."

"Ah. Shunning. What happened to your friend Julia."

"No, talking to someone who's Out isn't near the sin that breaking Silence is. We talk to outsiders all the time. But talking to someone who was once Elect and has lost their salvation is like talking to a dead person. It's definitely frowned upon."

"So Claire took a risk to tell you she'd done so."

"Yes." Matthew had concluded the same thing as she had. There was nothing to prevent Dinah from running to Melchizedek and deflecting the spotlight from herself by telling him what Claire was doing.

Nothing but this brand-new, fragile thing that might be friendship between them. Claire had put her own safety in Dinah's hands—something no one had done before.

All kinds of things were happening that had never happened before. How strange and wonderful and scary.

"Meantime, about your mother?"

"What about her?"

"Did you ever stop to think that perhaps it was more than just outrage over your accusations about Phinehas that upset her so much?"

"What do you mean?" What could be worse than accusing Phinehas in the way she had?

"I don't know. How long has she known him?"

Dinah thought back. "My whole life. Some of my earliest memories are of trying to reach the piano keys when he was playing. I couldn't have been more than three." Tamsen lost interest in Dinah's moving lips and latched onto her fingers instead. "But I think what did it is me accusing her of allowing it all this time."

"I can't imagine any mother doing so."

Dinah slanted him a wry look. "Try."

"Oh, I believe you," he said hastily. "But something must have driven her to it. Don't you think?"

"I really don't care if something did." Dinah got up and adjusted Tamsen on her shoulder. The baby saw Matthew by the mirror and made another cooing noise. "The point is she allowed it. She let it happen without doing a single thing about it."

"But don't you think that—"

"I'm going to make lunch." Dinah cut him off, too upset at his disloyalty on this topic to care how rude she sounded. "And then you'd better get yourself out to the barn while I break the news of your existence."

IF IT HADN'T been for Tamsen and her enthusiastic reception of solid food, lunch would have been strained and silent. Matthew's strategy for handling her, Dinah had learned, was just to be quiet and go away. Then he'd come back and take the problem up again when Dinah was calmer and could have a conversation instead of an argument.

On the topic of her mother, though, that wasn't likely. What did he know of the horror of those minutes before her bedroom door opened, when she had prayed that, just once, one of her parents would get up and come out into the hall and catch Phinehas in the act?

At ten minutes past three, Uncle John's big blue sedan rolled up the driveway and came to a stop by the front steps, where Claire had parked the other day. He helped Elsie out of the car and up the stairs as though she were fragile, as though Elsie's monumental selfishness wasn't already on the lookout for her own safety. Always the dutiful daughter, Dinah kept her thoughts to herself and kissed her mother on the cheek as she came in.

"Welcome back, Mom," she said.

Elsie's glance darted around the room, looking for—what? Signs that Dinah had thrown a huge party in her absence? Evidence of change?

The only changes were on the inside, and Elsie couldn't see those. She would hear about them, though. The days of Dinah's invisible, silent presence making everything comfortable and smooth were over. Dinah had found her voice in those long days of one-sided conversation with Matthew. Honesty felt good. It kept the air clear, to the point that she could actually feel the April sun when she went outside and breathed the cool breeze scented with the crocuses and snowdrops that had poked their shy heads above the soil.

Dinah planned to keep the air clear inside the house as well. No more forbidden subjects. No more suffering silence. And above all, no more lies and covering up.

Elsie sat on the couch with a sigh as heavy as if she'd climbed Mount Everest. Then she gaped at the sight next to her on the cushions.

Tamsen gaped, too, at the strange, horrified face above her. Then she burst into noisy, frightened tears.

"Who—is that—?" Elsie gasped.

"Yes." Dinah scooped the baby up and cuddled her in the easy chair, where she quieted at hands that had become familiar and that she'd learned she could trust. Tamsen hiccuped, gnawed her fingers, and gazed distrustfully at her elders.

"This is Tamsen Dinah Traynell, your new granddaughter."

"So it's true that she left the baby here." Elsie's voice was hushed. "I thought that Jezebel was just stringing us a line to upset us."

"If you mean Aunt Evelyn, she was just as upset as anyone. Tammy told her she was coming up for a visit, nothing more. Sit down, Auntie Meg. Uncle John, you too."

Cautiously, they sat in a row on the couch, where they all stared at the baby.

"She does have Tamara's eyes," Auntie Meg conceded at last. "Do you think she'd let me hold her?"

Dinah handed her over, expecting fireworks. But Tamsen was obviously a good judge of character. She settled into Margaret's lap and made a grab for her wristwatch.

"She came when I was gone?" Elsie asked, watching the baby with distress. Her fingers smoothed her skirt over and over, as if erasing defects in the fabric that only she could see.

"You were still in the hospital."

"She waited until I was safely out of the way before she forced you to break Silence?"

Dinah couldn't tell if her mother was angry over that or if it went deeper. Maybe she was disappointed that she'd missed Tamara's visit. She decided to err on the side of kindness.

"I don't think it was that at all. She wanted to visit you. At least, she said so. Then, when I got back from doing something on the property, she was gone."

"And no word?" John asked. Dinah shook her head. "What about the baby's father? Did she tell him anything?"

Here it was. Dinah took a deep, steadying breath. "I went to see Danny Bell and he says he's not the father."

"Of course he'd say that," Elsie retorted in disgust. "As soon as Tamara is located they'll have to get married. Quietly." She looked around the room. "It's probably big enough in here. Goodness knows who would come, but we have to make the effort anyway. Linda Bell will be happy about one thing: Danny will be Deacon, though he's not who I would choose for such a privilege."

"I believe him," Dinah said quietly. "He's not Tamsen's father. Don't plan the wedding just yet, Mom. He told me he never wants to see Tamara again."

"Well, if he isn't, then who is?" Margaret wanted to know.

The next ten seconds would change her life, Dinah thought. If she was brave enough.

"Phinehas," she said.

"Thank our dear Lord for Phinehas," Elsie sighed, clasping her hands. "If it hadn't been for his visits I don't know how I would have pulled through. He's been such an encouragement to us, hasn't he, Meg?"

Dinah tried again. "No, that's not what I meant."

"I'm exhausted." Elsie heaved her small frame off the couch as though it weighed three hundred pounds. "John, could you help me up the stairs to my room? I've had all I can take for one day. Dinah, maybe you can put together a tray for me. Just something light. Eggs and toast, maybe."

Dinah watched them go upstairs, one halting step at a time. *Have it your way, Mom,* she thought. *But we are going to talk about this, whether you want to or not.*

"SHALL I CATCH you up on what's been going on?" Dinah pushed open her mother's bedroom door with one hip and came in with the tray. On it were two pieces of toast, honey, and two boiled eggs with their tops already cracked off. Dinah had also added a small bunch of crocuses in a little vase, picked when she'd gone out to wave good-bye to her aunt and uncle as they'd driven off.

Elsie plumped up her pillows against the headboard and looked over the tray with interest as Dinah put it on her lap. "This looks nice. The crocuses are up already."

"We've had some sun lately. March went out like a lamb."

Elsie tucked into her eggs. "What else could possibly have happened besides Tamara bringing this baby home?"

"Tamsen's kind of cute once you get to know her, Mom. Eats like a horse. And she's really loud. But I think she's developing a sense of humor, so that's a good sign."

"I hope you don't get attached to her, Dinah. As soon as Tamara is found, she'll take her back and that will be that."

"How are you going to find her?"

"That woman—" Elsie paused and spread honey on a piece of toast. "Evelyn is making inquiries, apparently. And Uncle John is going to as well."

"Auntie Evelyn has been quite a lot of help, actually. I think she's nice."

"She might be, but she's a divorced woman living with a divorced man. She turned her back on the way of God and is living a sinful life. Don't forget that."

"Wearing color and having her nose done."

"Exactly."

"Mom, you know, if she decided not to stay in the Elect there's nothing intrinsically wrong with those things."

"She broke your grandmother's heart," Elsie pointed out, as if this were a good reason for a lifetime of shunning. "And your father's, too."

It was news to Dinah that her father even had a heart. It probably broke a few slats in the structure he lived in, though, and that would have hurt.

"Uncle John is going to put out the word among the Elect in various places," Elsie went on around her toast. "Tamara doesn't know any worldly people. She does know Elect families in Seattle, Spokane, and Richmond, though. We've been on the phone to all of them, so if she does turn up or they hear of her, they'll call us."

"Mom, she's gone Out. She's wearing color now. I don't think she's going to go to an Elect family and ask for a place to stay."

"We've told them she's confused, and to expect some odd behavior."

Confused was an Elect euphemism for a person who was undecided whether to stay in or go Out. It also meant a person who was unwilling to put herself on the altar as a sacrifice. If Tamara was said to be in that gray area covered by *confused*, the Elect would take her in and encourage her to do the right thing.

Dinah was no longer sure she knew what that was.

"I hope she turns up," she said mildly. "I just want to know she's all right."

"That's what we all want. Goodness knows the papers are full of what happens to young girls when they get off the train in some of these places."

"If she's smart enough to fool me into taking Tamsen, she's smart enough to avoid a situation like that."

"Let's hope so. And let's hope we find her quickly. I don't know what people are going to say. I tried to tell these families to be discreet, to consider the Kingdom, but I'm not sure how well it will succeed."

"Oh, they're already saying it. All of Hamilton Falls knows Tamara took off and the baby is here."

Elsie pushed the empty tray away. "So much for considering the Kingdom."

"You can't keep something like this quiet. The first time we show up in Gathering with Tamsen, people will talk."

"Oh, I won't take her to Gathering," Elsie said grimly. "Think of the disgrace Alma Woods could spread far and wide about our condoning sin."

"Mom, she's only four months old. It isn't *her* fault Phinehas raped Tammy and made her pregnant."

The words popped out of her mouth with all the force and surprise of a jack-in-the-box, a toy Dinah had always hated. Time ground to a halt in the room as her mother stared at her. The silence was deafening, a roar in Dinah's ears.

"Sorry," Dinah said at last. "I tried to tell you before. Danny Bell told me when I went over there to make him stand up to his paternal responsibilities. I had no idea."

Elsie's mouth worked, but no sounds came out.

Dinah felt the first prickle of alarm. "Mom? You're not going to have another stroke, are you?" She snatched the tray off her mother's lap and put it on the floor. Then she took her wrist and felt for a pulse. It seemed fast, but Dinah was no medic. "Mom?"

"Don't you dare," Elsie finally got out and pulled her wrist back, where she cradled it against her body as if it had been injured. "Dinah, for the love of God, you must never, ever say such a thing."

Dinah sat back on the bed, and Elsie moved her legs a few inches away.

"I believe it's true. If he's been raping me for ten years it's not that much of a stretch to believe he got to Tammy, too. Although I have to say I thought I was the only one."

"No—!"

"Yes, Mom." Dinah's voice held none of the shaking and fear that fluttered inside her like a frantic, trapped bird. But the words had to come out. She just prayed she wouldn't send her mother into a relapse. "He started when I was fourteen, but he'd been buttering me up for years before that. Since Tammy is only seventeen it's a good bet he started when she hit puberty. He seems to like them young." She paused. "I don't suppose it would do any good to warn Linda Bell not to leave her girls alone with him, would it?"

"Don't you dare speak of this!"

"Oh, I won't. But it isn't going to happen here again, Mom. Ever. If he comes back and tries it, I'll scream the house down. Matthew will come running and *he* certainly doesn't have a problem calling the police, even if you do."

Elsie stared at her again, her mouth opening and closing as sentences rushed to her lips and were bitten back.

"Matthew is our new hired man," Dinah explained. How was she pulling this off? A month ago she couldn't imagine taking charge like this. Making her mother listen. It was frightening, but in a way it felt good to stick by her resolution to keep the air clear. It felt like a gift to be able to stay calm and almost kind, leaving behind the brutal sarcasm that she might have used as a weapon in the past.

"He's staying out in the suite in the barn and he's very smart. He's a university professor on a walking tour, and I offered him a job to tide him over until he saves up a bit of cash." That was a good story. Nobody needed to know that they'd practically dragged each other back from death.

"A hired man," Elsie said faintly, evidently thankful to have something harmless to talk about. "That's good."

"I'm glad you agree. But I meant it about Phinehas. He's welcome here for your sake, but if he tries my door it's over."

To her surprise, instead of turning away, her mother's gaze pinned her in place with an honesty as new as her own.

"Not over," Elsie whispered. "Never over."

Silence fell again, the echoes of Elsie's broken whisper like the sound of fragile wings beating against a window.

"What do you mean?"

"It's never going to be over," Elsie repeated. "You, me, Tamara. Probably even the child, when she's old enough." Her gaze faltered and she looked down at her hands, lying palm up and empty in her lap.

Cold showered over Dinah's skin, soaked through her flesh and into her heart. "What?"

Elsie's hands closed into fists. "He'll never stop, Dinah. He used me, and then when I married Morton all he had to do was wait until I had girls. He knew I would never speak. Never. Not even when my heart broke and I wanted to jump out of the hay window in the barn. I never spoke."

Elsie's eyes were wide and dark and terrifying as she raised her gaze again to Dinah's face. "And you won't, either."

Chapter 16

"YOU, TOO?"

Dinah had never had an easy time with empathy. She had all she could do to control her own emotions, and as a result trying to imagine the emotions of others was too much for her.

But this . . . this was dreadful. The shock of it was still seeping through her veins, out to her fingertips, chilling them. She couldn't have moved off the bed if a fire had broken out.

"He abused you, too?"

All the fight had gone out of Elsie's body, but the warning still lit her eyes. "I was twelve. An early bloomer, as they used to say. He would come into our home and my parents would bend over backwards to make him comfortable, as we all do. So comfortable that he felt completely safe doing what he did in my dad's old Chevy, out in the garage."

"And you couldn't say anything." She felt as if she were speaking for herself, for her mother, and for Tamara. None of them could speak. Until now.

"He said the only thing keeping him in God's service was my service to him. That if I refused, hundreds of souls might go to hell because he couldn't carry on God's work."

"Sounds like he's been telling the same story for thirty years."

"He told me how difficult it is, how often he wanted to just disappear and give it all up."

"What, give up being offered the best people have? The best bed, the best food, their money, their cars?"

Dinah struggled to control her voice as her emotions see-sawed between shock and anger and simple, childlike astonishment at never having known. Of never having seen in her mother what she lived with daily in herself.

Or maybe she had seen it, she thought suddenly. That lack of emotion, that steely control. Was that what she'd been emulating unconsciously for the past ten years?

"But think what he had to give up," Elsie said. "His own will. The hope of a family of his own."

"That was his choice. That's no excuse to go preying on little girls."

"It's our service, Dinah."

"It is not, Mom, are you crazy? It's wrong. Criminal. I can't begin to tell you the damage he's caused."

"It's part of our sacrifice," Elsie said stubbornly. "If the gospel gets carried to one more seeking soul, then a little mortification of the flesh has been worth it."

"Mortific—" Dinah stopped before her voice spiraled out of control. "It's rape, Mom."

"No, it wasn't," her mother whispered.

"It was for me."

"I made myself be willing. It was my service. And . . . and it wasn't so bad, really. He's a much better lover than—"

"Mom!"

"Well, all right. When I was married, it ended. At least then I could welcome him into our home and serve in other ways. And then you were born."

"Your little preemie. I know."

"That's what I told people. My, what a trial you were. I was so unprepared to be a mother."

"Wait a minute. Back up. What do you mean, that's what you told people?" Dinah had always known she had been born prematurely. She'd consoled herself with the thought that at least back then she'd been wanted, even with her unexpectedly speedy arrival. That her parents must have loved each other to have wanted to start a family so quickly.

"Well, what else could I do?" Elsie asked simply. "I couldn't very well tell the Elect that I was already pregnant when Morton put the ring on my finger. I was marrying into a favored family, for heaven's sake."

"You and Dad . . . ?"

"No, dear. Me and Phinehas."

Dinah sat, stunned, as the last of her illusions about herself came crashing down around her.

IT WAS A miracle she didn't break her neck as she carried Elsie's supper tray down the staircase. Her body was functioning at some practical level while her mind was unraveling time, scrolling backward faster and faster, as if to locate the truth and put some kind of lens on it that would help her see her life differently, help her understand.

That's why Dad never loved me.

Phinehas doesn't know.

Dad knew. And he never said a word all those years. He was the one who allowed it. Not Mother.

I'm his daughter.

No, don't think about that.

Dinah stumbled through the yard and made it almost to the barn door when her stomach revolted and she lost everything in it. She gripped the doorjamb and breathed in and out, in and out, until her head cleared.

The door to the hired man's suite was closed, but a strip of light shone under it. "Matthew?" she croaked.

The old chair creaked, and in a moment footsteps crossed the kitchen. "Dinah?" He peered out, then blinked. "Oh, my dear, what's happened now? Come in."

She detoured into the bathroom and rinsed out her mouth, and stole a bit of toothpaste to freshen her breath. When she came out, feeling marginally calmer, she found him in the kitchen putting on the kettle for tea, that panacea for the world's ills.

"Tea?"

"Yes. Oh, Matthew, I've—" She stopped, staring into the living room. "What is Schatzi doing in here?"

His shoulders hunched a little bit, as if he were guilty of something. "I didn't mean to coerce her. Truly. It just happened."

"What are you looking so guilty for? With Sheba gone, she's the alpha hen. She can do what she wants."

He straightened and gave her one of his rare smiles, the kind that made his eyes glow and made something strange happen to her stomach. "I wasn't sure you'd be all right with it. I know how you are about your birds."

"You're the guy that shovels poop. You care as much as I do."

"Well, yes, but now that you don't have Sheba to cuddle with, I thought maybe Schatzi . . ."

"She's never been the cuddly type. But she's always liked you."

"She doesn't cuddle. She keeps me company. Our tea is ready. Do you feel better?"

Talking about the chickens and the prospect of tea hadn't made her feel better, but it had distracted her for a welcome moment. The sick, horrified anger at herself, at Phinehas, at her family was still there, lying under her ribs like a cancer, needing to be excised if she could only figure out how.

While Matthew poured them each a mug of tea and handed her the honey, she told him the secret Elsie had kept hidden in her heart for twenty-five years. When she was finished, Matthew sat down heavily in the kitchen chair, and Schatzi craned around from her comfortable perch on the back of the easy chair to look at them both.

He bowed his head.

"Dear Father, I come to you with a desperate prayer," he said quietly, while Dinah gazed at him in astonishment. "Please give Dinah the strength to deal with this revelation of her mother's. Give me the wisdom to help, if that is your will. And please, Father, help us all to learn to forgive."

Dinah was so amazed that she just stared as he lifted his mug and took a sip of hot tea.

"What?" he asked after a moment.

"Do you always start conversations with God in front of people?"

He exhaled sharply in what might have been a laugh. "No, only in moments of extreme stress or need on my part. And usually when I'm alone. But I didn't think you'd mind, being a praying person yourself."

"I'm not." Another reason she had always thought herself to be a misfit. The Elect were very firm that a person should pray twice a day, minimum, on one's knees if possible. But prayer brought you to the attention of God, and Dinah wanted to avoid that at all costs.

Besides, doing anything on her knees, even washing the floor, caused her excruciating pain. On the rare occasions when she did pray, it was face down on the bed, with her back toward heaven.

Matthew nodded at her bleak words. "It would be difficult to pray to that guy in the sky with the lightning bolts. I prefer to pray to the One who made Schatzi, there, and caused the crocuses to come up outside the tack room door. The One who gave his very self on the cross so that I would know grace."

It was going to be a long, slow process getting to know that God, Dinah thought. But Matthew was so quietly happy and trusting in his worship that maybe there was something in it. Certainly most of the Elect, with the possible exception of Rebecca Quinn, could not be said to be all that happy.

"So," Matthew said. "Tell me what you're thinking about this news of your mother."

Dinah took a sip of tea and shook her head. "I'm still reeling. I don't know what to think. Phinehas is like some horrible hereditary disease in the Traynell family, like sickle-cell anemia."

"He is a very disturbed individual. He needs to be incarcerated somewhere where he can get treatment."

"That will never happen." Dinah's voice was flat. "No one will believe it, least of all him. He is completely convinced of the rightness of what he does. Otherwise, how could he do it? And speaking of that, how could my father do it? All this time I thought it was my mom who was allowing this to happen to me—us, I mean. That she was handing me over to him because she hated me."

"Your mother must have a very difficult time with boundaries. Hers, her daughters', her husband's."

"I don't think Mom knows what boundaries are. As long as it's all in the family, it's okay with her."

"That's harsh," Matthew said.

"I feel harsh right now. Harsh and angry and confused. It's going to take me weeks to come to terms with this, and that's only possible because I can't fight the truth."

"If anyone deserves your forgiveness, it's your mother, don't you think?"

"Why? She still could have done something."

"Have you ever been able to do anything when your father didn't want it to happen? What sort of man was he?"

Dinah tried to slow her agitated breathing and think. "Immovable, I guess you could say. Hard. He ran Gathering with this sort of gentle authority that I know for a fact the other Elder tries to emulate. But to us he was cruel. If we wanted to do anything other than go to school, Gathering, or young people's meetings, he said no. The only thing that softened him up was getting cancer."

"Good grief, Dinah." Matthew sat back, looking a little winded. "That *is* harsh."

She shrugged. "He lived for the Elect, and traditions that say women have their place and men run the show. But since he was stuck with me and the financial situation had to be dealt with, he finally entrusted me with his banking and portfolios, right after we got the diagnosis. Mom just isn't capable of managing that kind of thing."

"So what do you think he felt when he found out Elsie was expecting you?"

"I assume it was after the wedding, when there was nothing he could do except cause a horrible scandal. And being from a favored family and already Elder, that would be impossible. So he took his revenge."

"Would a man who considered himself a godly man think of it in those terms?"

Dinah shook her head. "Who knows? But there is a lot in the Old Testament about the sins of the fathers being visited on the children."

Matthew got up to take the teapot to the sink. His back to her, he said, "It does have a sort of dreadful symmetry in an Old Testament way. Feed the child back to the man who fathered her."

Dinah winced, and the rocklike pain inside her throbbed as if someone had prodded it. "He used to quote that verse in Romans a lot. You know, 'Present yourself a living sacrifice.' I guess that was me."

Matthew slammed the teapot on the counter with such force she thought it would shatter. "Inexcusable. Dinah, I'm so sorry you've had to live this for all this time, like a toy batted between two cats."

She turned over a tired hand in a gesture of acceptance. "I got over saying 'Why me' a long time ago."

"Yes, well, from here on, things will be different, won't they?"

"I already decided that. No more hiding the truth and suffering in silence. I'm going to say what I think and you should, too. I told Mom about you, by the way."

"Since you can't talk about these things with your father"—Dinah laughed out loud at the very thought—"you're going to have to discuss them with your mother. If what we've been talking about is true and she wasn't the one who allowed Phinehas to do what he did, then perhaps some mending of fences might be in order, to use a ranch metaphor from these magazines I've been reading."

"She can mend them with me any time she wants." Why was she always the one who had to give and forgive instead of get and forget? It was time for someone else to step up and make her feel better for a change.

"She may not be able to, Dinah," he reminded her gently. "You have a pretty solid fence around yourself, you know, made of equal parts capability and contempt."

"Contempt? I don't know where you get that. I just feel sorry for her, is all."

"Pity is easy." His voice held the conviction of someone who knew what he was talking about. "True compassion and the forgiveness that goes with it is hard."

She set her half-empty mug on the table and pushed her chair back. "Come on, Schatzi," she said to the chicken on the chair. "It's time for you to roost up."

"Good night, Schatzi," Matthew said. "Good night, Dinah."

But she didn't answer as she closed the kitchen door. It took several minutes before her eyes grew accustomed to the dark, but she knew the way to the roosts by heart. When she finally let herself outside into the starlit yard, she realized that part of the problem was the tears that blurred the view.

IT WAS TURNING out to be difficult, if not impossible, for Elsie to ignore her granddaughter. For one thing, Dinah made no effort at all to spare her mother's feelings and keep the child hidden away in her room. On the contrary, if Elsie came down to breakfast, the baby was in her carrier, gurgling happily over pureed carrots. If she tried to do a little handwork in the after-noons, there she was in the middle of the carpet with Matthew, batting at the little wooden doodads he called carved birds.

In the end it was painfully obvious even to someone as self-centered as her mother had always seemed that the child was growing out of her clothes. Dinah smothered a smile as Elsie brought this to her attention with some irritation and pro-ceeded to take over the sewing machine in the downstairs guest room that up until now had been Dinah's domain.

Elsie, it turned out, had quite an eye for design. A day or two later, Dinah held up a little green outfit shaped like an apple, with two gathered openings for legs and a little white frill at the neck like a bit of leftover blossom. A pair of cocked leaves formed a pocket that had no earthly use except decoration.

"Mom, this is adorable. Tamsen will love it."

"I haven't worked with color in so long it made my eyes hurt trying to choose something in the fabric store." Her mother put away the spools of thread and swept the green scraps into the trash basket. "But of course she won't wear black until she goes to school."

"What pattern did you use?"

Elsie shrugged. "None. I've been sewing longer than you've been alive. Why would I need a pattern for something as simple as a pair of rompers?"

"Not everyone can make a pair of rompers look good enough to bite into."

Elsie said nothing, but when Dinah stole a look at her, the expression of pleased embarrassment spoke volumes.

Tamsen subsequently became the proud model for an outfit

resembling a pink strawberry and something white that Dinah couldn't identify, but that had folded arcs of yellow and purple fabric in place of the pockets.

"Those are crocuses," Elsie said shortly. "That one needs a bit of work."

When they went to Gathering Sunday morning, Dinah dressed Tamsen in her apple outfit and Elsie said nothing while she buckled the baby into the car seat. And once the women got over *oohing* and *ahhing* over the little outfit there was nothing more to be said. If Elsie Traynell thought her illegitimate grand-daughter should be in Gathering with the rest of God's people, then no one was going to argue with her, not with her recent loss and health problems. Dinah noticed that Rebecca Quinn, bless her, was right there in front after Gathering was finished, when it came time to have a look at the baby. With two such pillars of the church standing up for Tamsen, there wasn't much that old gossip, Alma Woods, could do except mutter to her cronies that it was a shame and a scandal and Elsie should know better than to display the fruit of sin like it was something to be proud of.

Dinah hoped no one paid any attention.

As for herself, she held her head high and smiled for all she was worth, sticking by her mother's side with the baby's carrier gripped in one hand so that Derrick Wilkinson couldn't get a word in edgewise about lunches or free time or anything else. Sticking by her mother was a bit of a novelty, too, but Dinah figured that if Elsie had come around enough to stand up for Tamsen, then Dinah would stand up for her.

Claire Montoya, she noticed, was missing, which caused her an unexpected pang. She asked Claire's mom where she was.

"The bank sent her on a weeklong training course in Seattle," Mrs. Montoya said. "I wasn't sure about her mixing with all those worldly people, not to mention getting a bunch of training in a job she'll give up when she meets the right man, but she was adamant."

"She had to go all the way to Seattle?"

"Yes, to their head office. But fortunately we have relatives there. She'll be able to get to Gathering and they'll have her for supper and such."

And Julia Malcolm was in Seattle.

Perversely, she hoped Claire would have the nerve to visit. They could all use a good dose of nerve and do some things they wanted to do just because they were right and good in themselves. The Elect didn't have a monopoly on right and good, though they certainly thought so.

Sunday afternoons were usually a mad rush of big meals and visiting and getting ready to go to the evening Mission service. But for once, they had an afternoon to themselves. Once Tamsen had gone down for her nap, Dinah let all the chickens out to ramble on the grass and took a garden chair out there herself.

She relaxed into the sun with a sigh. There was no sound except for the rush of the river across the road, behind the trees. The chickens conversed among themselves, punctuated by the occasional squawk as one was disciplined by a bird above her in the order. Schatzi queened it even over Joseph, their lone Wyandotte rooster, who tried to tread her and got a whack on the side of the head for his trouble.

Dinah grinned and closed her eyes, letting the sun warm her face.

"May I join you?"

Elsie stood a few feet away, carrying her own plastic garden chair. Dinah straightened.

"Of course. Should you be carrying that?"

"It's only a chair. Weighs hardly anything. And I don't need people to fetch and carry for me. Meg did that for two solid weeks. In the beginning, of course, I was grateful. But I don't need to be treated like a baby all the time."

Just most of it. Then Dinah squelched the nasty thought. Matthew had said she used contempt to fence people out. Well, there was a perfect example. And really, since she'd come home from the hospital Elsie had been unusually easy to live with, even to the point where she'd made breakfast this morning when Matthew was busy with the chickens and Dinah was occupied with the baby. In fact, her timely help was all that had enabled them to get to Gathering. Until someone was named Deacon to manage the Gathering here, Melchizedek had decided that Gathering would be at the Mission hall, with Owen Blanchard leading.

Elsie sank into the chair with a sigh of satisfaction, unlike her usual put-upon noise that gave the impression life was just too much trouble to manage. She, too, tilted her face to the sun.

"I feel as if I haven't felt sunshine in years," she said.

"It's been a long winter, hasn't it?"

" 'Now is the winter of our discontent.' "

Dinah glanced at her, puzzled. "Is that from the Bible?"

"No, dear. Shakespeare. *Richard the Third.*"

Dinah closed her mouth, which had fallen open in astonishment. Then she said, "I didn't know you knew Shakespeare."

"You'd be surprised what I know. We did *Richard the Third* for the senior class play. Well, I didn't do it, of course," she added hastily, as if Dinah would think she'd put on makeup and costume and go onstage in front of a crowd of worldly people. "I was excused on the condition that I wrote a two-thousand-word essay. So I picked Elizabeth and the ramifications of what would have happened had she not married Richard. And in the process I memorized quite a bit."

" 'The winter of our discontent,' " Dinah repeated slowly. And now the truth had come in like the sun and changed the way everything looked.

"That's what it's been like, you know," Elsie said. "When I was in the hospital convinced I was going to die or be a vegetable, it was like the ice breaking on the lake after a hard winter. I vowed that if God got me through it, I'd make some changes."

Elsie had been in no danger of dying, to Dinah's knowledge, but she could imagine what might have gone through her mother's mind in the long nights in the hospital. "What changes?"

Elsie gazed out over the river. "Where is the law of loving kindness in me?" she asked softly. "Where is the enlarging of my heart?" Dinah had the feeling the questions were not directed at her. Then her mother glanced at her. "I've lost half my family. And I'm in danger of losing you if I don't start treating you like a mother should treat her daughter. My world is small, and it's my own fault. I need to do something with the life God has let me have before everything I am implodes."

In the silence, Dinah tried to understand what was going on in her mother's head. She'd never spoken like this before. Never taken charge, most especially of her own direction. And most of all, had never confided how she felt.

In the distance, an osprey lifted off a snag and coasted on the breeze, following the river. "You're not going to say anything, are you, Dinah?" Elsie asked, her gaze following the bird's flight.

"About what?"

"About . . . well, you know. What we talked about the night I came home."

"About Phinehas using all of us to satisfy himself?"

"Yes." Elsie dropped her voice, as if it would encourage Dinah to speak more quietly. "That."

Dinah didn't answer her question right away. There was something else she wanted to know first. "When did Dad find out about me?"

It took her mother a moment to answer, as if she had to wrest her mind off the future and think back through layers of time and unhappiness to find the words. Or maybe she simply didn't want to.

"I told him when we got back from our honeymoon. I was so in love and I trusted him to forgive me, you see. I discovered that seeking forgiveness is an act of faith. One that was misplaced, as it turned out."

"He didn't?"

"Oh, no. And such a godly man, too, in other ways. He never let on to Phinehas, not once, that he knew. Never let it affect his service, though I know it cost him. But he never left me alone in his presence, either. As if I would have been unfaithful to him." She snorted. "The love may have been gone, but I took my vows seriously."

Her parents had been married twenty-five years, Dinah thought, dazed. And only two weeks of those years had been filled with love.

"So Dad never loved me either?" she asked at last. May as well have the obvious out in the open.

"I think he did, in his own way. He let you go to college, after all. Not many fathers would have done that."

"But not the way he loved Tamara." Who was his own child.

"Not like that, no. He never knew about her and—and Phinehas."

"So when it came to leaving me alone with Phinehas, he didn't have a problem."

"You were a child, Dinah. Phinehas isn't like that."

"But it has to start somewhere. And he gave me love, then."

"Yes, Phinehas did do that. Try to think of that during the dark times. Try to forgive."

"The problem was, Mom, he had an ulterior motive. He was priming the pump for what he planned to do later."

"Please don't say that, Dinah."

"It's true. Matthew says that's what abusers do."

"Matthew?" Her mother straightened in her chair, her hands gripping the arm rests. "Matthew knows about all this?"

"Oh, yes. His knowing is what saved me."

"Dinah, please tell me he won't say anything." Her mother leaned forward, her eyes wide with apprehension. "Please."

"He doesn't have anything to say. It's me that has to act."

"Don't. Please."

"Why not, Mom? Phinehas is a criminal. He has to be stopped. I told you that before."

The fear in her mother's eyes clouded over, and she slumped, her spine a curve of hopelessness. "He's the power in Washington State, Dinah. Nothing we say will do anything. And he can do everything to destroy us." Pain wrote lines on Elsie's forehead. "We're taught to lay up treasures in heaven. I don't know about you, but I don't have much else, and he can take away what I do have. Our place, our reputation . . . he can Silence us or cast us Out altogether. And then what?"

Dinah sat wordlessly. She knew it. If he were cornered, he could take away everything her mother had lived for and built up in the absence of love. Everything, in essence, that she had, except for the ground they stood on.

"One last thing, Mom."

"I hope so. This is the most painful conversation I've ever had with you."

Dinah cocked an eye at her. "It's the only valuable one we've ever had, too."

"Honesty is a hard virtue. But we have to start somewhere. What else?"

"Did Dad allow it? Did he even think about stopping Phinehas once he started coming to my room? Even once?"

Elsie sighed, a long, troubled sigh that ended in a hitch. When Dinah glanced over, she saw a single tear track its way over the cheek that had once been smooth and smiling.

"No, sweetie," she said at last. "In fact, he locked me in the bedroom to prevent my going out into the hall and diverting Phinehas away. He was afraid that if he didn't let him have you, he'd come after me. Not that I meant anything to him by then." She paused, and swallowed. "He said he was doing what Jesus commanded, and rendering unto Caesar the things that were Caesar's."

Chapter 17

*B*E CAREFUL WHAT *you wish for.*

For years, Dinah had wondered what could possibly have kept her parents from protecting her. Now that she knew, the long-awaited confirmation just made her sick.

Not throwing-up sick, though that in itself was unusual. She hadn't been losing her meals as much lately, and consequently was feeling stronger and able to catch herself before she said hurtful things. Her vow to honesty didn't, after all, include contempt and sarcasm, those weapons that came easiest to hand.

In the spaces that contempt had once filled came compassion. She supposed she had Tamsen to thank for that. The next day, as she was giving Tamsen her bath in a plastic tub on the kitchen counter, the baby laughed out loud at some soap bubbles and clapped her hands to make them fly. Dinah felt a helpless sinking in her heart that she recognized some time later as the moment she fell completely and unreservedly in love with her niece. Half-sister, she amended to herself. She was no longer a burden to be kept clean and fed, but a person, a member of their household with likes and dislikes and the ability to love right back.

Dinah had loved Sheba without reserve, but it wasn't like this. She knew Sheba loved her, but of course a bird had no way to express it except by taking what Dinah had to give. Tamsen showed it every day by greeting her in the morning with a big smile and a screech of joy.

Unfortunately, love didn't make the baby any quieter. Sunday Gathering and midweek prayer meeting were turning out to be quite a trial, because Tamsen saw no reason why she shouldn't vocalize along with the men, and she was a lot louder than they were. Dinah spent most of the time standing out in the parking lot of the hall with the baby in her arms.

For a kid who hadn't been wanted by anyone, she sure knew how to love. Matthew had been under her spell from the first. And with the apple rompers and her determination to make changes, Elsie seemed to have succumbed as well. As she dried the baby and dressed her in a pair of terry sleepers that were so small they'd cut the feet out of them, Dinah took a moment to marvel at what Elsie had done.

Because her mother hadn't stopped with rompers. Her sewing machine hummed every morning, and cream slipcovers piped in blue appeared on the couch and chairs in the living room, covering up the ancient, dark print that had been the choice of her mother-in-law back in the fifties. The brass lamps that had to be polished once a week gave way to lamps with china ginger-jar bases in Blue Willow colors. And the oval portraits of grim Victorian ancestors—the first fruits of the gospel that Morton had so prized—came down and were relegated to the attic, where Elsie unearthed a landscape with a lot of blue sky that went up in their place.

The UPS man began to call, bringing fabric that Elsie said came from a catalog, since the tiny shop in Hamilton Falls didn't stock the materials she wanted. And she wanted a lot. At this rate, Tamsen was going to have enough clothes to dress an entire nursery of babies. When Elsie pieced a tablecloth in a cheery Irish chain pattern in pink, green, and cream for the kitchen table, Dinah realized there was a revolution going on right under her nose.

"Mom, are you sure this is right?" she finally asked, when Elsie spread the cloth on the table with a snap and put the butter dish down in the middle of it.

"I am sick—" Down went the salt and pepper shakers. "—to death—" *Clack* went the napkin holder. "—of living in a funeral home!"

Dinah gaped at her.

"This is the most depressing house in all of Hamilton Falls," Elsie snapped. "My mother-in-law had awful taste, and Morton wouldn't let me change a thing. But if Rebecca Quinn can have pink roses on her armchairs, then I can have blue-and-white lamps!"

"Absolutely," agreed Matthew, holding Tamsen and looking ready to run.

"Get used to it, missy." She fixed Dinah with a look. "The living-room drapes are next."

"It's your house," Dinah said, holding up both hands in mock surrender. "You can do anything you want with it."

"No one is going to want to buy a place that looks like a mausoleum. What do you think of pulling the carpets up and seeing what shape the hardwood floors are in?"

"Buy?" Dinah said with a gasp.

"Are you thinking of selling?" Matthew asked.

"I can't run the ranch, Matthew, and let's be realistic—neither can you or Dinah. Hamilton Falls is growing and Linda Bell tells me a big chain store might be looking to build where the apple factory was on the edge of town. If that happens, chances are good I could subdivide this place and sell off luxury lots. We have three facing the river, after all, and the views from up the hill are pretty good, too."

For the second time in a week, Dinah had to pick her jaw up off the floor. "Are you serious?"

"Do you want to stay here?"

For how many years had she wished hopelessly to get away? "No." She thought of the stock portfolio. And the shares of General Electric and Microsoft. "But I wouldn't mind having first dibs at one of your river lots."

Now it was Matthew's turn to gape at her.

"Well, I'm not going to rush into anything," Elsie said. "But there needs to be change around here and I wanted you to know."

"Why?" Dinah asked. She had never seen so much change in so short a time. It was one thing to change inside yourself. But it was quite another to get a shock every time you walked in the door and saw that something else had disappeared or been added.

Elsie sat at the table and smoothed a hand over the carefully pieced seams of the cloth. " 'The winter of our discontent,' " she said. "Remember? Winter is over. Don't you feel it, Dinah? Don't you feel as though you're going to burst if you don't change things, do them differently, open yourself up to something new?"

Dinah had the feeling things were building up to an explosion no matter what she did or felt. Change was in the air the way the scent of softening earth filled it when she went outside.

"If we move, what about Gathering?" Dinah thought to ask, fixing on something solid, a problem that would have to be solved. "People have been coming here for Gathering for a hundred years."

"I'm not sure about that. We still don't have a Deacon. I'll need to talk it over with Phinehas and Melchizedek."

Elsie got her opportunity after lunch, when the phone rang. Dinah knew who it was immediately, from the soft, deferential tone that crept into her mother's voice. Blue-and-white lamps and declarations of independence notwithstanding, the habits of years would not change so easily.

"Of course you can come, Phinehas," she said into the phone. "Our home is always open to the servants of God. I'll make up your room and we'll expect you for supper."

"I CAN'T DO this," Dinah moaned, and tilted over until her face was buried in the cushion in the corner of Matthew's couch. "I can't face him. Everything's happening at once. It's too soon."

"If not now, then when?" Matthew went to sit beside her. "Is there ever going to be a time when you are ready?"

"Maybe." Her voice was muffled. "A year from now."

"There has to be a first time. And better now, when you're surrounded with people who know the secret. He won't have anywhere to hide."

"Mom will never let on she knows. Despite what she's been saying, everything will be exactly the way it's always been, and he'll come tonight the way he always does."

"But tonight will be different. Tonight you'll tell him no."

"And he'll have me Silenced."

"Let him. Tell him your mother and I know, too, and if he even thinks about retaliating, I shall go to the police."

Dinah wasn't sure she had the strength to stand up to the most powerful man in the state. She no longer believed he had any kind of connection with God, and it was difficult to believe that disobeying him would send her straight to hell. But the fact remained that he had every power over the society she lived in, and could take away everything that made life worth living for her mother. Friends, family, respect, all of it. With just a few words, Phinehas could reduce them to outcasts—and in Hamilton Falls, that left them with nothing.

On top of that, even if she did speak, she had no physical proof there had been years of abuse. She hadn't gone to see the doctor, so there were no medical records. She'd never spoken of it to a living soul, so there was no history. All she had was Tamsen and a white nightgown, and even that could have been bought anywhere, by anyone. It was Phinehas's word against hers, and without documentation it was pretty obvious whom the Elect would believe.

Documentation.

IN THE BABY'S room, Dinah hunted out the manila envelope that contained the letter Tamara had left. She'd been so shocked and dismayed by it that she hadn't bothered to look at the other papers in the envelope, and had been too busy since to think about them. The second piece of paper bore the address of a pediatrician in Spokane and a list of the shots Tamsen had had. There were blanks next to upcoming dates.

Shots. She needed to get Tamsen registered under their medical plan. As what? An adoption? Was she Tamsen's guardian or something else? Did she plan to be her aunt, her sister, or her mother?

Oh, that was too hard. Dinah set the vaccination schedule on top of the letter. She'd deal with that later.

The third paper was a birth certificate. Under "Mother," Tamara's name was listed. Under "Father" . . . Dinah frowned. *Philip Leslie?* Who on earth was Philip Leslie?

Danny had said that Tamsen's father was Phinehas. Or had it been a lie of the worst order and Dinah had been maligning him for something he hadn't done?

If it were true, somehow Tamara had found out the name Phinehas had been born with. Dinah couldn't imagine how— Phinehas had been Phinehas as long as the family had known him. It never occurred to anyone to think about the Shepherds' birth names. They were irrelevant to the call to preach, and it was tradition that they took the name of a biblical prophet, as befitting modern-day preachers of the gospel.

But it all added up. Tamara had not slept with Danny, and with her mother's story adding weight to his sin, she had no doubt Danny had told the truth and Phinehas had been raping Tamara as well.

She wondered if he carried anything in his wallet or suitcase under his birth name. He must. The State of Washington wouldn't register a driver's license to a man with no last name, prophet or not.

Tonight, if she could find a connection in his things, she would have her proof and he could never hurt her again. If she confronted him with the birth certificate, maybe he would even agree to leave them alone and not punish them all for her refusal to cooperate.

Maybe pigs would fly, too, but it was worth a try. She could no longer sit and let this happen to her. She may not have the most effective weapons to fight him, but she had to do something to defend herself.

Armed with a sense of purpose, she was able to greet him when he arrived just before supper as if there were nothing wrong. Just as she always did, she shook his hand and took his coat, then offered him a cup of coffee. And just as he always did, he sat in her father's easy chair with his Bible on the end table beside him and allowed her and Elsie to serve him.

At dinner, they made conversation about the number of strangers in the last mission he'd preached in Spokane and what their prospects might be for conversion. While Matthew looked from one woman to the other in confusion and growing disbelief, Dinah fed Tamsen her cereal while Elsie handed Phinehas the potatoes and urged him to another helping of Irish stew.

Dinah caught Matthew's eye and shook her head, the smallest of motions, which caused him to drop his gaze to his plate and sigh.

She'd explain later.

After dinner, she picked up Phinehas's suitcase and took it upstairs, just as she always did. He and her mother were talking in the living room, where, it seemed, he had just noticed nothing was the same as it had always been.

Get used to it, Phinehas.

In the front guest room with its view of the river, she put the suitcase down on the window seat. But instead of fluffing the pillow and going away as she had always done, she popped the case's latches open. She'd have to be quick.

With shaking hands, she rifled through his belongings. Slacks, shirts, ties, a sweater, all of the finest quality. A toiletry kit, a couple of books, socks, underwear. The ministers of God traveled light, with only the necessities of life in a single suitcase. Everything else was provided by the Elect as part of their service.

Ears straining for the sound of a footstep on the stairs or a change in the tenor of conversation, Dinah ran her hands along the pockets lining the sides of the suitcase.

Aha.

She reached in and pulled out a passport. The room below had gone silent. Hurry. Fanning the passport's pages, she found the one bearing his name and photograph.

Philip Arthur Leslie. Date of birth April 21, 1946. Place of birth Fraser, Michigan.

Bingo.

The fourth stair from the bottom creaked like an alarm, and Dinah slipped the passport back in the pocket, glanced hastily at the contents of the suitcase to make sure it looked the way she'd found it, and closed it. The latches snapped when she pressed them, but with the footsteps on the stairs, chances were good the sharp sounds wouldn't be heard.

She whirled as the footsteps reached the landing. It was Phinehas. She knew that step intimately, knew the pressure the weight of his elegant body put on their wood floors. After ten years of listening with despair for that very sound, oh yes, she knew it. And now she'd waited too long. He'd reached the landing and if she tried to leave his room, he'd see her.

She whirled and ran to the bed. Bending over the pillow, she was straightening the bedspread like a well-mannered chambermaid when he pushed open the door and came in.

"Well," he said with a mix of greeting and gratification.

She straightened. If it was a greeting, she wasn't going to reply to it.

"Getting it ready for me, I see." He looked her up and down, as if looking for the same kinds of changes in her as he'd found downstairs.

"Yes." She rounded the bed and made to move past him. "Enjoy your rest."

He put a cool hand on her arm, crumpling the black batiste of her sleeve. "I'd enjoy it more if you shared it with me. Since I find you in my room, I take it you've gone before the Lord and begged forgiveness for your unwillingness the last time I saw you?"

"I came to make sure the room was ready," she said steadily. Only Phinehas would read *sex* into someone coming in to make up the bed. "Nothing else. Let go of my arm, please."

He did, as though he'd meant to all along. "Still unwilling. Dinah, what does this say about your spirit? What happened to the girl I loved who was always so willing to serve her God?"

"I'm perfectly willing to serve God." She stepped away, but he still stood between her and the door, well dressed, well fed, and predatory. Her heart pounded and she felt the hot blood of desperate courage flood her cheeks. "But it's not going to be by letting you rape me any more."

He gazed at her for a long moment. Shock at her unexpected defiance fought with sadness and a kind of calculation, as if he were planning how to counter an opponent's bold move. "Is that how you see your service to God? Calling your wonderful, loving service that awful thing?"

"It isn't loving. It isn't even service. You raping me has nothing to do with God and everything to do with you. I want it to stop, Phinehas. Now."

"Do you?"

She took a deep breath. "I found out who I really am. I found out you had sex with my mother and my sister, too. And you want to know what else I found out?"

Oh, it felt so freeing, saying the dreadful words to the one who had spoiled her life. Throwing them back in his face where they could sit there, dripping with bile, making him as ugly as she had felt for years.

"I'm your daughter, Phinehas. You've been raping your own daughter all this time. Just imagine what the judge will say when he hears *that*."

She didn't know what she'd expected. That he would shudder and collapse somehow, fold up and beg her not to tell anyone. That he would be surprised, at least, that he had been committing an even worse crime than rape all this time without knowing it.

But he just stood there, in his tasteful wool suit and his shiny designer shoes, and gazed at her with sad affection.

"Poor Dinah," he murmured. "What dreadful wickedness have you allowed to take root in your soul?"

They always blame their victims, she heard Matthew's voice say in her memory.

"The only wickedness here is you," she retorted, keeping her voice as steady as she could. She took one step to the left, hoping he would move, but he did not.

"I am a servant of God, Dinah," he said gently. "And who are you? A deluded, isolated spinster under a lot of strain. It's obvious your father's death and your mother's illness have affected your mind."

"There's nothing wrong with my mind. You haven't answered me."

"About what? You've said so many things."

"You're never coming to my room again. If you do, I'll—"

"What? Tell me, I'm very interested."

She'd give anything to be a man, and smack that look of gentle amusement right off his face. But then she'd be dragged down to his level of physical violence, and she was too good for that.

"I'll go to the police. I have Tamsen's birth certificate with your name on it as the father, *Philip Leslie.*"

"Tamsen? That bastard child of a Silenced girl? Why would the police be interested in that?"

"Because it's proof you raped her, too," Dinah said furiously. "Me, my mother, my sister. How dare you, you beast!"

Her barely contained rage had no effect on him at all. "The ramblings of a spiteful runaway teenager. Who would believe it?"

"The police would believe it."

"And how can you prove it?"

Dinah thought fast. "DNA testing."

He stared at her as though she were speaking a foreign language. Perhaps, to him, she was. "What?"

Thank goodness for the Internet and their forbidden laptop, out in the barn. Thank goodness for Matthew, whose research skills turned up all kinds of helpful information. "A simple blood test can determine that you're Tamsen's father and mine, too. And then your career as senior Shepherd is over. You'll be disgraced and sent to jail, *Philip.* You'll be the one who loses everything, not me."

"Are you threatening the Shepherd of your soul, Dinah? What does that say about you, exactly?"

He was doing it again. Turning the ugliness on her. She batted it back at him. "I'm just telling you what the consequences of your actions will be if you don't leave me alone."

"And if I do? If I allow you to flaunt your unwillingness in front of your family, and disobey the commandments of God?"

"Not just me. If you're abusing anybody else, that has to stop, too."

"And in return, what?"

"In return, nothing. You stop, or I go to the police. It's as simple as that."

He gazed at her the way one would gaze at a puppy, idly wondering if it will bite. Then he shook his head.

"Think carefully, Dinah. Think what your behavior will mean to the Kingdom. How it will affect me and my service. How it will affect you and your service. How it will endanger your salvation."

She knew better now. She knew that accepting his abuse wasn't going to earn her anything but more abuse. And he . . . he had no control over the salvation of her soul. In a blinding moment of clarity she saw him as he really was. Not as the Shepherd, guiding lost souls to the heavenly pastures, standing in the gate deciding who would and would not come in. But as a power-hungry man who was willing to manipulate and hurt to get and keep that power.

She owed nothing to that man.

"I have every confidence in my salvation," she told him. "It's God's to give, not yours."

"But is he going to give that precious gift to someone so unwilling and disobedient?"

"You just don't get it, do you, Phinehas? Salvation can't be earned. It isn't a prize to be handed out to the person who works the hardest. It's a gift. Jesus made it possible, not anything I can do. Or anything you can do, for that matter." A strange feeling bloomed under her breastbone, like the feeling she got when the clouds split over the mountain and the sun came beaming through. Joy and awe and a heady sense of freedom. "You can't take my salvation away from me. No one can. Because God has given it to me freely and I've accepted it."

His eyes were cold and blue and very sad. "I'm sorry you feel that way, Dinah. I'll pray that you won't be deceived by a world that makes the heavenly prize sound so easy. And now, if you don't mind, would you please leave my room?"

He stepped aside and she darted out the door without a second's hesitation.

Now she knew. He wouldn't come to her room any more. He didn't control her, either physically or spiritually.

Now she was truly free.

Chapter 18

MATTHEW LEANED ON the doorjamb of the hired man's suite and listened as Phinehas's sedan purred down the gravel drive and onto the road that led to the highway. A few minutes later, he heard Dinah talking to the chickens as she made sure they were secure for the night.

"Do you think she'll want a cup of tea?" he asked Schatzi.

The hen fluffed her feathers, making herself comfortable on the threadbare pillowcase he'd laid on the back of the chair for her to sit on, and made her bubbling-water sound in reply.

"Yes, I thought so, too."

In a moment he heard Dinah's quiet knock and let her in. "Did Phinehas have other plans for this evening?" he asked.

Dinah took off her barn jacket and subsided onto the couch. Schatzi clucked softly in greeting. "Hello, darling. Aren't you pretty up there. No, he decided not to stay. He's gone to Blanchards' for the night."

"And what brought that on, I wonder?" When the kettle boiled, Matthew filled the teapot and set it and the two mugs they usually used on the coffee table in front of her.

With a sigh that seemed to come from a place deep within, Dinah leaned over and let him fill her mug. "Me. I found Tamsen's birth certificate this afternoon. Her father is listed as Philip Leslie."

"Who on earth is that?"

"Phinehas. I rifled through his suitcase to find something to confirm it, and found his passport. Of course, he then proceeded to catch me in the act."

"Oh, dear." Matthew wasn't sure he wanted to hear what happened next. "What did he do?"

"He assumed that since I was in his bedroom waiting for him, I'd come to my senses and was ready to take up where we'd left off."

"Oh, Dinah." Dread pooled in his veins. "He didn't—tell me he didn't—"

If Phinehas had come within touching distance of her, Matthew could not bear it. Something inside him, some slowly tightening tension that had begun to build after the other man's phone call, would snap.

"No." She shook her head and took a sip of tea. "I confronted him. Told him I wouldn't let him do that to me any more. And to make sure of it, I told him if he touched any of us again, I'd go to the police with my proof of what he'd done."

The strain inside him released in a wave of relief and admiration. "Well done, Dinah. That's brilliant." With the last ounce of his self-control, he stopped himself from hugging her. Now was not the time.

Could her long nightmare finally be over? Could it be possible that this girl who had been through so much might actually have a chance at a normal life? So what if she had used blackmail to extract the promise. In this case, Matthew was sure the end justified the means.

"You'll be safe, then," he said.

"For now. You just never know with Phinehas. He's angry, but I've seen him angry before. And he always comes back expecting to take things up just where he left them. Maybe he took me seriously. Maybe not."

He took a seat beside her, and set his mug on the coffee table. "The point is you've set the boundaries. You've stood up to him, told him no."

"I've told him no before and it never did any good."

"But it's different this time. This time you don't need him. He has nothing to offer you spiritually, so that means he has no hold on you any longer."

She gazed thoughtfully at Schatzi on the chair opposite, the warm mug of tea cradled in her hands. "It's true, isn't it?" she said. "I always came crawling back before so that I could have his approval." She shook her head. "Isn't that pitiful? I probably never really had it. It was all in my head. He probably despised me the whole time."

"Who knows what went on in his mind? He came to you for something he needed. Now that he can't get it, I wonder what he'll do."

Dinah nodded, and her forehead creased. "I worry about the Bell girls. They're thirteen and fourteen, and Linda would be nothing but delighted if the senior Shepherd started staying with them more. It's a mark of favor, you know. A sign that you've been doing something right."

"Can you warn her?"

Dinah laughed. "Linda Bell? Are you kidding? That woman cares more about social standing than either of the favored families. She could walk in on Phinehas doing his worst with Melanie and Tracy and tell herself he was praying with them."

"We'll just have to pray for her. That the Lord will give her discernment."

She gave him a doubtful glance. "If you think it will help."

"Oh, I think it will." That was progress, wasn't it? The last time they'd discussed prayer, she'd made a fool of him and walked away. "When I haven't been cleaning up after the ladies out there, or working on the leases, or researching the eating habits of babies, I've been pestering the Lord about you. Perhaps it did some good." He smiled at her. "Something is working. The changes around here are quite amazing, as Phinehas remarked at supper."

"If you say so." She didn't sound convinced, but at least she wasn't laughing.

"Speaking of researching, I came across something on the 'net this afternoon."

"Oh?" She sipped her tea and eyed him curiously.

"It's about Tamsen. I think you ought to do something about her. Legally, I mean."

"Why? We'll find Tamara."

"Even if you do, from the tone of that letter it doesn't seem likely she's going to want to take up motherhood again."

"She'll have to." Dinah's voice was grim.

"But say she doesn't. Now Phinehas knows Tamsen is his. Legally, he has parental rights."

"What are you saying?" She put her mug down next to his, as if to free up her hands to . . . what? Fight?

"I'm saying he could take her away from you."

"He's a Shepherd. A missionary." She gripped the arm of the couch. "He lives out of a suitcase. How is he going to take care of a baby?"

"Maybe he wouldn't. But he could take her from you and give her to a family with what he considers a better attitude. More complaisant. A family that would allow her to be brought up in an atmosphere where she'd be raised to worship him, as you were."

"Oh, no. And then Mom would be right. The cycle would start all over again." Her lower lip trembled. "I won't let that happen. I just won't. He doesn't have any rights at all, including the right to just hand her off like a piece of livestock, to be fattened up for the auction."

"The question is are you willing to go to court for her?"

"Of course I am! Do you know what I have to do?"

"As a matter of fact, I do." His research skills had paid off in spades in the last day or two. "You apply to the court for non-parental custody."

"But what if I want to adopt her? Isn't that a better idea?"

He held up his hands, as if to slow her down. "That's one of your options, certainly, but the difficulty is that both parents are still alive. You have to hunt them down and have them declared incompetent—"

"I can do that in Phinehas's case, no problem."

"—and get them to relinquish all rights."

"Tammy did that in her letter."

"Well, according to my information, the letter helps, but it isn't enough."

She sighed again. "Okay. What does this other thing involve?"

Now came the delicate part. "I took the liberty of contacting an attorney in Pitchford, which I understand is the county seat. Just for information purposes, mind," he added hastily. "I apologize if I'm treading on your toes."

She stared at him. "Treading on my toes? Good grief, Matthew, this is wonderful. I've been trying not to think about it, and you've been doing all the work. It's almost like—" She stopped. He could see her throat working.

"Like what?" he prompted gently.

"Like you want me to be her guardian," she whispered. "Or . . . something."

"Is that a good thing?" He certainly didn't want to lay more burdens on her. In fact, had he been in her place, he would have booted this nosy Cornishman out of here long ago.

"I want to be a mom, some day," she confessed quietly. "But I couldn't see how it could be possible. Phinehas wouldn't let any of the young men get close to me, not that many tried. And even if they did, I'm used goods. There are ten women to every eligible man in the Elect. No one in his right mind would choose me over some pretty virgin with all her options open."

It broke his heart that she saw herself this way. Phinehas had far too much to answer for.

"Only a man in his right mind would choose you," he assured her softly. Gently, so as not to frighten her, he smoothed a tendril of hair from her temple. "You have an enormous capacity for love. Look at you, arranging to care for Tamsen under circumstances that would frighten most people away. You cared for a starving, homeless man. You're supporting your mother. You're as capable in the house as you are in your business affairs, and you know all there is to know about chickens and cattle. What man wouldn't want a woman like you?"

With every word, her cheeks got a little more scarlet. Or perhaps it was his touch. Maybe she didn't like it. Heaven knew she had no reason to value the caress of any man.

"That's all very well," she mumbled, "but most men want to marry a woman they're attracted to. And I don't compete very well in that department."

"You're used to seeing yourself through other people's eyes. How about seeing through mine?" he suggested with a smile. "I see a woman who smiles rarely, but when she does, it's like the sun burning away the clouds. I see a woman with dark eyes that a man could fall into, and skin so soft and fragile he's almost afraid to touch it. I see a woman with hands capable enough to drive a Jeep yet gentle enough to comfort a crying baby or cuddle a frightened chicken."

His voice dropped as he saw her lower lip tremble. "I see shoulders that bear other people's burdens as well as her own. I see dark hair always trying to work its way out of imprisonment, and feet that would leave but that stay for love's sake." He paused. Her eyes were wet. "Why would any man not want a woman like that?"

She made a choked sound, and pitched forward into his arms.

He pulled her closer, fitting her against him. He hadn't truly held her since that dreadful day when she had lost Sheba. But this wasn't a simple offering of comfort. He held her because he needed to. Because he hadn't just been saying these things to build up her confidence and make her feel better.

He meant every word.

Under the black fabric of her dress, her arms and shoulders were thin, but not as thin as they had been. One arm curled around his neck and she hung on as if someone were going to grab her around the waist and tear her away. But no one was going to do that, he swore silently to himself. He may not have much in the way of worldly prospects to offer her, but he could offer support and friendship and loyalty.

And more, if she would allow it.

Matthew realized that his world had just rocked on its axis and had begun spinning in a different direction. A direction that had a sense of purpose.

Dinah Traynell had given his life meaning. For months he had been wandering in a fugue state brought on by disgrace and disappointment, traveling because there was a road in front of him, not because he had any desire to set his course there. He was convinced God had brought him to this ranch on the lonely side of a mountain for a reason, and now he knew what it was.

He'd brought him here for Dinah.

They were both battered and damaged. He might look like a soldier ready to topple over on the field of battle. He might have lost his sword and have no idea where the rest of the army was, but he still had his shield of faith. And maybe, just maybe, there was room under it for two, at least in the short term.

All that remained now was to convince Dinah that not every man on the planet was out to hurt her. That some might even have something to give.

He wanted to give. Badly.

The storm of weeping against his chest had subsided to an occasional sniffle. "Do you want a tissue?" he whispered.

"No, I'm okay. Can you . . . can you just hold me for a minute?"

It was on the tip of his tongue to say, *No, I'd rather hold you for a lifetime,* but he didn't want to frighten her off. Instead, he adjusted them both so that she cuddled into his side.

He marveled at how good she felt there. How very right. As if both of their long journeys had culminated in this warm, safe spot where there was just the two of them, drawing comfort from each other where they could not find it anywhere else.

Which, he suspected with a sense of dawning joy, was what the Father had had in mind all along.

For only the second time in her life, Dinah stayed home from Wednesday night prayer meeting without the excuse that she was sick or dead. Tamsen had been cranky all day, and between her and going grocery shopping and spending a fruitless hour on the Internet trying to put the baby on their medical plan, Dinah was worn out. The thought of dressing a screaming child and taking her to Gathering, where she'd spend the entire time standing outside in frustrated embarrassment, was just too much.

"Are you sure?" Elsie asked, when Dinah managed to keep Tamsen quiet by putting her in her plastic tub for a bath. "You might get something for your spirit if you go."

"How can I do that when I'm standing in the parking lot?" Dinah sighed. "You go ahead, Mom. You can tell me what helped you when you get home."

"Maybe she's got colic." Elsie eyed Tamsen as the baby took a deep breath. "Should we take her to Dr. Archer?"

"I have to get her on the medical plan first. And they require official paperwork because she hasn't been born or adopted into our family. Matthew says that once I have this thing called *non-parental custody,* I can do everything an actual parent can do."

"Why would you do that?" Elsie paused in the middle of tucking a tissue into her Bible bag. "As soon as we find Tamara the baby will go back to her."

"I can't count on that, Mom. I have to do what's best for Tamsen, and right now that seems to be getting her some sort of official status. I can't even take her in for her shots right now."

"I think you're wrong." A harsh note Dinah hadn't heard in a long time crept into her voice. "You're letting Tamara get away with her irresponsible behavior. And now I need to go or I'll be late for Gathering, but we'll talk about it when I get back."

Dinah didn't reply. Instead, she ran the warm cloth over Tamsen's wriggling body, devoutly grateful that she seemed to like this, if nothing else.

The kitchen was silent but for Tamsen's enthusiasm about the bubbles in the tub and the hum of the fridge. Matthew had invited her to take a ramble along the river's edge with him, but she had declined. If she went into the living room and looked out, she would probably be able to see his long frame through the trees, poking at piles of leaves and turning over rocks. Professor or not, he had that in common with small children and chickens. Everything interested him, no matter how insignificant.

For about the hundredth time since last night, her mind went back to that perfect moment with him on the couch. The lovely things he had said to her—and more, the tone of absolute truth in which he'd said them. There was no doubt in her mind that he meant every word.

Instead of running away or discounting and deflecting what he said, the way she might have done a month ago, she had let his voice pour over her like water, its warmth cleansing away the layers of dirt on her self-esteem.

It had been a long time since she'd opened her Bible out of

more than a sense of duty, to get herself in the proper frame of mind for Gathering. When she'd finished bathing Tamsen, she dressed her in her sleepers and settled into the easy chair. Morton's Bible, the gilt edges worn gray from constant thumbing, sat on the lower shelf of the end table. Dinah cradled Tamsen in one arm and picked the Bible up.

In Psalm 139, she read, "If I take the wings of the morning, and dwell in the uttermost parts of the sea; even there shall thy hand lead me, and thy right hand shall hold me."

There was a time when she'd seen that verse as a threat. Now it seemed comforting. No matter what she'd been through, no matter how far she'd run or how many walls she'd thrown up, was it really possible that God would pursue her with His love until she accepted it?

Dinah could hardly believe such a thing, but both Matthew and the psalmist seemed to think so, and they were fairly reliable authorities.

Dinah flipped to the New Testament, where Paul told the Romans, "For I am persuaded, that neither death, nor life, nor angels, nor principalities, nor powers, nor things present, nor things to come, nor height, nor depth, nor any other creature, shall be able to separate us from the love of God, which is in Christ Jesus our Lord."

She'd never believed that, either. Now the words held a kind of limitless grandeur, a wonderful hope that picked up her worries and concerns in great big arms and gave her a place to put them.

Maybe it was so.

Dinah exhaled and relaxed into the depths of the comfortable chair, the baby warm and drowsy in the crook of her arm.

If it's so, Lord, please forgive me. Help me to learn what you're really like. Help me to love you. Help me to know you as you really are, because Lord, it's a fact that I don't know you at all.

Twilight fell, and she heard the crunch of gravel under

Matthew's feet as he walked up from the river and went around to the barn. She smiled at the thought of him feeling guilty about entertaining Schatzi in the evenings. She of all people knew the healing power of a chicken on a mind full of worries. He was lucky Schatzi liked him.

IT WAS FULLY dark when her mother came home. When she saw the lights of the car on the highway, Dinah carried the baby, worn out from a day of fussing, upstairs and put her to bed.

When she came down, Elsie was hanging up her coat in the closet next to the front door.

"I just put Tamsen down," she reported.

"Good." Her mother sounded a little distracted. Had the news that she was going to go the legal route to protect Tamsen disturbed her that much?

"How is everyone?" Dinah asked. "Did you have a good prayer meeting?"

Elsie stopped fussing with the scarf around the hanger and looked Dinah in the eye. "Have you been talking to Alma Woods lately?"

Dinah avoided talking to Alma Woods whenever possible. Between her and Linda Bell, gossip was a finely honed art in Hamilton Falls. If you told either of them anything at breakfast, it would be all over not just the town, but the entire state by lunchtime.

"No," Dinah said. "I haven't spoken to her other than to say 'How are you?' in weeks. Why?"

Elsie led the way into the kitchen. "I overheard her talking to Owen Blanchard. Something about it being no wonder there was no Deacon at the Gathering in our home. That you had turned down Derrick Wilkinson in favor of someone else. Are you seeing somebody, Dinah?"

Dinah stared at her. "Of course not. I don't have time to see anybody, even if anyone were interested."

"It sounds like Derrick is interested."

"If he is, it's only because he wants to be Deacon. With Julia McNeill out of the picture, I'm his only candidate."

"Has he asked you out?"

"For lunch, a few weeks ago. I said no. I have more important things on my mind than having lunch with him."

"You should think about the Kingdom, Dinah. If we're to keep Gathering here, we're going to need an Elder."

"What happened to the subdivide and sell plan?"

Elsie made a motion with her head halfway between a nod and a shake that seemed to indicate she was undecided. "That's an option. But no matter where we lived, we'd still be a favored family. Still need an Elder to preside at Gathering."

"Mom, I'm not going to marry Derrick just so you can have an Elder."

"You could apply your heart to it."

Dinah snorted. "If I were going to apply my heart to anyone it would be—" She stopped, a second too late.

Elsie gave her a long look. "Who?"

"No one."

"I've seen you and that Matthew together," her mother said slowly. "I've seen the way he looks at you."

He had already told her how he looked at her. Was it so visible? "There's nothing going on, Mom."

"He's an Outsider, Dinah. He could endanger your soul."

"If anything, he helped rescue it," Dinah retorted, goaded into defending him. "If it weren't for him, I'd have killed myself a month ago."

Elsie drew in a quick breath, as if the words had hit her, and gripped the back of the nearest kitchen chair. "Don't talk like that, Dinah."

"It's true. He pulled me out of the river the night Uncle John killed Sheba. I owe him more than I will ever owe the Elect."

Her mother gazed at her, pain etching furrows in her forehead and at the sides of her cheeks. "You really tried to kill yourself?" she whispered. "Oh, Dinah." She reached out, and before Dinah had time to react, wrapped her in a fierce hug. "Promise me you won't do it again. I couldn't bear it. Promise me."

Dinah was so astonished that she felt herself hugging her mother back, as if there were some natural reflex in her arms.

"I promise."

Displays of affection from Elsie came few and far between. There had been the time when she was twelve and had stood up in Summer Gathering, indicating that she wanted to be part of the Elect congregation and give her life to God. There had been the occasional pat and maybe a word or two of praise when she'd done well at school, but that was about it.

But Elsie was a changed woman. They both were. Maybe this was a good place to start changing the way they related to each other. Maybe she could learn to know her own mother the way she wanted to learn to know God.

Nor height, nor depth, nor any other creature . . .

"I didn't think you'd miss me," she said into her mother's gray hair.

"Don't ever think that." Elsie pulled away enough to look up into her face. "I'm down to half a family. I couldn't bear to lose you, too."

Dinah stepped back. "You miss Tammy, and yet you and Dad sent her away."

"How can you say that? You know how your father was. He wasn't such an angry man when we were married, you know, but it certainly all came out when I told him I was pregnant with you." She paused. "You know what? When he was diagnosed with the cancer, he told me he was glad to die. That living with the three of us was more than any man should have to bear."

"Dad said that?"

Elsie nodded, and stepped away to straighten a dish towel hanging from the oven door handle. "I tried to be a good wife, under the circumstances. I did everything he wanted me to do, hoping I could make up for—for—"

"Me," Dinah said flatly.

"No, not for you. For deceiving him. I could have said no when he proposed, and he could have married Alma Woods."

"Good grief. He should have been thankful."

Elsie smiled, with a glint of impish humor. "Alma says she's forgiven me, but I know perfectly well she hasn't." The glint faded, and the pain flowed back in. "I could have let her have him, but I just didn't have the courage. It would have meant being Silenced for fornication. I took the easy way out, and we all suffered."

"Yes. We did. But the thing is we don't have to now. We can make our own way, do things differently. I mean, this house is a completely different place." She waved an arm at the living room, with its slipcovers and cheery lamps. "It's a place to start. We can work outward from here."

Elsie gazed at her, the fondness she seemed to be finally allowing herself to feel in her eyes. "When did you learn to be so positive, young lady?"

"Matthew taught me," Dinah said simply.

"So there is something going on."

"Yes." Dinah thought of his kind eyes and ragged cuffs and the chicken manure on his shoes. And of the strength in his arms when he held her. And of his unshakable faith in the God he loved. "I just don't know what it is, yet."

Chapter 19

THE ATTORNEY IN Pitchford, in Dinah's opinion, didn't look old enough to drive, much less represent Tamsen's interests in court. But Matthew seemed to think he could do the job, and Dinah certainly didn't want to go to the law firm in Hamilton Falls where Derrick Wilkinson was a paralegal. All she needed would be for Derrick to have access to the papers she was filing on Tamsen's behalf. The less anyone at home knew about her business, the better.

The brass plate on his desk said William Chang, and the framed diploma behind him said he'd received his *juris doctor* from the University of Washington five years before.

"Your research is correct," Chang told Matthew. "Adoption isn't a good route to take right now, since both parents are alive and well, and you'd have to terminate their parental rights. Either of them could contest it, and then where would you be?"

"They're not going to contest it," Dinah said. On her lap, Tamsen gazed curiously around the office, especially at the way the sun hit the brass desk set and made it sparkle.

"We don't know that. So as Mr. Nicholas suggested, I'm going to go for a petition for nonparental custody. This way you just have to serve notice on the natural parents that you're filing the petition. Since we don't know where the mother is, we'll put a notice in the county paper. And since you do know where the father is, we can serve him personally."

"We?" Dinah didn't want to be anywhere near Phinehas when he was served with the papers. Who knew what he would do?

"*We* as in our case. A representative of the court would do it, or I can do it, if you like."

Dinah nodded. "Then what?"

"Then we have what's called a *guardian ad litem* appear on Tamsen's behalf and recommend custody. With your sister's letter and the clear case of sexual abuse, I can't see any guardian doing anything but awarding custody of Tamsen to you." Chang paused. "What you choose to do about the abuser is, of course, your business. I recommend filing charges, of course."

"Yes, I know," Dinah mumbled.

"One other thing you should know," Chang went on.

"Yes?" Matthew said.

"This nonparental custody action doesn't terminate the father's parental rights; it just limits them as severely as the guardian believes is in the best interests of the child. You would have the right to recover child support from him."

This was such unexpected information that Dinah laughed. In her arms, Tamsen smiled and grabbed for her face. "Child support? He's an unpaid missionary. How could I get child support?"

"Unpaid?"

"It's a long story," Dinah said. "But the ministers in our church live off charity. The provision of God, in other words."

Clearly this was way outside the realm of Chang's experience. "O-o-kay. But I just wanted you to know you had that option."

"I'll keep it in mind."

Chang said he would file the notice with the paper and the petition with the court that week. They gave him Tamara's letter and the birth certificate, as well as the Blanchards' address in

Hamilton Falls. As they left the office, a woman came in pushing a stroller. Matthew held the door for her while Dinah glanced down at the baby.

"How old is your baby?" she asked the woman while she put Tamsen's little coat back on.

The woman took off the blanket covering her child. "Nine weeks tomorrow."

Dinah blinked. The baby wore a pair of apple-green rompers with a white frill around the neck. "Where did you get that outfit?" she blurted.

"I ordered it online," the woman replied. "Isn't it darling?"

"Where online?"

"It's a Web site, but I can't remember the name. Something to do with fruit."

"Dinah?" Matthew was still holding the door.

"Coming." She thanked the woman and carried Tamsen outside. How strange. Maybe Elsie had seen the rompers somewhere and decided to make a copy for Tamsen. Goodness knows they were cute enough.

She dismissed the woman from her mind and got back to more immediate problems. "I know this is necessary," she said as she buckled Tamsen into the car seat, "but I can't help feeling I've started something I'm not going to be able to stop."

She climbed into the passenger side and Matthew backed the car out of the lot. "Why would you want to stop it?" he asked. "You're doing this for Tamsen."

"Oh, I don't want to stop the custody thing. That's necessary. In fact, it's the only thing I can do under the circumstances." She looked out the window, where the houses and businesses of Pitchford were giving way to the rolling, grassy ranch land that would soon become the foothills surrounding Hamilton Falls. "It's what will happen with Phinehas that scares me. I know he's going to do something awful when he's served with those papers."

"But he won't take Tamsen away from you. You heard what Mr. Chang said. There's no reason the guardian would allow that. So hang onto that thought. We don't want to borrow trouble quite yet."

It seemed to Dinah that trouble had been on loan to her for so long that she'd never need to borrow it again. Maybe Matthew was right, though. She had to stay positive.

"I wish I could pray for stuff like this," she said, startling herself. She never talked about spiritual things in public.

"Why shouldn't you?"

"Matthew, God doesn't have time for things like custody and serving people with papers. He's busy running the universe."

"I've found him to be intimately involved with every aspect of my life," Matthew said mildly. "He knows everything about me. Why would we not pray about something like this? Go on. Give it a try."

"What, now?" Dinah looked around, as if the fields and trees on either side would eavesdrop. At the very least, she couldn't pray in front of someone. Not sitting in a car in broad daylight. It was too personal.

"Certainly." With his eyes fixed on the highway and both hands firmly on the wheel, he said, "Dear Father, thank you for guiding us to William Chang, and for giving us the means to protect Tamsen and keep her safe. Give us wisdom, Father, and courage to deal with whatever is ahead. We know it's part of your plan for our lives, and whatever it is, help us to accept it with the love in which it's given." He glanced at her. "Anything to add?"

His simple faith humbled her. If only she could have an attitude of love and appeal like that. "Thank you for Matthew, Lord," she whispered to the grassy expanse outside the window. "And help me to trust you."

"Amen," Matthew said softly. "Amen."

———

OVER THE NEXT week, while they waited for William Chang to call and tell them he'd filed the petition, and for the notice to Tamara to come out in the county paper, Dinah began to wonder if somehow the news of what she'd done had leaked out. No one in the history of the Elect had ever brought a Shepherd's name into court. Many wouldn't recognize the name Philip Leslie anyway, but some of the old-timers might. She didn't want to think about what would happen once the word got out. No matter how discreet Chang was, this was the Elect they were talking about. The harder you tried to keep something quiet, the faster people would find out about it.

Except for Phinehas and what he had done to her family. That had been kept quiet because they were all too afraid to fight for each other. Well, that was going to change. No one had stood in the breach for her, but she was going to do it for Tamsen, no matter what the consequences.

She tried to remind herself of that after Gathering on Sunday. She'd half expected Derrick to approach her again, but after catching her eye during the second hymn, he ducked his head and—she turned her head to look more closely—blushed.

What did he have to blush about?

People shook her hand more as a formality than because they were glad to see her, but Dinah had become used to that. But the best news of all was that Claire was back. She touched the other girl on the elbow as she was talking to Tracy, the second of Linda Bell's daughters.

"Dinah! Oh good, I've been meaning to call you. Come on, let's go outside."

On the lawn, some of the younger kids were playing tag while their mothers tried to round them up and get them into their cars. Claire pulled her over to where her parents' car was parked.

"How was your class?" Dinah asked. "Did all the junior tellers go?"

"There were about twenty-five of us, from all over the state. Charlene Fox from Richmond said to say hello."

Dinah smiled, pleased. She and Charlene had gone to a training class together back when Dinah had first started at the bank.

"But who cares about work?" Claire hurried on. "Guess who else says hello."

"Who?" Dinah couldn't imagine there was anyone else at the bank who would remember her.

"Julia Malcolm says there's room enough in Rebecca's suite for you and me to room together, and if you don't say yes, she's going to send Ross's partner down here to convince you." Claire laughed. "And believe me, you don't want that to happen."

"Who is Ross's partner?"

"His name is Ray Harper. He came over for dinner one night when I was there."

"I knew it! I knew you'd go over there. Good for you. How are they?"

"Happy," Claire said simply.

"What's it like, being with them when she's Out? I wouldn't know what to say. What to talk about."

"I just remembered to put our friendship first, and everything seemed to follow from there," Claire said. "There was no awkwardness at all. She's just the same, only happier. More at peace somehow. You know, inside."

"How can that be?" Dinah couldn't imagine being Out. Her world was so circumscribed by structure and rules and expectations that going outside and having to make the right choices among a bewildering array of possibilities was at once tempting and frightening. In the Elect, choices were easy. They had been made thousands of times before by everyone around you, and the results either measured up to expectations or they didn't. You could see right away how good your decisions were by people's behavior.

And in Gathering this morning there had been a whiff of that very thing, telling her something was wrong. It made her a little nervous.

"I don't know," Claire admitted. "They go to church."

"You can't find peace in a worldly church. Everybody knows that."

"Do we know it?" Claire asked. "Or are we just told that? I mean, has any of us actually gone and seen what happens in a worldly church?"

"Melchizedek went once. He said it was empty of the Spirit and full of noise. They even had a rock band up front." Dinah had a sneaking suspicion that it would have been in Melchizedek's best interests to say so, in order to keep his flock from going and experimenting with other churches themselves, but there was no way to say such a thing aloud. He was probably just speaking the truth as he saw it.

"Well, regardless, Julia is happy and there was no wall between us. We talked about everything and everybody, same as always. She sends her greetings."

"Thanks. What did your relatives say when you went over there?"

Claire shrugged. "It's not like I was staying with them and I'd have to tell them where I was going. I was in a hotel. I didn't see them every night, and it's really none of their business who I visit anyway."

But it was something to conceal. And something concealed from God's people was by default something wrong, as Dinah knew only too well.

"They live in Ross's condo," Claire went on. "It has this little grass courtyard and the complex has a pool where Ross takes Kailey to swim every day. It's a whole different life for her now."

Dinah had heard a rumor that the child had been kidnapped by her now-deceased mother and brought up in a cult. "Is it true she'd never seen her father before last summer?"

Claire nodded. "They're making up for lost time, let me tell you. He's a cop, right, so his time isn't really his own, but he's involved in her school doing talks and field trips and stuff. So is Julia."

"How does she like being a mom?"

"It seems to suit her. Want to know a secret?" Dinah grinned, amused at the way Claire's voice dropped. "Her family doesn't even know yet, but she missed her period while I was there."

"No kidding." So Julia was to be a mother twice over. Dinah could tell her a thing or two about formula and baby food.

"Don't say anything. I'm sure she'd want to tell them herself."

"I won't say a word."

Claire eyed her. "I believe that. You don't say a word about a lot of things. Tell me, what's this I hear about you and Matthew?"

"Me and Matthew? Not this again. What's to hear?"

"I overheard Julia's mom and Rebecca inside just now. Apparently Phinehas is staying with Blanchards because he didn't have freedom of spirit at your house. That doesn't sound like the Traynells I know."

"No freedom of spirit?" People lost their freedom when they mingled with worldly people. That was why Dinah had been so surprised when Claire had said there were no barriers between herself and Julia. Freedom of spirit was a mark of fellowship among the Elect, and when it was missing, it meant something had gone seriously wrong with one party or the other.

"Yes," Claire said. "He says it's because of you and Matthew. 'Fess up. What's going on?"

How dared Phinehas say he'd lost freedom of spirit, implying there was something wrong with her and her mother? Blaming the victim. He was doing it again. What he'd lost was his freedom with her body, and just as she'd feared, he'd chosen this way to retaliate. And Dinah couldn't say a word in her own defense.

Even though Claire had shown every sign that she could be trusted as a friend, Dinah still couldn't tell her the truth. Not only would Claire not believe her, she'd be Silenced for saying such a thing of the senior Shepherd in public. He could say he'd lost freedom because, really, who could prove he hadn't? It was spiritual, ephemeral, and totally damaging—and it was doing its work.

That, she realized suddenly, was why Derrick had blushed.

"Dinah?" Claire said, tilting her head to look into her downcast face. "Did you hear me? Or are you thinking of a nice way to tell me to mind my own business?"

In spite of herself, Dinah smiled. "Matthew is our hired man. That's it." The only man she'd ever allowed to see into her damaged soul. Who looked and didn't run, but instead made her think and act in ways she never would have dreamed of before.

No, it wasn't even that. He didn't *make* her do anything. He spoke his mind and allowed her to see he cared, and because of that she was free to think and act in new ways.

Scary ways. Ways she was probably going to regret. But new and exhilarating and adult ways nonetheless.

"Oh, my." Claire's gaze was frank and a little penetrating. "He's a nice guy, but not everyone could put a look like that on your face."

A flush flooded Dinah's cheeks. "A look like what?"

"The look a woman gets when she thinks about her man. The look Julia has when she talks about Ross."

Her man. *Oh Lord, can it really be true?* "You're seeing things," she mumbled.

"I don't think so." To Dinah's astonishment, Claire slipped an arm around her shoulders and squeezed. She'd never touched the other girl, outside of shaking hands after Gathering, and for a moment she didn't know whether to pull away or hug her back. Before she could decide, Claire dropped her arm and faced her again.

"You're lucky," she said fiercely. "I'd give anything to feel that way about someone. But in this town, unless you want to marry a boy of twenty-one or somehow get adopted into a favored family and become Mrs. Derrick Wilkinson, there are no prospects at all."

"You can be adopted into mine if you want." Dinah's tone was wry.

"You know what I mean. I'm twenty-six and no closer to finding someone than Melanie Bell."

"You need to get out of Hamilton Falls."

"I need something." Claire gazed, unseeing, at the cars in the parking lot. "Or I'm going to go nuts here." She glanced up. "Julia's right. We should room together at Rebecca's. Do weekends in Seattle. Forget to put our hair up. Wear red pajamas. Be wild and crazy."

"I can't, Claire. Don't forget Tamsen and the chickens."

"Oh, right. Boy, you should hear Linda Bell on *that* subject. No matter where I go these days, people are talking about you."

Oh, great. "Good or bad?"

"Just talking. Nobody really knows you, Dinah. Half the time people just gossip about what little they know."

"I've never given anyone anything to talk about." She fiddled with the zipper on her Bible bag, and ran a finger along the little pocket for her pen.

"I'll say. Time was, I really disliked you for being so perfect."

Perfect? The word was like a hammer blow. "Don't say that."

"Oh, I know none of us are, me most of all. But my parents were always saying, 'Why can't you be more like Dinah Traynell? Her hair is always *this* way. Her clothes are always *that* way.' Blah, blah, blah."

Dinah shook her head, a little bemused. "I always thought Julia was perfect. And look what *she* gave the gossips to talk about."

"Isn't that the truth. I guess maybe I don't want to be in a favored family after all."

"Everyone is always staring at you, wishing they were you.

And here we are, wishing we were somebody else. Anybody else."

Claire gazed at her, a clear gaze that demanded the truth. "But you're not really who everyone thinks you are, are you?"

"No," Dinah said. "Not anymore."

WHO SHE WAS didn't seem to matter. Who she had been didn't seem to matter either. Twenty-four years of trying to be the perfect daughter, perfect woman, perfect representative of the favored family, and what did she have for all her efforts?

The beady eye of Alma Woods watching her, waiting for her to do something wrong so she could pick up the phone and tell someone about it.

At least, that was how it felt after the notice came out in the Friday paper and people got wind of it. Elsie fielded a couple of dozen phone calls from the women in her circle, demanding to know what on earth Dinah was thinking of to take Tamara's baby away from her, before she gave up and let the answering machine screen the calls. By Saturday afternoon, they stopped. Except for one.

"Dinah, the phone's for you," Elsie called from the back porch. "It's Melchizedek."

"He probably wants to have a young people's meeting here or something," Dinah said to Matthew as she crossed the floor of the barn to where the extension hung on the wall next to the door. Three of the chickens followed her, convinced she was going to get cracked corn for them.

But a young people's meeting was the last thing on Melchizedek's mind.

"Dinah, I just had a very disturbing conversation with Phinehas. So disturbing, in fact, that he wasn't able to speak to you, and he asked me to call you in his place."

"What is it?"

Oh, Lord, be with me now. This can't be good. I know now it's not you who's been throwing bolts of lightning at me all this time. It's Phinehas. And it looks like he hasn't lost his aim. Help me, Lord.

"A young man came to the Blanchards' this morning and gave Phinehas a document. Do you know anything about it?"

Play dumb. "Who? What kind of document?"

"I don't know who it was, but Owen said he was Chinese or Korean. And the document was a legal notice."

"Of what?"

"Of your intention to petition for the custody of your niece."

"Oh," Dinah said.

"Is this true?"

"Yes."

"But Dinah, why on earth would this—this notice be given to our senior Shepherd?"

"Did you read it?"

"It upset Phinehas to the point where he couldn't even pray, and he has to lead two Gatherings tomorrow."

"But did you read it?" she persisted. Maybe he hadn't. Maybe she could be vague and he would go away.

"Yes, I read it." His voice was heavy with years of the knowledge that he had stayed in her home, eaten meals with her, comforted her in her grief, and advised her in her distresses. "I can't tell you how much this grieves me, Dinah."

"What does?" Was he talking about Phinehas's fatherhood or her daring to get custody of Tamsen?

"Please don't play games with me. This is serious."

"I honestly don't understand, Melchizedek. What is wrong with me trying to get some kind of legal status for my niece?"

"There's nothing wrong with that. What's wrong is the name on the document. Philip Leslie."

Oh. Any hopes that this might have been done quietly and with the least amount of pain evaporated with those two words. Her one hold over Phinehas vanished when he'd allowed Melchizedek to read the document. She should have known this would happen. She should have predicted that Phinehas would find some way to turn his sin back on her.

"How could you do it, Dinah? How could you name a godly man, a Shepherd who leads a flock of hundreds, who has sworn himself to celibacy for the gospel's sake, as the father of this child?" His voice broke.

"I didn't name him," she said as steadily as she could. "It was on the birth certificate."

"A lie," he said in a voice so hushed it was almost a whisper. "By a girl whose sins led this congregation to Silence her. A girl who is not worthy to serve the Shepherd even a cup of cold water."

"That girl is my sister, Melchizedek. Be careful what you say."

"Threats and accusations," he retorted. "But I am armed against the darts of the wicked. Dinah, I must tell you the purpose of this call."

There was a purpose? "Yes?"

"My first reaction when I saw what you had done was to ask Phinehas if we should call the Testimony of Two Men."

The bottom dropped out of Dinah's stomach. The Testimony was only called when someone was to be Silenced. When it happened to Tamara, it had begun the nasty work in their father that the cancer had put an end to.

"You're going to have me Silenced?" she whispered. "But I haven't done anything."

"You are very fortunate in the loving heart of Phinehas, Dinah," Melchizedek told her. "He held me back from picking up the phone and calling it for this very evening. As it is, I'm going to be spending a good long time on my knees asking God to take this anger out of my heart. It grieves me that one of our Shepherd's own flock should turn on him this way."

"But I—he—"

"In the spirit of truth, he left me a message to give you."

Here it came. The final lightning bolt. Maybe she wouldn't

be Silenced, but the sick, rolling feeling in her stomach told her that Phinehas wouldn't let this go without a fight. "What's that?"

"He believes you're in danger, Dinah. His first care is for your welfare."

"In danger from what?"

"Not what. Who. That hired man you have. Information has come to light that he's more than a university professor, Dinah. He's a predator. An animal."

"What are you talking about?" Dinah's voice had risen in trepidation. Her gaze locked on Matthew, who was busy with bucket and rake under the roosts.

"Phinehas believes that the truth will set you free," Melchizedek said with all the authority of the law and the prophets. "This Matthew Nicholas that you've given a home to was arrested just a few months ago for the sexual abuse of one of his female students. That's why he's no longer a teacher. He can't get a job anywhere in California."

Chapter 20

"THAT'S NOT TRUE," Dinah retorted in a voice so harsh it was almost a whisper. "Phinehas is l—is misinformed."

"I'm afraid it is true," Melchizedek said. "I have the newspaper clipping here in front of me. 'Prof Arrested in Sex Scandal,' it says, naming Matthew Nicholas, professor of English literature, who abused a student in his office under the pretext of prepping her for her exams."

"Where did it come from?" The notice had only been served this morning. How on earth had Phinehas dug up this information? She leaned against the barn wall, hoping it would hold her up. In the chickens' area, Matthew murmured to a group of curious birds who were hoping he'd share some corn while he was raking up droppings.

Pain needled under her breastbone, and she turned away.

"Sometimes we have to use the tools of the Devil in order to beat him at his own game," Melchizedek informed her. "Phinehas went to the library and in minutes Satan presented him with evidence of his work."

Any other time Dinah would have been amused at the thought of Phinehas, who preached fire and brimstone against television, music, and the Internet, being reduced to hunching over the little terminal with its thirty-minute limit in the Hamilton Falls Public Library and trying to figure it out. But at the moment all she could do was marvel at the lengths to which he would go to destroy her life.

"Good-bye, Melchizedek," she said.

"Wait, I have more."

What more could there possibly be? Phinehas had taken Sheba. He had taken Matthew. The only thing left was Tamsen, and he would probably contest the notice and take her, too.

"What is Phinehas going to do about the notice, do you know?"

"Do? What is there for him to do but pray that you are forgiven for your malice?"

"But is he going to contest it?"

"Why would he? The child's future has nothing to do with him. His care is for souls."

Thank you, Lord. "What more did you have to tell me, then?"

"Only this. Phinehas charged me to advise you that he will not call the Testimony if you make three sacrifices. You must cleanse your home of this criminal so that the women of our congregation will be safe. You must promise that only the three of us will ever know about the document he received. And you must restore freedom of spirit in your home."

"Consider the first two done." She glanced at Matthew again, and winced at the spurt of fresh pain. "But the third is up to him."

"I understand that for his freedom of spirit to be restored, you must be willing to sacrifice your own self-will. In his words, to render again the service of love as you once did."

No. No. I'd rather be Silenced. I will never, never—

"Dinah, are you all right?" Matthew laid down the bucket and rake and walked over to her. "You're as white as your rooster over there."

Pain lanced through her knees and arrowed up through the

muscles of her thighs. She hung up on Melchizedek in mid-sentence before she dropped the receiver altogether and pressed both hands flat against the smooth Sheetrock of the barn wall.

"How could you not tell me?" she breathed. "Me, of all people?"

"Tell you what? Dinah, please sit down. You're about to drop. What did he say to you?"

" 'Prof Arrested in Sex Scandal.' " She threw the headline bitterly into his dear, worried face. "No wonder you know so much about sexual abusers, Matthew. Just when were you planning to tell me that's exactly what you are?"

⌣

"SOMEONE'S BEEN DOING a bit of detective work, have they?"

Matthew tried to slip an arm around her, but Dinah spun away from him. "Of all people to tell me, it had to be them, Melchizedek and Phinehas. Tell me they're lying, Matthew. Tell me it was some other guy in the paper."

He'd wondered if this day would ever come. Wondered how he would bring it up, because of course he had to do so if they were going to move on to the kind of relationship he hoped for. But the longer he had let it go, the more she learned to trust him, and the more impossible it became for him to risk saying the words.

"Yes," he said at last. "It's true I was arrested."

"Oh, lovely. Maybe you'd like to explain, before I write your last check and you go."

He had a little money now, enough to get back to California. The very last place he wanted to be.

"I was arrested, but it turned out the girl had a history of abuse, and of making such accusations in order to get attention."

"Once again, we blame the victim," Dinah snapped. "You told me yourself that's what abusers do."

"I'm not an abuser, Dinah. I'm just a little shortsighted. I didn't see it coming. I sincerely thought she wanted tutoring for a paper about the plays of Aphra Behn."

She snorted in disbelief.

"Yes, the police agreed with you. At first. But I was completely cleared. I see that Phinehas neglected to search the newspaper archives for the articles that reported on my exoneration."

She turned away and opened the barn door. "I'll go write your check. Feel free to take my dad's—Morton's—clothes if you want. I certainly don't need them."

"Dinah, please." He reached for her arm, but she jerked away.

"You could have told me," she choked. Her face was twisted with distress. "You could have explained. But oh no, you let me go on and on about my own problems and completely shut me out of yours."

"Why would I burden you with all that ugliness?" The words burst out of him. "You had enough to bear."

"Let me be the judge of how much I can bear, Matthew. Let me do the thinking for myself."

"And what would have happened? Exactly this. You getting upset and asking me to go."

"Maybe. But maybe on those long nights when I was crying on your shoulder, you could have shared a little. Could have talked things out with me."

He gazed at her, completely at a loss as to why she would want such a thing. "I don't understand. What happened in California is irrelevant to us now. I was innocent. I'm still innocent. Don't let that mistake come between us, Dinah. Please."

"It's not that." Her voice shook. "It's the fact that I gave you everything and you gave me nothing. You know everything there is to know about me and what do I know about you? Friends, family, education, history? Next to nothing."

"I can tell you all that. I thought we had time."

She made a sound of frustration. "It's not the facts that make the difference, Matthew. It's the willingness to share them. To exchange pieces of ourselves, don't you see? It's happened to me again. I give my pearls away and I get nothing back. I suppose I should thank you for not throwing them on the ground, at least."

He had no idea what she meant.

She opened the door and jerked her chin in the direction of the hired man's suite. Her face was set, with fear stamped on it the way it had been when he'd first arrived. "Go on. Pack your things and I'll drive you to the bus station. And make sure you close the door behind you. On top of everything else, I'm going to have to break Schatzi of the urge to visit you now."

With that she marched outside and swung the door shut. The chickens, seeing him as their last hope, gathered around his feet and looked up at him, murmuring encouragement.

"What am I going to do, my little friends?" he asked them, his voice thick with despair. "How am I going to make her see?"

The chickens had no reply. But there was One he could turn to when the waters of loss threatened to overwhelm his soul.

Lord, you've brought me to this place and to this woman for a reason. Give me wisdom. Give me guidance, please, Lord. Help me know what your will is, and oh Lord, give me the strength to do it.

Shortsightedness had been the least of his mistakes. He had blithely told his friend Paolo that he thought he could help Dinah by listening. So he'd just sat there like the God she had once believed in, accepting everything she brought to him and giving nothing back. It had never occurred to him that he might have allowed her to listen, that in sharing his pain she might be able to alleviate it. Instead, he'd been all wisdom and benevolence, dishing out advice as though it were his place to do so, setting himself up as another selfish father figure in the long line she'd already had to deal with.

Oh, Father, forgive me. I have no idea what I'm doing.

Outside, the door slammed on the family's Oldsmobile, and

someone started it up and backed out of the yard. On the other side of the barn, he heard the doors slide open and then the truck engine fire up. Everyone, it seemed, had somewhere to go today. Meantime, he had not done what she'd asked him to.

It took only a few seconds to pull his few shirts off their hangers and to roll up the pair of pants that had belonged to Morton. His books went into the pockets in his backpack they had become used to, and his toothbrush and comb into a plastic bag.

When he took a last look around the cozy kitchen and living room he'd begun to think of as his little harbor of peace in the wilderness of the world, he saw that Schatzi had followed him in the open door from the barn.

A lump formed in his throat as he knelt down to stroke the soft golden feathers. "Good-bye, little friend," he said softly. "Take care of her for me as best you can."

Then, mindful of what Dinah had said, he slung the pack over one shoulder and picked the bird up. He closed the door carefully behind him with one hand, which put Schatzi off balance. Her normal contented bubbling sound became a squawk of distrust and she leaped from his arm, flapping to a landing on the floor of the dark passageway. Then she took off at a run for the rest of her flock, who were milling around the feeder on the other side of the barn.

The lump in his throat swelled in fresh pain.

He had no way to make amends for his clumsiness with her, either.

DINAH KEPT HER mouth shut and her foot jammed on the gas pedal as they sped down the highway toward town. Matthew had tried to speak once or twice, but with Tamsen in the back trying out her vocalization skills it was easy to freeze him out. If she let him say anything, her heart would melt and she'd beg him to forget what she'd said and stay.

But she'd made up her mind. He'd broken her trust and now he had to go and that was that. She couldn't even think about the howling pain in the region of her heart, or the sick dread in her stomach at the thought of having to face Phinehas's third condition alone. She even felt as though she ought to apologize to Schatzi for sending him away, but some childish jealousy held her back on that one. Schatzi could just get used to the real alpha bird in the flock—Dinah.

She parked the truck outside the bank, where she could see Claire at the counter through the picture window. Next door, the coffee bar was doing a rousing trade, some brave souls even drinking their lattes at outdoor tables. Across the street, people browsed in Rebecca Quinn's bookshop, Quill and Quinn.

Everyone looked so normal, while her world was splintering all around her.

"It will just take a moment to cash this and close the account," Matthew said before he slid out the door.

Dinah looked out her own window and caught sight of her mother going into the post office on the corner. Her arms were full of red, white, and blue "Priority Mail" boxes, and someone held the door for her while she maneuvered them all inside.

What was going on? Was she sending presents to everyone she'd ever met? In the middle of April?

Dinah popped Tamsen out of her buckles and locked the truck. Holding the baby, she crossed the street and pushed open the post office door with her hip. Her mother was already at the counter with her pile.

"Mom," she said in a low voice, "what's going on?"

Elsie looked her up and down, and nibbled the inside of her lower lip. Then she seemed to come to a decision.

"I'm mailing my things to my customers," she said.

Dinah stared at her. Tamsen waved an arm and grabbed a pen

out of the postal guy's pen holder, and she took it away from her without looking. "What?"

"The baby clothes. I've been selling them for a couple of weeks now. Well, Matthew has. These are all going to the people who ordered them."

"Selling them?" Dinah was getting tired of sounding like a parrot, only able to mimic, not think.

"Our hired man has many talents, in case you haven't noticed. I took pictures of the clothes on Tamsen—yes, you're Granny's pretty model, aren't you, love?—and Matthew had them scanned at the stationery store. Then he made a Web site and is selling them on something called eBay, too. He looks after all that, though. I just fill the orders."

"Matthew?" *Come on, Dinah. Get your brain in gear.*

"Yes. He's got a little computer in the barn, you know. I know we've been taught that the Internet is a window into wickedness, but it sure is handy when a woman has to make a living and all she knows how to do is cook and sew."

"Mom, I just fired Matthew." There. That was something sensible to say. Besides, technically it was her little computer. And it was still sitting in the hired man's suite.

Now it was her mother's turn to stare in astonishment. "Fired him? Why?"

Why? It was completely impossible to explain why. She finally settled on the easiest part. "He was arrested for sexual abuse earlier this year."

"Good heavens. Well, was he guilty?"

"No."

"So what did you fire him for?"

"I just don't want him around any more. He broke my trust." *And my heart.*

Elsie took her change from the postal employee and led the way out the door. "You don't. Well, goodness, missy, some of us might. How am I going to run my business without his brain, not to mention his computer?"

"That computer is mine."

Now it was Elsie's turn to stare at her. "Is it, now. And here I was feeling guilty about letting Matthew talk me into this. Not that I'm not enjoying it," she added. "But I felt I had to hide it from you. I guess now I don't."

"I think we're done hiding things from each other. The truth has set us free, hasn't it?"

They had reached the Oldsmobile. "But for some reason that doesn't apply to Matthew?" her mother asked. "Where is he? I'm going to tell him he isn't fired after all. I don't know what you were thinking. If he wasn't guilty and he's been a good friend to you, what would you want to get rid of him for?"

"Mom, don't."

But it was too late. When Elsie marched down the street to the truck, Matthew was nowhere in sight. Dinah went into the bank while Elsie put Tamsen into her seat.

"Claire, did you see where Matthew went?"

The customer at Claire's window gave her a dirty look for interrupting his transaction. "He said he had to catch a bus. I told him he'd better hurry—the one to Richmond went through at three o'clock."

Elsie was right. What was the matter with her? She had pushed Matthew away the way she pushed everyone away who got close enough to really see her. She had branded him with the same label the newspapers had. She was quick to judge when he had not judged her. And she had been unkind when he had been nothing but gentle toward her.

She was an idiot and she needed to fix that, right now, before it was too late.

Dinah looked at her watch. Three fifteen. But the bus station was just on the next block and around the corner. There might still be time.

As she pushed the bank's glass and steel door open, she heard a roar and the Richmond bus accelerated down Main Street and picked up speed as it passed the old apple-processing plant where the discount store was going to be.

Dinah stood on the sidewalk and watched her only chance for happiness roll down the highway, leaving nothing behind but the choking smell of exhaust.

HAD IT NOT been for Matthew and the gifts he'd given her during those black nights when she'd emptied herself of ugliness the way she had purged her body of food, Dinah wouldn't have been able to bear it when Phinehas called. Of course, Elsie did the expected thing and invited him to dinner. If not for Matthew and his unselfish acceptance of the horror that had been her life, she would not be able to sit across the table from her abuser and make small talk while her mother served Dutch apple pie.

She had accused Matthew of keeping himself from her, but maybe, she thought now, it was more a case of the poor man not being able to get a word in edgewise. Had she asked him about his family and friends? Had she shown interest in his passion for seventeenth-century literature? Had she made even the smallest attempt to enter into his life the way he had wholeheartedly entered hers?

No.

No wonder he had left without a word in his own defense. She hadn't given him a chance to do that, either.

But if God had given her Tamsen as a reason to live, then Matthew had given her the tools to live by. Courage, honesty, and above all, the knowledge that she was worthy of love. Not the twisted reflection of his own ego that had passed for love with Phinehas. But real, unselfish, generous love that reached out, even when it wasn't wanted.

The kind of love God showed when he sent his son to an

earth that didn't know him and didn't care to. But God did it anyway. And Dinah was determined to as well.

"I got your message from Melchizedek," she said calmly to Phinehas when Elsie went out to the kitchen to start a pot of coffee. "I've fulfilled two of the conditions." To her own detriment and sorrow.

"And what about the third?" Phinehas cleaned the last of the vanilla ice cream off his plate with the tines of his fork. They were using Grandma Simcoe's silver—she of the Simcoe Schnozz.

"I'm afraid not, Phinehas. There will only be the two. You don't have the right to ask the third of me."

"And you have the authority to tell the Shepherd of your soul what he has the right to do?" His voice was as calm and smooth as oil on water.

"The only authority I have is over my own body," she replied steadily. "And I choose not to allow you to rape me any more."

Silence fell in the dining room, punctuated only by the sound of running water from the kitchen as Elsie filled the reservoir in the coffee maker.

"It grieves me that you still view your service this way." Phinehas laid his fork carefully on his plate, so that it didn't clink. "It used to be a willing service. Now you heap ugliness on it."

"Let's call a spade a spade, Phinehas. I was never willing. Never. I told you I would not make it public if you never touched me again."

"You broke your word. So anything you 'told' me is null and void, my dear."

"How did I do that?"

"You had that attorney serve me with the notice, as if I had any connection with that child."

"You can deny it all you like, but it doesn't change the facts. You chose to show the notice to Melchizedek. Our deal still stands. I won't make the third sacrifice. And I will go public if you don't stop."

"Are you threatening me again?" All the music had leached out of Phinehas's voice, leaving it harsh and flat.

"No, not at all. Just telling you the truth. I take it our discussion is closed? Would you like some coffee?"

"Our discussion is *not* closed. It's obvious to me that you have forsaken God and given yourself wholly to Satan. I have no choice but to call the Testimony of Two Men. This very evening, in fact."

GOOD THINGS COULD take a whole lifetime to come. Bad things, however, could be arranged in half an hour.

If ever there was a time when Dinah could have used love and support, it was now. But Elsie had retired to her room in tears after unsuccessfully begging Phinehas not to make those calls. And Matthew? Well, her selfishness had done a fine job of chasing him away just when she needed him most.

It's not God throwing lightning bolts at you, she reminded herself as Owen Blanchard's car rolled into the driveway, joining that of Melchizedek. *It's Phinehas. You can fight this. Only the truth is spoken in this house now. You have nothing left to lose, so you may as well say it out loud. God is a God of truth, not lies and covering up. He is with you.*

He had to be. Otherwise, how could she sit here in this dining room chair so calmly as Phinehas, Melchizedek, and Owen filed into the living room and seated themselves in three chairs facing her? In fact, she was more than calm. She was filled with a quiet joy brought on by the knowledge that she had done the right things all along, and with the shield of her newborn faith, she could take on anything they had to throw at her.

Owen Blanchard looked unutterably weary, she thought as he seated himself. His suit was as crisp as ever, his shirt and tie impeccable, a nice contrast with red-gold hair that had faded over the last year or so to a sandy gray. It couldn't be easy for him as Elder. All the girls from the two favored families except one were either Out or Silenced, and the one remaining, his wife, Madeleine, was at some kind of asylum getting treatment for a disorder no one wanted to talk about.

Strange that it was the girls this was happening to, Dinah thought suddenly. *Is it because we're the only ones able to struggle free of generations of tradition and open our mouths to speak the truth?*

Phinehas pulled Morton's Bible from the end table next to the easy chair, opened it, and began to read.

"Jesus said in the eighth chapter of John, 'And yet if I judge, my judgment is true: for I am not alone, but I and the Father that sent me. It is also written in your law, that the testimony of two men is true.'" He looked up at her. "Dinah Traynell, we have called the Testimony in response to your unwillingness to support the leadership of the Elect of God. You may choose two of us to decide your case. Who will you have?"

"Melchizedek and Owen," she replied. That was a no-brainer. Why should she choose Phinehas when he had engineered the whole thing and was determined to get his revenge for her daring to tell the truth? Not that either Melchizedek or Owen would go against what he wanted. Her "case" was probably already decided. She pressed her knees together and tried to invite the spirit of peace into her heart. She was going to need it.

Phinehas handed Melchizedek the Bible, open on both hands, and the latter flipped further along in the New Testament. "Paul's first letter to the Corinthians, chapter five. 'But now I have written unto you not to keep company, if any man that is called a brother be a fornicator, or covetous, or an idolator, or a railer, or a drunkard, or an extortioner; with such an one no not to eat.'" The Shepherd's voice was heavy, the way he said grace at the table. As a little girl, Dinah had always thought he had a stomach ache. Maybe he did now. " 'For what have I to do to judge them also that are without? Do not ye judge them that are within? But them that are without God judgeth. Therefore put away from among yourselves that wicked person.' "

He closed the Bible. "You are brought before us because of your actions toward the senior Shepherd of Washington State. You have railed on him, implicating him in a legal matter by naming him the father of your sister's illegitimate child."

Owen looked up and his sandy lashes flickered in surprise. Dinah saw his jaw clench, as if he were biting back an exclamation.

"You have professed yourself to be unwilling to serve the Shepherd with the love and care appropriate for a sheep of the flock. As a result he and the Elect have no freedom of spirit in your home, damaging the possibility of your family, the first fruits of this pasture, having Gathering here again. How do you answer these charges?"

"Phinehas *is* the father of my sister's child," she said. "It says so on her birth certificate."

"Danny Bell is the father of her child." Owen seemed to force the words out. "It's all over town."

"I'm afraid not." Dinah smiled at Owen, whom she'd always liked. "Phinehas has been raping both her and me since we turned fourteen. And our mother before that."

Owen turned as white as the pages of the Bible in Melchizedek's hands, and glanced at Phinehas in appeal. "I can't hear this," he said.

An expression of patient grief for what Dinah assumed were her dreadful delusions crossed Phinehas's face. "For the sake of our brother's spirit, Melchizedek, we should make this as speedy as possible."

"Oh, but I'm not finished yet," Dinah said. Her heart began to pound at her own temerity, yet something in her chest, some urgency, was forcing her to speak at last.

"Yes, I'm afraid you are." Melchizedek raised a hand to stop her, but Dinah disobeyed the gesture and plowed on.

"Tamsen isn't Phinehas's only child. I am the product of his rape of my mother. I am Phinehas's daughter, too, though Morton Traynell's name is on my birth certificate. A simple blood test will prove it."

Owen, who had never been anything but urbane and kind, was looking at her as if she were a slimy thing that had crawled out from under the couch.

She opened her mouth to say more, but at that moment the tires of a car crunched on the gravel outside.

"Dinah," Phinehas said, enunciating her name as though it made his mouth dirty, "please see who it is and tell them to come back another time."

Personally, she was glad for the interruption. It would give her five more minutes as a member of the Elect. She had a feeling they were going to do more than Silence her. They were going to cast her Out altogether. They could not suffer her to be in the congregation now, with what she knew and was prepared to say. But once she was Out, anything she said would be discounted as the mutterings of a lost and bitter soul, and no one would pay any attention.

She opened the front door and found a stranger standing on the porch under the light.

"Dinah Traynell?"

"Yes. I'm afraid there's a meeting going on here at the moment. Would you care to come back tomorrow?"

"No, that's not possible."

The man was young, in his early thirties. He wore a polo shirt under his denim jacket, and black jeans. His hair was a little on the long side, brown and wavy over the ears and on the nape of his neck. Was he selling something?

"My name is Raymond Harper. I'm an investigator with the

Organized Crime Task Force based in Seattle. I understand that one Philip Leslie is currently at this address?"

"Yes." Ray Harper? The name niggled in her brain and she finally unearthed where she'd heard it before. "Are you Ross Malcolm's partner?"

"I am. May I come in?"

She couldn't imagine what he was there for, but neither was she about to refuse a law enforcement officer. She stood back and Harper stepped into the living room.

Ray Harper. The one Claire had said was the kind of man you wouldn't want coming after you.

His gaze went to the three men sitting motionless on the row of her mother's dining room chairs. "Which of you is Philip Leslie?"

"There is no one here by that name," Melchizedek replied. "As the young lady said, we're having a meet—"

Harper pulled a notebook out of his back pocket and consulted it. "All right. Which of you goes by the name of Phinehas?"

Phinehas stood with dignity. "I do. I am the senior Shepherd of this congregation. How can I help you, Investigator?"

"I doubt you'll be in a position to give anybody any help, Mr. Leslie. I'm arresting you for the sexual assault and rape of Tamara Traynell, formerly of this address. You have the right to remain silent. Anything you say can and will be used against you in a court of law . . ."

Chapter 21

ELSIE PUT HER Bible case on the table and sat in one of the kitchen chairs to put her shoes on. "I'm beginning to sound like a broken record, but are you sure you're not coming to Gathering?"

Dinah slipped another spoonful of baby food into Tamsen's mouth and shook her head. "They never got around to Silencing me, but the intent was the same." And outside of Elsie, only Owen Blanchard and herself knew it. "With Melchizedek sick, who do you suppose will lead?"

"Owen, I imagine," her mother said thoughtfully. "Though his mother-in-law says he's not doing too well either. I have to say, Dinah, you've really put the dog among the chickens, haven't you?"

Dinah wondered if Owen would speak or shake hands the next time she saw him, or if he would uphold Silence. "Mom, you know as well as I do that the dog has been preying on the chickens for thirty years." Tamsen swallowed another spoonful of food and beat joyfully on her knees for more. "I'm just glad the truth has finally come out."

"I am, too, in spite of everything. So maybe I'll get a few of the mud balls now that I would have fielded had I spoken out back then. Alma Woods will no doubt have a stockpile of them.

But what worries me most is what we're all going to do now. Spiritually, I mean."

"God is still leading," Dinah suggested.

"Well, yes, but everyone is used to him leading through the Shepherds."

"Mom, I think the Shepherds were all too happy to let people believe that. Maybe God is doing a bit of housecleaning so people will look to him instead of ordinary men. As we know all too well, it's not healthy when people do that."

Elsie's gaze was fond and a little admiring. "How you've changed, my Dinah."

"I hope so. This whole house has changed. You, too."

"I just wish Tamara were here." Pain flickered across Elsie's eyes. "She might find it easier to live with us now."

"All we can do is pray for her," Dinah said. "And that's everything."

She finished up the baby food and put a towel over her shoulder so Tamsen could spit up on it.

Elsie lifted the baby up and gave her to Dinah. "And what about this little one? No one is going to contest the notice and your Mr. Chang seems to be on your side as far as convincing the judge this is the place she should be."

Dinah nodded. "I'm not her mother. And I'm only half her aunt. We're half-sisters, so that's how I'm going to bring her up." She glanced at the clock. "You'd better get going. It's already five past."

When the Oldsmobile purred out of the drive and down the highway, Dinah went out to the barn. After all that had happened, there was no reason she couldn't have the laptop in the house. She was no longer a member of the Elect in name or spirit, so why should she trap herself inside its structure? Maybe she'd even go to town and buy something outrageous, like the beautiful bronzy-brown tunic sweater she'd seen in the dress shop's window.

But for now, she'd start with the laptop. She had something important to do.

She let the chickens out onto the lawn, since it was such a beautiful spring day, and went into the hired man's suite. It was as dim and antiseptic as it had always been, now that Matthew's gentle presence was no longer there to make a haven out of it. The laptop sat on the kitchen table. She picked it up and brought it into the main house, and when it booted up and she logged on to the Internet, she gazed in surprise at the home page.

What on earth was www.firstfruits.com?

In a couple of seconds she had her answer. There was Tamsen in the apple-green rompers, in a pair that made her look like a peach, in a white set with pockets that clearly looked like crocuses. There was ordering and pricing and a PayPal account. Matthew had designed a beautiful Web site for Elsie's clandestine business, Dinah had to admit. Love and color and humor were there on every page.

Shaking her head in amazement, Dinah opened her e-mail account and scanned the incoming mail. With a gasp, she saw a familiar name, and a date of two days before.

> To: Schatzi@hotmail.com
> From: TamaraT@hotmail.com
> Re: what's happening
> Hi Dinah,
> You probably haven't forgiven me yet, so I'll skip all that and cut to the chase. You should expect a guy named Ray Harper to show up. He's Ross Malcolm's partner, and I've told them everything. Sorry I didn't let you know where I was before. I'm in Seattle, working part time and going to the U. I stayed with Ross and Julia at first but now I'm in the dorms. Ross's church has a program for abused women called Beauty for Ashes, so I'm going to that, too. It seems to be helping. I think social work is the

place for me. The weirdness that is my life has to have some kind of point.

Hope you're well. Kiss Tamsen for me and tell her I love her, even if you don't believe me.

Love, Tamara

Dinah sat back with a sigh. The mystery of Ray Harper's sudden appearance on her doorstep was solved. Tamara had spoken out, just as Dinah had done, and between the two of them they'd seen to the downfall of Phinehas, just as if they'd been working together.

Matthew had told her once that he thought God had been weaving a strange and wonderful design to bring him to the ranch. At the time Dinah had thought he was just grasping at straws in order to make some meaning out of his life. But now she, too, saw the beauty of the pattern. She and Tamara and Julia had been able to speak at last. All the threads had woven together and Phinehas had been enmeshed in them, as unable to escape God's plan as they had been unable to prevent it, even if they had wanted to.

Father in heaven, your power and wisdom amaze me. Thank you for using us all. Thank you for working in my heart. Father, you know what I want most of all. If you're weaving this grand and lovely design, Lord, you wouldn't want to leave these last threads hanging, would you?

God, she hoped, could take a hint.

She closed out of Tamara's message and when the mail screen had refreshed, saw that another one had come in.

The address wasn't familiar. Despite the risk of spam, curiosity made her open it.

To: Schatzi@hotmail.com
From: Paolo_Martinez@ucca.edu
Re: home
Hello, Dinah. I'm back in California, staying temporar-

ily with a friend, Paolo, who is letting me use his e-mail account. I've done a lot of thinking lately, and praying, and feeling sorry for myself, and praying some more. The thing is I'm not going to let you chase me away. We've been through too much, both separately and together, to allow pride and selfishness to separate us. I'm speaking of my own, of course.

I should have told you about Torrie Parker. I should have counted on your generosity of spirit to give me the same comfort I have been able to give you. I was wrong to think that I was some kind of infallible counselor. There is only One who is that, and I pray he will be able to work in both our hearts so that together we can glorify him. Yes, together.

This is my dream, Dinah. An e-mail is a poor way to express it, particularly when I know you don't check it all that often, but like me, this message will be waiting for you if you decide to respond.

My love and admiration always,
Matthew

Dinah bit her trembling lip and blinked several times. The Lord certainly *could* take a hint. And he'd made it clear it was up to her to knot her own threads and finish the design herself.

Upstairs, Tamsen's fire-engine noise began, telling the world that naptime was over. Dinah climbed the stairs and lifted her out of the crib.

"What do you say we make like the chickens and go outside for a bit?"

She couldn't reply to either Matthew or Tamara right now. Her heart was too full and her throat ached with the need to either cry or sing. So she dressed the baby in a pair of warm overalls and her coat, pulled on her own barn jacket, and walked down the slope and across the road to the river.

The sun fell on a curve of sand and grassy hillocks that the river had carved out of the bank this past winter. The sand was dry and warm to the touch, so Dinah put Tamsen down on it and sat next to her.

She was neither mother nor wife, she thought, as she watched the clear water roll past with a chuckling sound. She was aunt and sister and daughter . . . and now, beloved. But most of all, she was herself, a self she was still getting acquainted with as she learned to walk in newness of life.

At her feet, a wavelet purled up on the sand, forming ribbons of foam like a necklace of pearls. In seconds, another wave had overtaken it and washed them away, throwing up new strands of glistening bubbles. They never really went away. They were renewed moment by moment, over and over, as long as the river was there to replenish them and the sun to give them beauty.

Sitting in the sand, the baby kicking happily by her side, Dinah smiled at the rush of water and decided that, all things considered, she would rather sing than cry.

And then she'd go back up to the house and send Matthew his answer.

1. Matthew 7:6 ("Neither cast ye your pearls before swine, lest they trample them under their feet, and turn again and rend you") has a lot of meaning for the heroine, Dinah. What do you think it means to her? To the theme of the book? To Christian women in the larger sense? What does it mean to you personally?

2. Even in their darkest moments, Dinah and Matthew discover small pearls of beauty that help to make life worthwhile. How many of these can you find? What moments of beauty in your own life have been like finding loose pearls?

3. *Pocketful of Pearls* deals with sensitive issues of sexual abuse. In the beginning, Dinah handles the abuse by becoming bulimic and by fencing people out of her emotional life. She even sees suicide as a solution. Do these ways of dealing with abuse seem realistic? Sympathetic? If you were in her place, with her strict and insular upbringing, what would you do?

4. According to the book *The Wounded Heart: Hope for Adult Victims of Childhood Sexual Abuse* by Dr. Dan B. Allender (NavPress, 1995), there are three stages of healing using a Christian model: honesty (acknowledging the truth of what has happened), repentance (making changes and admitting the need for God), and bold love (confronting the abuser). How does Dinah work through these stages? What steps does she take? How does Matthew help her? Do you think it's possible for her to be fully healed?

5. Have you ever heard the expression "toxic church"? What

do you think this means? Are the Elect a toxic church? Have you ever been involved with a toxic church before? If so, what was your experience?

6. One of the issues the book deals with is salvation by grace versus works. Paul advises the Philippians to "work out your own salvation with fear and trembling" (Phil. 2:12). And James 2:17 says: "Even so faith, if it hath not works, is dead, being alone." What do these verses mean in the context of grace? What are the signs of a belief in salvation by works versus one that bases its faith on grace? How is salvation and grace manifested in your own life?

7. Dinah has been a member of the Elect all her life, and believes she is a Christian. At what point does she realize she is not? What does it mean for her to become a Christian? Where does she begin a real relationship with God? And how does this fit into the healing process for her?

8. For Dinah's sister Tamara, the solution is to flee the unsafe family, so she abandons her baby with Dinah. Is Tamara a sympathetic character? Why might she have done this? Have you ever had to make a decision to leave something in order to save yourself?

9. At the end of the novel, the Elect's leadership is in ruins and there is a vacuum at the top that must be filled. If their tradition has been to filter God through their leaders, what will they do now? Have they learned their lesson after seeing that the head Shepherd has feet of clay? What happens when people put their trust in their leadership instead of in God—in other words, to put their faith in the "way" (meaning a system) of worship instead of in the Way (meaning Jesus)?

IF YOU ENJOYED *Pocketful of Pearls* . . .

A SOUNDING BRASS

Shelley Bates

Claire Montoya's life doesn't fit her anymore. Brought up in a toxic church in the small town of Hamilton Falls, Claire has watched her friends leave the church and has seen the leaders she trusted disgraced. It's time for a change—if she can just figure out what that is.

When Luke Fisher, radio evangelist, is invited to preach at one of their gatherings, Claire decides this is what she has been waiting for. She goes to work for him as bookkeeper at the radio station. Although she initially enjoys taking part in the ideas and changes Luke wants for the community, she soon discovers there are things about this charismatic visionary that just don't add up. And Investigator Ray Harper of the Organized Crime Task Force is hanging around the station too, asking questions and disturbing her . . . in a completely different way.

But who is right? The nationally known evangelist or the nonbelieving cop? And, more important, whom can Claire trust with her heart?

AVAILABLE AUGUST 2006

"I'd like to present Mr. Luke Fisher," Owen said, "evangelist from our very own KGHM Radio, right here in Hamilton Falls."

What?

People turned in their seats to stare at one another and gaped at Owen as if they couldn't believe their ears. A worldly evangelist? To speak to them? Someone who wasn't even Elect?

"Is he completely mad?" Rebecca said aloud, forgetting to whisper.

No one heard her. Everyone was busy talking, speculating, wondering the same thing.

"Please, folks, listen to me." Owen's voice rose above the noise, and out of habit, the congregation quieted enough that he could be heard. "We've all been praying without ceasing that God would save us in our hour of need. And I believe the reason he hasn't is because we've strayed away from him. We've put our trust in our leadership—in man, in human frailty—and the result has been disaster. We've looked inward to ourselves instead of looking outward at what God is doing in the world."

People murmured, and Claire nibbled her lower lip, wondering where on earth this was going.

"Folks," Owen said, "let's listen to Mr. Fisher's message and then do what Paul exhorted us to do—try the spirit and see if it's of God."

He yielded the microphone to Luke Fisher and returned to his seat. Every eye in the auditorium was riveted to the front.

Claire drew in a breath as Luke Fisher spoke. That melodious voice that had sounded in her car—announcing songs, exhorting people to come to God, talking with people who called in—filled their humble auditorium with his particular brand of music.

"Those of you who listen to the radio," he said, "may have heard a number of your hymns being played and wondered how it could be that worldly artists could sing the music and words that mean so much to you."

He paused, and all the young people in Claire's row looked at each other, eyebrows raised. Obviously they'd thought the very thing she had. Maybe some of them had even been listening to the radio on the way to Mission and had heard "Just As I Am."

"Well, here's the thing." He paused, then said, "I grew up in the Elect."

An audible gasp swept through the room.

"I did, and I lived a life of sin and suffering brought on by my own headstrong will. But God had a plan for me, and you know what that was?"

Claire found herself shaking her head, as though he had spoken directly to her. She wished he would. She wished those eyes would seek her out in the midst of this crowd and see that there was a mature, reasonably attractive woman who was currently single and very much available, right here in the seventh row.

"God's plan was for me to preach the gospel, but not as a Shepherd. No, his plan for my life reaches further than that. Radio isn't a sin, my friends. It's a way of reaching the heart of the sick, the shut in, those who aren't as fortunate as we are in this hall tonight. It's a way of bringing cheer to your soul as you drive to the supermarket, of focusing your mind on Christ while you work in the office. It's a way to reach the soul on the other side of the cube divider who doesn't know which way to turn in a life that looks like a maze."

The crowd was utterly silent.

"God gives us all our talents, my friends. And what have we been doing with them? Have we been burying them in the backyard of our own little group? Or have we been lending them out to others, and participating in the body of Christ?"

"Backyard," Claire heard someone say.

"Nonsense," snapped Elizabeth McNeill, Julia's mother, and then blushed scarlet at having actually spoken aloud in a Gathering, where it was forbidden for women to raise their voices except in song.

Luke Fisher smiled at Elizabeth, and Claire lost her ability to breathe.

If only someone would smile at me that way.

Remember Me
Deborah Bedford

Pastor Sam Tibbits has everything he wants or needs. But when his brother unexpectedly dies, he finds himself questioning God, searching for the meaning in it all. In an effort to work through his doubts he takes his nephew on a road trip to Piddock Beach, the small coastal Oregon town where he spent his childhood summers. In those innocent, adventurous years, he'd lived every waking moment with his close friend Aubrey. They knew each other as only young kids can, sharing confidences year after year as they explored the coast and sea. Until the summer Aubrey's family unexpectedly moved away with no forwarding address.

Sam returns to Piddock Beach in an effort to reach out to his nephew and to untangle his own emotional turmoil as he reflects on those long-ago joyful days. How like God, then, to return Aubrey there the very same week, as she seeks to work through her own personal problems. Together Sam and Aubrey face their inner demons and in the end each finds a way to peace on their own terms.

COMING NOVEMBER 2005